continued . . .

French Kiss

SUSAN JOHNSON

BERKLEY SENSATION, NEW YORK

THE BERKLEY PUBLISHING GROUP
Published by the Penguin Group
Penguin Group (USA) Inc.
375 Hudson Street, New York, New York 10014, USA
Penguin Group (Canada), 90 Eglinton Avenue East, Suite 700, Toronto, Ontario M4P 2Y3, Canada
(a division of Pearson Penguin Canada Inc.)
Penguin Books Ltd., 80 Strand, London WC2R 0RL, England
Penguin Group Ireland, 25 St. Stephen's Green, Dublin 2, Ireland (a division of Penguin Books Ltd.)
Penguin Group (Australia), 250 Camberwell Road, Camberwell, Victoria 3124, Australia
(a division of Pearson Australia Group Pty. Ltd.)
Penguin Books India Pvt. Ltd., 11 Community Centre, Panchsheel Park, New Delhi—110 017, India
Penguin Group (NZ), 67 Apollo Drive, Mairangi Bay, Auckland 1311, New Zealand
(a division of Pearson New Zealand Ltd.)
Penguin Books (South Africa) (Pty.) Ltd., 24 Sturdee Avenue, Rosebank, Johannesburg 2196,
South Africa

Penguin Books Ltd., Registered Offices: 80 Strand, London WC2R 0RL, England

This is a work of fiction. Names, characters, places, and incidents either are the product of the author's imagination or are used fictitiously, and any resemblance to actual persons, living or dead, business establishments, events, or locales is entirely coincidental. The publisher does not have any control over and does not assume any responsibility for author or third-party websites or their content.

FRENCH KISS

A Berkley Sensation Book / published by arrangement with the author

PRINTING HISTORY
Berkley Sensation trade paperback edition / June 2006
Berkley Sensation mass-market edition / May 2007

Copyright © 2006 by Susan Johnson.
Cover art by Stanley Chow.
Cover design by George Long.
Interior text design by Kristin del Rosario.

ISBN: 978-0-425-21634-7

BERKLEY SENSATION®
Berkley Sensation Books are published by The Berkley Publishing Group,
a division of Penguin Group (USA) Inc.,
375 Hudson Street, New York, New York 10014.
BERKLEY SENSATION is a registered trademark of Penguin Group (USA) Inc.
The "B" design is a trademark belonging to Penguin Group (USA) Inc.

PRINTED IN THE UNITED STATES OF AMERICA

10 9 8 7 6 5 4 3 2 1

One

OKAY, NICKY HAD TO ADMIT, SHE WAS INTIMI-
dated. Even though she'd told herself she wouldn't
be. So Johnny Patrick had produced the most top-
ten records in the last decade. So he'd been married to
the most beautiful movie star of the century. So he
could have been a movie star himself—you know the
tall, dark, silent type that could get any woman he
wanted. It wasn't supposed to matter.

This was a potential new client.

Nothing more.

It wasn't as though she was going to sleep with him
this afternoon—although she and every woman in the
world with breath in her body might be tempted.

For sure, she wasn't going to act like some idiot.

She'd worked for lots of rich people.

Her tree houses could get pretty pricey.

Not that she didn't build inexpensive ones, too, but

let's face it, ever since that article about her tree houses had appeared in the *L.A. Times*, she'd been swamped with top-bracket people wanting her to build them the tree house they'd never had as a kid. They always pretended little Madison or Skip Junior wanted a quarter-million-dollar tree house. And in return, she always pretended that those little kids did.

But even in her more rarified world of customers since that article, Johnny Patrick was right up there in the stratosphere of celebrities. And the locked gates at street level, not to mention the long drive up the Berkeley hills, with gardeners manicuring the landscape on every side, were doing a number on her intentions to stay calm.

Oh, Christ.

She'd reached the top of the hill.

Was that a house, or had Versailles been transported stone-by-stone to California?

AFTER PARKING IN THE HUMONGOUS CAR PARK TO the left of the entrance, it took her a moment to compose herself. Leaning on the steering wheel of her small hybrid car, she went through that old saw of Burns'—"A man's a man for a' that"—and reminded herself as well that she was here because she'd been asked. Johnny Patrick was interested in her expertise.

But really, how confident could one be in the presence of this—no shit—French palace. She felt like she was a fucking long way from Black Duck, Minnesota.

Nicky found herself relaxing when the door was opened by a little girl instead of a stately butler or French maid. And when the towheaded girl, dressed in shorts and a Shrek T-shirt, asked excitedly, "Are you the tree house lady?" the atmosphere shifted closer to normal.

"I am," Nicky said, holding out her small portfolio of plans.

"Oh, great! Hey, Daddy, the tree house lady is here!" And spinning around, she ran away down a cavernous hallway, shouting, "Come on, follow me!"

Keeping the blond hair in sight, down the hall and through a large room with museum-quality furniture and floor-to-ceiling French doors, Nicky found herself outside on a veranda that bordered an Olympic-sized pool. And swimming in that pool was none other than one of *People* magazine's "Sexiest Men Alive."

Her towheaded guide was hopping up and down on the hand-painted red and blue tile pool surround, screaming, "Hurry, hurry, Daddy! I've been waiting all day!"

When Johnny Patrick pulled himself out of the water in a spectacular display of toned muscle and grace, Nicky didn't know where to look. He was really built— lean with heavy-duty muscles, his tanned skin sleek and wet, his Speedo not doing a lot to cover what looked to be a real noteworthy package.

"I'll be right with you," he said, reaching for a pair of faded shorts on the tiled edging. "Sit down." He waved toward a pool-side table and chairs. "Jordi, go find Maria. Tell her we need some lemonade."

The sound of a zipper zipping was a distinct relief, as Nicky moved toward the table and chairs. The word *charisma* was tailor-made for a man like Johnny Patrick. He was a frigging babe magnet without even trying.

Fortunately she had a moment to gather her wits before he sat down. This was a business appointment, she reminded herself sternly. Don't screw up because he happens to be God's gift to women. A man like him knows it.

He dropped into the chair opposite her, ran his fingers through his hair to slick it back, slid down on his spine in a comfortable lounge and looked at her with a penetrating gaze. "You're an architect, right?"

"Yes." She sat up straighter, his tone all business. Although it would have helped the businesslike atmosphere if he'd worn a shirt.

"A friend of mine had you build his son a tree house. Kyle Jeter."

She nodded. "We just finished it." *Don't, don't, don't look at his buff upper body.* Deliberately fixing her gaze on his face, she said in her best professional tone, "We came in under deadline, too."

"So I heard. Kyle was pleased. He said you're really good."

"Thank you." Those cool gray eyes; she felt as though he was gauging her against some internal criteria.

"You're familiar with keeping a low profile, I understand."

"If necessary. Certainly."

"I don't want Jordi's tree house to wind up in some scandal sheet. I'm trying to give her as normal a life as possible."

That was a big assignment, she felt like saying, with a celebrity mother and father who had been featured on every tabloid cover known to man, as a couple and then singly since their divorce. "I understand," she said instead. "Everything can be kept under the radar if you wish."

"How did you end up in tree houses?"

"Long story."

"I've got plenty of time."

That chill glance again, as though he was overfamiliar with interlopers. "I came out here with a boyfriend. We both had degrees in architecture and wanted a warmer climate for our designs."

"Not tree houses."

"No. Small houses for people with simple lifestyles."
She smiled faintly. "That didn't exactly work out."

"Did the boyfriend work out?"

"Does it matter?"

"It could if I'm trying to keep this from the tabloids."

"He's gone. He took a trip to Thailand and never
came back."

"Ah."

"Meaning?" Her voice took on a small edge.

"Nothing." He smiled for the first time. "Forgive me.
One gets paranoid in my line of work."

"Too many groupies?" she said, figuring she was allowed after his damnably personal queries.

He seemed not to notice her pique. "Lots of stuff,"
he said, his shoulder lifting in the smallest of shrugs.
"Did you bring something to show me?"

As Nicky slid her portfolio across the table toward
him, a girlish voice shouted, "I wanna see, too! Wait!
Wait!"

Jordi was running toward them, followed by a
middle-aged woman in slacks and a U2 T-shirt carrying
a tray of glasses. As Jordi neared her father, she leaped
at him with total abandon from at least six feet away. He
caught her easily, as though they'd gone through that
drill once or twice before, and settled her on his lap,
drew up the portfolio, and opened it.

"Oh, I want *that* one!" Jordi cried, brushing her long
blond hair away from her face so she could see better.
"Look at that cute tower and that rope ladder!"

"Wait till you see them all, baby. There might be another one you like more." His voice was low key, his
smile doting, as he gazed at his daughter.

Nicky's stomach did a sudden little flip-flop at that
look of adoration from the rock world's major player.

He'd produced every big name album in recent history.
And there he was—not the bad-ass magnet of every star-
let and serious musician in the world of rock-and-roll,
but fucking DADDY. Oh, Christ, he must have asked her
something because he was looking at her expectantly.

"Alcoholic or non?"

Clearly, he'd repeated the query. "Ah . . . non is
fine," she quickly replied as though she hadn't been in
dreamland.

"Me, too, Maria." He smiled at his housekeeper.
"I'm on the wagon."

Maria grinned and shot a glance at Nicky. "Mr.
Johnny watches his drinking. He's a real good father."

Wow. That shot down the public image of sex, drugs,
and rock-and-roll.

"How 'bout some of those big cookies?" Jordi
looked at her father. "It's still hours till supper."

"Why not. Some of those Rocky Road cookies,
Maria. You like chocolate?" he asked, looking up at
Nicky.

"I doubt there's a woman who doesn't."

"Really?" His dark brows rose slightly.

Apparently Lisa Jordan, ex-wife and star of important small films adored by the critics, didn't like chocolate. "I probably like it more than most," Nicky said,
trying to be polite.

His brows dropped, his attention back on the portfolio and his daughter's enthusiastic appreciation of each
and every tree house Nicky had ever built.

When Maria returned with a plate of mouthwatering
cookies studded with chunks of dark chocolate, creamy
marshmallows, and huge pecans, Nicky had to restrain
herself. She'd forgotten to eat lunch, breakfast hadn't
been exactly filling—unless three cups of espresso
counted—and the temptation to grab two or three cook-

ies was almost overwhelming. Rocky Road was her favorite kind of ice cream, and the Dean & Deluca catalogue always had Rocky Road cookies that required overnight delivery.

Really, she was suddenly feeling a kind of immediate rapport.

It was amazing how chocolate could make one overlook even blatant discrepancies like Versailles-like homes and rock-star personalities.

Ohmygod, he reached for a cookie almost before the plate hit the table.

How could you *not* get along with a man who liked chocolate?

They all ate their cookies in a companionable silence, agreeing between chews on several characteristics necessary to tree houses. Like rope ladders that pulled up. And the need for electricity for a TV. And a small fridge for sodas. And a room large enough to bring up a ton of friends.

Nicky jotted down Jordi's favorite construction elements as they ate, not even refusing when Johnny offered her a third cookie. So she looked like a pig. So what, when these cookies were to die for.

"Bring up the plans when you have them finished," he said, after they'd cleaned the plate and drunk their lemonade. "I think we have a go here."

"Is there some budget number for the project?" She'd learned early on to let her clients know that if they wanted the Taj Mahal of tree houses, it would cost them more than a nickel.

"Not really. As long as Jordi's happy with the plans, I'm on board."

"I could show you something say—by the end of the month."

"I need it sooner."

His smile was meant to dazzle, and it did, a distinct sensation of pleasure zipping through her senses in spite of his outrageous demand. "How soon exactly?" she asked, dubiously.

"Real soon," he said, ignoring the reservation in her tone. "We have a birthday coming up, don't we, baby?" he cheerfully added, ruffling his daughter's hair. His gaze swung back to Nicky. "I apologize for such short notice, but I just finished work on an album and came out into the sunlight again, as it were. Then Jordi decided she wanted a tree house for her birthday, you were recommended as the best and"—he shrugged—"and here we are. Naturally, I'd be happy to compensate you for whatever inconvenience this rush project will entail."

"Jeez, I don't know . . ." She had work up the gazoo, and she wasn't sure she liked his blasé money-will-buy-anything attitude.

"I'm good at expediting things," Johnny offered. "Whatever you need, I could see that it was on site ASAP."

"Can I *have* my tree house for my birthday?" Jordi murmured, looking up at her father with a soulful gaze.

His daughter had picked up on her uncertainty, Nicky thought, although the father clearly hadn't—or wouldn't. Right now she could practically see the wheels clicking in Johnny Patrick's head—giving his daughter what she wanted was priority one for him. The question was: How much did she want to make it her priority, too?

It wasn't as though she were starstruck or impressed with money; she'd worked with lots of prominent, wealthy clients. But Johnny Patrick had a couple of things going for him that those other clients didn't— like a face and body to die for. Not that she was interested in turning into a groupie, but she had to admit, it *would* be fun just *looking*. So, call her shallow, along with all the other ladies who drooled over him, if the titillating stories in the tabloids were true.

And seriously, he was offering her the store, moneywise. So what did she have to lose? She'd charge him big-time, make her accountant happy, make his daughter happy, and derive a modicum of enjoyment herself from an up-close-and-personal view of the man whose New Year's Eve party in St. Barts was still generating gossip in the scandal sheets. "When is the birthday?" she asked.

"August fifteenth."

A fucking month? Was he crazy? "Are you crazy?" she said, as though her frontal lobes that were charged with self-censorship had gone on vacation.

He smiled faintly. "Probably. But, look, make it small. We can add on to the tree house later. What do you think, baby?" he queried, glancing down at his daughter. "Will you settle for something small to begin with?"

"Sure, Daddy! I don't care what size it is! I just want a rope ladder to climb up into my *very own* tree house!"

Apparently neither one of them were used to the word *no*. "Even a small tree house takes time to construct," Nicky cautioned. A month was almost out of the question.

"I could hire whatever men you need—and gofers to fetch and carry for you. Do you need a driver, extra draftsmen? Someone to cater food for the crew?"

Not only was she in Versailles-on-the-hill, but apparently the Sun King mentality that brooked no dissent had come over to sunny California with the building materials. Not to mention, Jordi was watching them both intently, like a spectator at a tennis match.

"Say yes," Johnny said, softly, his gaze no longer cool but warm and enticing. "And name your price."

"Puleeeese!" Jordi pleaded.

Whether it was Johnny Patrick's sex appeal or his daughter's pleading, whether she was taken in by his extraordinary good looks or his more or less unlimited offer of money, Nicky heard herself saying, "Okay, I'll try."

"Yessss!" Jordi exclaimed, smiling broadly.

"Thanks," Johnny said. "I really appreciate it."

His simple reply seemed to strike some pleasure center she hadn't known existed—somewhere deep in the recesses of her psyche. Luckily, her more rational senses took charge a second later and reminded her that this was about building a tree house and making money—not about anything else. "I'll take a look at the site and get working on a plan, then," she said in a deliberately neutral tone to compensate for her momentary lapse in judgment. "The design won't be anything complicated though."

"Fine. We're good with that, aren't we, baby?" Johnny said, smiling at his daughter.

"Any kind of tree house will be PER-FECT!" Jordi announced.

Johnny nodded. "Absolutely. We'll take a look at the site. Then, give us a call when the plans are ready, and we'll set up a meeting."

"I need a chair big enough for you, Daddy." Jordi glanced at Nicky. "So he can watch sports with me. Is that okay?"

"I'll make sure there's room."

The first few bars of U2's "Vertigo" suddenly resonated in the spring air.

Johnny pulled a cordless phone from his shorts pocket, glanced at the caller ID, frowned, and pushed his chair back. "I have to take this call," he said, easing

Jordi off his lap. "We were thinking a tree house would be good at the end of the terrace. Over there," he said with a wave toward the bay side of his house. "Do you mind looking it over yourself? Jordi, it's Mommy. Run into the house and pick up one of the phones."

He turned and walked away before Nicky could answer, but not before she heard him ask in a pissed off tone, "Where the hell are you? You were supposed to come and see Jordi yesterday. She's running for a phone, so get your damned story straight. I don't want you fucking up her head."

Okaaay. Trouble in paradise, Nicky decided as she came to her feet. Not that the tabloids hadn't dished out what all the inquiring minds wanted to know ten times over already—like Lisa Jordan's drug use, her three times in rehab, the rumors of Johnny's extra-curricular women on the side, the last screaming match between the loving couple in Paris, and the details of the divorce settlement that supposedly had Lisa Jordan trying to overturn her prenup she claimed was signed in Bali somewhere and didn't count.

It made one appreciate the boredom of a normal life where one worked nine to five—ostensibly . . . and considered recreation a drive up the coast highway or a flavored martini at some new night spot. No paparazzi, no prenups, no rehab—unless she was going to be put in someday for overconsumption of chocolate.

On the other hand, people like Johnny Patrick had enough money to offer her an open-ended contract to build his daughter a tree house. So rather than make judgments on people's lifestyles, she should count her blessings, keep her mouth and eyes shut, apropos of celebrity scandals past and present, check out the tree house site, and design Jordi Patrick the best damned tree house possible.

* * *

AS SHE BRAKED HER WAY DOWN THE STEEP DRIVE
some time later, she was already planning the house in
her mind. And she was thinking, too, how lucky she was
to be making a living doing what she liked to do.

She could thank Theo for dragging her out here
when she was all set to open a shop in Minneapolis. Although she wasn't about to forgive him for cleaning out
their bank account and selling all their furniture to finance his trip to Thailand.

The jerk.

It had taken her a couple years to move on from a
hand-to-mouth existence.

But the gravy train had come into town after the first
tree house she'd built for a friend for nothing. She'd had
to hire three extra crews lately to keep up with her
clients.

It just went to show you, you could plan and plan—
six years of nose-to-the-grindstone in college, internship at a top firm, and then voilà—gypsy fate hits you
over the head, and you find yourself in California—
broke, then not so broke—building some of the more
creative structures in the universe.

Two

$\mathbb{A}$ THE NEXT TIME NICKY ARRIVED AT VER-
sailles-on-the-hill, her plans completed, Maria escorted her to the loggia with views of San Francisco Bay and Jordi's tree house site and left her in the
little girl's care. "Daddy said he'll be off the phone in a
minute," Jordi explained, gesturing at her father, who
was pacing back and forth under a flowering wisteria at
the end of the loggia. "We were waiting for you, and
then Mom called. Are those the plans?" She jabbed at
the roll of blueprints Nicky carried.

"Yup. They've got your name on them."

"Wow! Like for *real*? My very own *name*?" Jordi's
eyes were huge. "Show me, show me—over here . . . on
the table!" Running to a large teakwood table used for
outdoor dining, Jordi shouted, "Hey, Dad! My tree house
plans are here!"

The phone still at his ear, Johnny swiveled around and waved.

"He said he'd stop talking when you came, but they're probably in the middle of a fight. They always fight," Jordi said with casual acceptance. "My friend Betsy's parents always fight, too, and she says I have it better 'cause my mom and dad aren't in the same house, and I don't have to *listen* to them scream."

Too much information, Nicky thought, beginning to unroll the plans on the tabletop. On the other hand, Jordi Patrick didn't seem distraught by the irreconcilable differences between her parents. The resiliency of youth, Nicky figured, or maybe Jordi had a different comfort level when it came to family discord.

"Ohmygod—there's my name!" Jordi cried, gesticulating wildly at the heading at the top of the first page. "Jordi Patrick's Tree House. Awe-*some*!"

"How about we take a look at the drawings, and you let me know what you think?" Quickly flipping over the page, Nicky pointed at one of several elevations on the second page. "This is what the tree house will look like on the side facing the bay." She slid her finger to a second drawing. "And this view"—she paused as a sharp expletive resonated from the far end of the terrace—"will face the terrace," she quickly went on, trying not to acknowledge the round of curses drifting their way.

Jordi looked up, but instead of registering consternation, she cheerfully said, "O-*kay*! Daddy's done now!"

Maybe Jordi was into gratitude therapy—you know, like always looking on the bright side of things, Nicky thought, surreptitiously checking out Jordi's dad. Johnny Patrick was slipping his phone into his shorts pocket as he strode toward them, but unlike his Pollyanna daughter, he was frowning.

"Sorry about the wait," Johnny said as he reached them. He nodded at the plans. "How's it looking, baby? Is it something you like?"

"It's awesome, Daddy!" Jordi said, tracing the rope ladder with her fingertip. "Look at the ladder! And look at this!" she added, moving her finger upward. "It even has a fabulous, perfect, pointy-top tower like I wanted!"

Despite Jordi's exuberance, Nicky could see that Johnny Patrick's thoughts were elsewhere. While he was doing his best to be attentive, he wasn't entirely succeeding.

Jordi tugged on her father's hand. "Hey—Earth to Daddy!"

From the mouths of babes, Nicky thought.

"I heard everything you said, baby—pointy tower and all." He squeezed his daughter's hand. "I love it."

His effort to refocus was so patently forced, Nicky decided the lives of the rich and famous sucked at times like everyone else's. "I tried to incorporate all the elements Jordi liked best," Nicky interposed, talking fast to fill the sudden silence. "I'm glad the tower and rope ladder works for everyone, but if you want any changes just say so. The main room is large enough for a chair for your dad, Jordi. So we're good there. Any questions so far?" Although after one look at Johnny Patrick's blank stare, she was sorry she'd asked.

"Do I have a TV?" Jordi piped up.

Thank God for children's egocentric worldview. "Yup, sure do."

"How big?"

"Whatever you want, although I'd suggest something semimodest. The rooms aren't all that big."

"It's perfect then. Betsy's gonna be soooo jealous. She's my best friend, though, so she'll really like it, too.

Hey, Dad!" Jordi jerked on her dad's hand. "Do you like it?"

"Absolutely." Johnny's smile was more real this time.

Maybe he'd snapped out of whatever weird mood he'd been in, Nicky decided, although she hoped he wasn't going to be out of things on a regular basis. The tabloid rumors about drug use had always pointed at his ex, but one never knew.

"It sounds as though Jordi is on board," he said, his tone all business, like it had been at their first meeting. "And I want to thank you for your promptness. Jordi's been bugging me mercilessly, so I appreciate your quick turnaround. Let me take a closer look at what you've come up with," he added, leaning over the table and studying the elevations. "Nice," he murmured a moment later. "Terrific. The design is unusual." He flipped over another page and glanced at it briefly. "We won't be seeing a dozen of these anywhere," he added with a grin as he stood upright. "Baby, did you thank Nicole?"

"Nicky, please."

"Nicky it is. What do you say?" he prompted, glancing at his daughter.

"Thank you, Nicky. It's fab-u-lous," Jordi declared. "More fabulous than anything!"

"I agree." Johnny arched his brows. "So when can you start?"

"Don't you want to see the rest of the plans?" Nicky thumbed the edge of the thick stack of blueprints.

"I've seen all I need to see. How about you, Jordi?"

"A birthday party in my own tree house is gonna be GUUUR-ATE!"

Johnny's grin shifted from his daughter to Nicky. "I'd say we're ready to go if it's okay with you."

"I knew you were in a rush—so whenever you want to start we'll schedule you in."

"Yesterday, if I know my daughter." His gaze was amused.

"How about tomorrow morning? Then—with luck, if we don't run into any snafus, we'll bring this project in on time."

"Don't worry. I'll take care of any snafus."

He spoke with such assurance, she almost believed he might be capable of such a daunting task. "Things come up sometimes. Unavoidable things," she cautioned. "Materials don't come on time, something you've ordered has been discontinued and they forgot to tell you, even the weather can be a problem, although this time of year weather probably won't be an issue."

"Whatever crises come up, consider them handled."

Wow. He sounded positively commanding—like he should be wearing combat gear or general's stripes instead of shorts and a T-shirt. "Sounds good," she said in lieu of her reflections. "I'll have a crew here tomorrow morning. We start early. Will that be a problem?"

"I *always* get up early," Jordi said. "Don't I, Dad?"

He smiled. "Oh, yeah."

"You're gonna have to get up early, too," Jordi teased.

"We can manage without supervision," Nicky quickly interposed, not sure celebrity music producers wanted to be awakened early. "Really—unless we run into a situation that requires a change order you have to authorize, don't worry about us."

"I don't sleep in often. Occasionally I work in my studio all night. When everything's clicking, I take advantage of it." He shrugged faintly. "But that's rare, so assume I'm available should you need me."

"Will do." Now, if she weren't trying real hard to ignore the fact that he was tall, dark, and handsome—not to mention sexy—that *I'm available* line might have been super-enticing.

"I'm *always* available," Jordi announced. "'Specially in the summer."

"Sounds good," Nicky said, coming back down to earth. "We start at seven. With a rush job like this, I'll be coming by to check things out more often than usual, but I'll try not to get in your way."

"You won't be in *my* way!" Jordi exclaimed with her usual enthusiasm.

"You'd better see that you don't get in Nicky's way," her dad admonished. "But seriously, if you need anything," he added, turning to Nicky, "and can't find me, check with Maria. She'll know where I am."

"I look forward to the project," Nicky said, putting out her hand.

Johnny took her hand in a firm grip. "I'm pleased you could fit us into your schedule."

Nicky wondered how many times Johnny Patrick was denied anything with his money-is-no-object stance. But she knew better than to voice her thoughts. "The pleasure is mine," she murmured, slipping her hand free.

He was really tall, she thought, apropos of nothing, as she took a step backward. And really rich apparently. This was one of those win/win situations. With the profit from this tree house, she'd be able to pay off the balance on her office mortgage. How cool was that? Thank God for the world's love of music and even more for rich music producers. That little Green and Green bungalow she used as her office was gonna be hers free and clear real soon.

Nicky was in the midst of building castles in the air, and it took a nudge from Jordi to bring her back to earth. Not that the little girl wasn't used to adults going off into the ether, she thought, looking up and trying to figure out what Johnny had said to her.

"Care for a glass of bubbly to close the deal?"

His query was polite as hell, but he was smiling, and rather than explain her lapse by saying something inconsequential—Nicky decided on the truth. "I was counting my money."

"Reason enough to zone out," Johnny said with a grin. "Do you have time for a glass? We'll toast our new project. Jordi's looking forward to a Shirley Temple."

"I *love* Shirley Temples—'specially the way Maria makes them with lots of cherries. Come on—sit down." She pulled out a chair. "Come on!"

Nicky hesitated—not because her life was so busy she couldn't take time to have a glass of champagne, but mostly because she was thinking it would be more prudent to maintain a professional distance with God's gift to women. Not that she expected to be hit on, but she didn't want to get too close to his potent force field. Especially if she was going to be around him a lot in the coming month; a certain circumspection would be politic. "Sure, why not," she heard herself say, as though reason and logic had left town. "I'd love a glass of champagne."

"Great. I'll be right back. Jordi, tell Nicky about that song you wrote for me. Not that I'm prejudiced, but my daughter has talent," he said with a grin.

"And he should know," Jordi asserted, smiling broadly.

He winked at Nicky. "When Jordi makes the charts, then I can start counting my money, too."

As if he didn't have accountants keeping busy doing that already, Nicky thought, mentally ticking off his material assets the tabloids loved to disclose: the yacht, the various homes around the world, the fast cars. But well-mannered, she said instead, "Way to go, Jordi. Tell me about your song."

AS JOHNNY STRODE AWAY, HE WAS FORCED TO acknowledge he hadn't planned on extending an invitation for drinks. In fact, he was super-wary of making new female friends for a thousand cogent reasons. So why had he? Good question. Maybe it was because Lisa had pissed him off more than usual. Maybe he needed some time with a normal woman to remind him that every female wasn't as selfish and demanding as his ex.

One of Lisa's rants today had been about the price of tea in China. Literally. No shit. She was on some new kick, and apparently she thought it was up to him to find her some rare handpicked tea from some goddamned special mountain in China. As if he fucking cared. But no matter how many times he told her he wasn't her go-to man, she still expected him to take care of every fucking little thing for her. Fortunately, he had people who could handle shit like that. But Christ, when would the constant haranguing end?

Now that he thought about it, he probably needed a drink after talking to Lisa and just didn't want to drink alone. Maybe it was that simple.

No doubt.

(Male introspection or lack of it at work.)

Before Johnny returned, Jordi not only sang her song, but explained how she'd composed the music first, then the lyrics in the space of an hour. Now, it wasn't a complicated song, but it was impressive nonetheless. The girl was only nine. And Nicky knew, because she'd asked when Jordi had finished singing.

So much for genetics.

Three

NICKY DIDN'T STAY LONG FOR CHAMPAGNE.
Before she had drunk less than half a flute,
Johnny pulled his phone out of his pocket, although it must have been on vibrate, because it hadn't
rung. Glancing at the screen, he said, "Sorry, my
phone's my office; I have to take this call." Rising to his
feet, he smiled at Nicky. "Tomorrow at seven, then?"

"I'll be here."

"Me, too," Jordi said. "I'm setting my alarm just in
case."

As Johnny walked away, Nicky heard him say, "Your
album's going platinum next week," and was struck by
the casual demeanor of this man who created one successful career after another for musicians on his small
indie label. Talk about the golden touch. Yet he seemed
immune to the deification syndrome suffered by so
many famous people. He was dealing with a tree house

for his daughter like any other suburban dad would. He didn't have handlers or an entourage, unless Maria counted. And he was raising his daughter to be as unpretentious as he.

"Can I keep these?" Jordi asked, tapping the blueprints. "I'm gonna call Betsy and have her come over. Maybe she can stay with me tonight, and we'll both be here when you start tomorrow."

"They're yours. Keep 'em." Coming to her feet, Nicky smiled. "And I'll see you bright and early tomorrow."

"I'll make sure Dad is awake."

Nicky could have said she didn't need Johnny Patrick around to begin construction, but maybe his daughter did. "Sounds good."

"I'll walk you to your car." Gulping down the last of her Shirley Temple, Jordi ran around to Nicky's side of the table. "And if Betsy's here tomorrow we'll sing our duet for you." She fell into step alongside Nicky. "Betsy's even a better singer than me. It figures though—her mom used to sing in a band. That's how her dad met her, but now that they're married, he doesn't want her to see any of her old friends, Betsy says. He calls them burnouts, her mom says they're not, and then—"

"Does Betsy write songs, too?" Nicky interrupted, thinking Betsy's parents would probably prefer not having the troubles in their marriage broadcast to the world.

"Uh-uh. But she plays the piano pretty good—almost as good as me. But no one's as good as my dad on the piano. He can play anything. He can do just about anything else, too."

And before they reached Nicky's car, Jordi had chronicled a formidable list of her father's accomplishments, including his ability to stand on his head for *just ages and ages.*

Yoga, Nicky thought. A California lifestyle. That

explained his lean, supple body and the way he carried himself. Unfortunately, images of those really
sexy Tantric yoga contortions sprang to mind when
she thought of Johnny Patrick and yoga. Which
would never do. Professionally speaking. With construction about to begin. Struggling to shut down her
lurid imagination, she seriously focused on Jordi's
monologue, which had somehow segued into Maria
teaching her how to swim. "She's from Hawaii, you
know, and swims like crazy. I'm getting better all the
time, she says. Next year, I'm gonna take lessons in
school. Hey, you have one of those hybrid cars," she
exclaimed as they entered the limestone paved car
park. "I told dad he should get one, but he likes to
drive too fast, he says. Hybrids go fast though, too,
don't they?"

Nicky glanced at the flashy black sports car next to
hers. "Hybrids probably don't go as fast as your dad's
cars." *Nor do they cost the equivalent of some third-
world country's domestic GNP,* she thought, quickly
scanning the low-slung race car.

"But you're saving the environment, that's for sure."

"I hope I'm making a difference." Nicky opened her
car door.

Jordi took a step back and waved. "See ya tomorrow."

"My crew and I will be here early."

"I can *hardly* wait!"

Nicky smiled at the young girl as she dropped into
her seat. "Me, too," she said and found she really meant
it, although she chose not to examine the reasons why.
With a wave, she shut the car door and fired up her lime
green hybrid.

She could see Jordi still waving as she drove down
the serpentine drive to the street below. If only all her
clients were so personable, she thought—and willing to

pay the premium price Johnny Patrick was to see that his daughter had the birthday of her dreams.

It looked as though this tree house project might be sunny skies as far as the eye could see.

Fingers crossed.

Four

A
THE NEXT MORNING WHEN NICKY ARRIVED
on-site, the pattern for the days to come was set.
Johnny Patrick was there to greet her (with both
Jordi *and* Betsy that first morning), and after a brief
conversation concerning the construction schedule and
some friendly comments to the crew, he disappeared
into his studio.

Jordi wasn't so reclusive. She was, in fact, the complete opposite of her father, following Nicky around,
continually asking questions, her curiosity about every
facet of the construction more adult than juvenile. On
days when some difficult design element was taking
form, or there were questions only Nicky could answer,
she'd stay at the tree house for more lengthy periods.

They'd respected the site, doing the least possible
excavation in order to ensure the integrity of the hillside
and old-growth trees. The design itself was an organic

concept of cantilevered levels, suspended from a minimum of large timbers and steel guylines, the delicate structure giving the appearance of a bird about to take flight. The engineering was complex, but that was the beauty of the design—the experimental and pragmatic coalescing into a single goal.

On occasion, if her schedule allowed, Nicky would join Jordi for lunch. Maria's cooking was definitely an added incentive.

On even rarer occasions, Johnny would join them for lunch.

Nicky thought it might have something to do with the hand-rolled tortillas and lime-marinated snapper that Maria made on Tuesdays. Maria may have come from Hawaii, but she'd learned the art of fine Mexican cuisine somewhere, and apparently Nicky wasn't the only one who appreciated her expertise.

Even the wine sangria she served was out of this world, and in Nicky's opinion, that was hard to do with sangria.

On those infrequent times when Johnny joined them, Jordi carried most of the conversation. Her father would speak if spoken to, but was generally reserved. But not in an intimidating way, Nicky decided, although it might be that she was used to a father and brother who mostly let others talk. With Jordi around, however, no one had to worry about keeping the conversation going. She was an outgoing, gregarious child.

As the construction proceeded, Nicky and Jordi enjoyed an increasingly easy camaraderie. She and Jordi had just clicked, and they'd taken to having a tea party from time to time just to take a break in the afternoon. Nicky collected tea sets, so it wasn't a question of indulging a child. She was enjoying herself as much as Jordi.

Johnny had come out of his studio one day to find Nicky and his daughter laughing hysterically over a SpongeBob SquarePants joke, and at their invitation joined them. He soon became the object of their teasing as he tried to manipulate the tiny teacups with his large hands. He even drank several thimblefuls of tea, although he wasn't a tea drinker, because Jordi was having so much fun.

"Mommy drinks stuff from teacups, but it's not always tea," Jordi announced blandly. "I know it's something else, 'cause she won't let me have any."

A sudden silence fell.

"Maybe your mom doesn't know you like tea that much," Johnny quickly noted. "I'll tell her you do next time I talk to her."

Jordi rolled her eyes. "I'm not a baby, Dad."

"You know, I bought the most beautiful tea set in Japan. Why don't I bring it next time I come?" Nicky suggested, undertaking a politic shift in conversation. "The set was made at a monastery that's eight hundred years old."

"No kidding? Wow!"

"We can pretend we halfway understand the Japanese tea ceremony." Nicky smiled. "It's kind of complicated."

"I'll help out," Johnny offered. "I have a friend who's a master of the art, so I've sat through one or two." Or one or two hundred actually. His friend Kazuo had been a fanatic about tea ceremonies at one time.

"Do I know him?" Jordi asked. "Has he been over?"

"Uh-uh. He lives in Japan now. I knew Kazuo when we both lived in L.A.—before you were born."

"Can we do the tea ceremony thing tomorrow?"

Jordi looked from her father to Nicky. "Can we? It sounds super-fun!"

Her father always said yes to her, and today was no exception. "It's okay with me, if it's okay with Nicky."

Johnny was giving her a look that said she should agree. "Tomorrow sounds fine to me," she said. "I'll make sure I bring my tea set."

Five

THE NEXT AFTERNOON WHEN NICKY STOP-
ped by, she found two black Mercedes pulled up to
the door—as in right up to the base of the entrance
stairs.

Things didn't look quite right.

And apparently for good reason, she realized after
seeing Maria standing fixed in the open doorway, a suitcase in her hand and tears streaming down her face.

Jumping from her car, Nicky ran up the steps and
took the suitcase from Maria, although the older woman
seemed not to notice. Bending low to meet Maria's va-
cant gaze, Nicky said, "Is there something I can do to
help? Are you going somewhere? Could I drive you?"

Nothing.

The housekeeper was in a trance.

Figuring she'd interrupted some family drama that
was no business of hers, Nicky was about to set the suit-

case down and continue on to the tree house site in back, when Johnny Patrick's voice rang down through the entrance hall from the second floor. Looking up, she saw him racing down the massive curved staircase, flanked by two men who looked like bodyguards. Black T-shirts, black slacks, dark glasses, hair cut so short their skulls gleamed, and Hulk bodies.

"Let me know as soon as you find out when they took off. If they're on their way to Paris"—he looked at one of the men, who nodded—"then we'll be right behind. Get the pilots out to the airfield. We'll meet them there in an hour. We need Lisa's flight plan. Pay whomever you have to, to get it. Fucking loose cannon addict. She can't stay off the dope. A half hour now," he said as they reached the bottom of the stairs. "I'll see you out there. Oh, crap—we need someone who speaks French, too, someone who can be discreet. The last thing I want is the tabloids nosing around."

As Nicky stepped out of the way of the two burly men racing out the door, Johnny saw her for the first time. "*You* speak French, don't you?" Familiar with making things happen in an industry that could find itself out of fashion overnight, he reverted to form, intent on making things happen *his way* right now. "You said your grandmother spoke French to you." The subject had come up one luncheon when they had debated various French wines and their appellations.

"I also said my French accent was pretty quirky." Her grandmother's French Canadian patois was essentially eighteenth century. And if she needed another excuse not to go, people who traveled with bodyguards made her real, real apprehensive.

"Got a passport?"

Apparently quirky hadn't cut it. "I do, but—"

"Look, I'll make it worth your while. We're going to

Paris. I need someone who speaks French to come with me—someone I trust."

"I'm really sorry, but I can't. I mean . . . I have crews working and an office to run and clients—well . . . let's face it, screaming at me every day."

"How about fifty grand—a hundred—fuck, I don't care? Don't you have an office manager?"

"Well, yes . . . but."

"They took Jordi," he said, grimly. "It's not as though my fucking ex hasn't done this before. But she's never taken Jordi out of the country before, and the people she hangs with aren't exactly high-minded churchgoers. So I'm in a real fucking rush. Can you help me or not?"

His gray eyes were drilling into hers. Despite his cavalier outlook on her business, she *did* have a business that required her presence. Like all the time. But now she was also upset over Jordi's situation. She realized being a scion of the rich and famous had some serious pitfalls. And despite Jordi's acceptance of her mother's habits, she was probably a frightened little girl right now.

"I'll send my accountants to run your office. I must have ten of them. How's that?"

The man knew how to negotiate.

"And with satellite phones, you're never out of touch. You can leave a number with your office. Or two or three. There's a drawerful of phones on the plane. Look," he said, his distress showing for the first time, "Jordi might be in danger. I could really use your help."

"When would you leave?"

His smile lit up the cool, dim foyer. "Right now. And thanks."

"Don't say thanks yet. I'm still not sure, and *right NOW* sure as hell doesn't sound good."

"How about after we pick up your passport?" he said

with a faint smile, feeling as though something might be finally going right in his day from hell.

"I'd have to pack if I went."

"I'll buy you whatever you need."

"I'd have to call my office at least."

"You could call them from the car and settle whatever you have to settle or call them later from the plane. You'd have twelve hours of flight time to talk. Is your passport at home or at the office?"

"Jeez, I don't know you very well," she blurted out, voicing her most serious reservation. She'd actually be flying out of the country with a relative stranger—the stories in the *Enquirer* and a few lunches notwithstanding.

"What do you need to know? Tell her I'm trustworthy, Maria. Tell her I used to be a Boy Scout."

Christ, she'd forgotten the housekeeper was even there. Maria's soft sobs melted into the background of her own incredulity and doubts.

"Mr. Johnny's the best, Miss Nicky. Good and kind, the best father—" Maria broke down into racking sobs, her words undistinguishable wails.

The fact that Jordi liked Nicky was a distinct plus in this fucked-up situation, Johnny decided. Although he wasn't particularly keen that Jordi had formed a friendship with a woman he barely knew. But Jordi came before everything. That he *did* know. "Would you come with me for Jordi's sake if nothing else? She could very well be scared to death." He grimaced. "Her mother hasn't taken her out of the country before, so she could be worried as hell. And what with you two laughing a lot—and, you know . . . getting along so well, you'd be another friendly face, if you know what I mean. Like you'd bring a bit of normalcy to all this bizarre crap." At the thought of Nicky and Jordi laughing together he had

an uncomfortable moment: Jordi liked people so easily;
somehow he'd lost that ability. "Look," he said, his
voice husky and low, "I'd be damned grateful if you'd
come."

"If I went," Nicky said, slowly, knowing she didn't
actually have a choice unless she wanted to look like the
most uncaring bitch, "I couldn't be gone long."

He hadn't realized he'd been holding his breath. He
exhaled softly. "I'll see that you're not. My word on it.
Hey, Maria," Johnny exclaimed, moving toward his
housekeeper, feeling decidedly more upbeat. "I've got a
helper. We'll be back with Jordi in no time." Guiding
the housekeeper to a chair, he eased her down and patted her shoulder. "Have your mother come stay with
you until we get back. Joseph will pick her up. I'll let
him know. Stay here now, and he'll come for you." With
a last pat on her shoulder, he nodded to Nicky and
strode toward the door.

"If we had more time, I'd wait until Maria's mom got
here, but"—he shrugged as they moved outside and he
picked up the suitcase—"time I don't have. My car's
over there," he said, stabbing his finger at a black Lamborghini and pulling his cell phone from his jeans'
pocket. "I just have to call my driver, and we're out of
here."

Six

JOHNNY WAS DIALING HIS CELL PHONE AGAIN as Nicky left his car and walked up the path to her front door. After ransacking her desk and the junk drawers in the kitchen, she eventually found her passport where she'd left it after her Tokyo trip—in the bottom of her carry-on that was still lying on a chair by the door. There wasn't even time to feel guilty that she hadn't moved the bag in a month. Grabbing the green leather tote, she ran upstairs to her bedroom.

She jerked open several drawers on her semanier, tossed a couple changes of underwear into her bag, moved to her dresser, and emptied the cosmetics tray— sum total, four items—into the tote on top of her underwear. Sending up a brief prayer that her perfume bottle didn't leak, since it cost more than a person from Minnesota would normally pay for frivolity, she pulled two

T-shirts from her closet, added a pair of slacks to complete her minimum packing, and was back downstairs in record time.

Grabbing a chartreuse suede jacket from a hook by the door, she spun around in the foyer of her restored California craftsman cottage, as though one last look would afford her sane counsel, or lacking that, some sign that she was doing the right thing.

The stuffed moose head she'd inherited from her grandpa stared back at her with its usual transcendental expression.

Shit. She needed advice, not a blank stare.

A trumpeting car horn brusquely intruded into her moment of doubt.

Okaaay. If not a sign, it sure as hell indicated urgency.

Probably a kidnapped daughter trumped doubt anytime.

Pulling open the front door, she walked out.

As she moved toward the sleek, black car idling at the curb, she wondered, was this really happening? Was she about to fly to Paris? Was this all insane?

Like seriously?

Just then the car door swung open, and there was Johnny Patrick leaning over and smiling up at her.

What the hell.

How many women had the chance to be up close and personal with the gorgeous, fabulous, more-beautiful-than-Brad-Pitt Johnny Patrick?

"Sorry for rushing you, but I'm uptight as hell." He put his hand out for her bag.

"I was just having a moment of indecision," she admitted, handing over her tote.

"Call your parents, your friends, whomever. Let them know where you're going." He tossed her bag next to his in the small storage area behind the seat. "Give them my phone number. It works everywhere." He held her gaze as she dropped into the seat beside him and pulled the door shut. "How's that?"

"What's the number?"

"Here's a pen." Reaching above his visor as he hit the accelerator, he cranked a tight U-turn in the narrow street. Steering with his knees as he ran through the gears like a race car driver and held out an expensive Mont Blanc with his other hand, he eased them at rocket speed past a delivery truck like a champion multitasker. Shooting through the stop sign at the corner, he downshifted, grabbing the wheel a split-second later as the gears caught, and he wheeled a right onto the main thoroughfare.

Paralyzed by fear, Nicky braced herself against possible lethal impact. But moments later as Johnny smoothly wove through traffic, she decided perhaps she wasn't about to die that precise second, and her ability to speak returned. "I don't need the pen," she said— something she should have mentioned a block and a half ago, so he could have had two hands on the wheel instead of one or none. "My memory's good."

He shot her a skeptical look.

"Keep your eyes on the road. I'm not sure my insurance is paid up. I'm even less sure if I ever changed my beneficiary after Theo took off for Thailand and more or less left me at the altar with ten payments left on my engagement ring. No way do I want him to live in comfort on my dime. So what's the number?"

It took him a moment to digest her blunt assessment of her former fiancé. And another to decide the guy didn't know when he had a good thing going. Not that any of it was relevant to his life, he quickly resolved, and recited his cell phone number—slowly . . . just in case.

"Jeez! Eyes on the road *please*!" she shrieked. He'd practically taken the paint off a Hyundai as he threaded his way through a very small opening between cars. She wasn't ready to cash in her chips *yet*.

"Don't worry. I raced Le Mans once."

At which point she shut her eyes. He'd switched lanes again, easing the Lamborghini between two cars with barely an inch to spare. A second later, he punched the accelerator, veered right across two lanes of fast-moving vehicles, hurtled up an exit ramp, catapulted out onto the freeway, and apparently indifferent to California traffic laws, put the speedometer into the red zone.

Johnny was more or less driving on automatic, his mind a tumult of emotion. The thought of his daughter in the hands of that lowlife crowd his ex hung with had him completely unnerved. Jordi might be scared as hell—wondering what was going on. She always called him if they went out of town. But she hadn't this time, and the fact that she hadn't disturbed him. If one of his friends hadn't seen her with Lisa at the Oakland airport, he wouldn't have even known she'd left San Francisco.

Silently running through every expletive known to man, he raged at his ex's selfish indifference to everyone but herself. She might not even remember Jordi was along once she was strung out. Not to mention the fact that those men his ex had been partying with of late were definitely operating outside the law. He'd had them checked out, and they were third-generation, big-time drug dealing families, Ivy League degrees, custom tailors, and all the right addresses notwithstanding. None of them were the kind of men he wanted around his daughter.

He felt like strangling Lisa.

Sure, she had a drug problem.

Sure, she needed help.

Again.

Three sojourns at Malibu House and the weekly therapy sessions he paid for apparently weren't doing the job. But, dammit, he didn't care how messed up she was. She had no friggin' right to involve their daughter in her druggie life.

This was the BLOODY . . . LAST . . . TIME.

No more Mister Nice Guy, no more goddamn shoulder to cry on.

The minute he had Jordi back, he was suing for sole custody.

Seven

"VERNIE, THE MUSIC'S TOO LOUD," JORDI MUM-
bled, half asleep.

"I know." The elderly woman grimaced faintly.
"Try to sleep, sweetie." Laverne Maxwell was nanny to
the stars, so she'd seen it all. But she didn't have to like it.
Gently massaging Jordi's small back, she softly hummed
a favorite Disney song and hoped the party in the main
lounge would soon wind down. Not that she was overly
optimistic, knowing her employer as she did. But they
would land in Paris by morning, she'd been told. At least
then, she and Jordi would be in their own hotel room.

At the moment, they were in a small bedroom on the
Gulfstream jet, the door shut—and locked. The nanny
didn't like the look of the crowd outside. But the driving
beat of the music echoed through the door, and the raucous sounds of voices trying to make themselves heard
above the music remained a persistent din.

Pulling the quilt higher, she covered Jordi's ears and prayed for a speedy landing.

Laverne had first met Lisa Jordan right after her much-reported divorce. She'd been one of two nannies who was nominally interviewed by the beautiful Miss Jordan. Even that first day, she'd recognized the signs of drug use. Lisa Jordan's face had been pale, her forehead beaded with sweat; she'd been agitated, constantly wiping her nose and sipping water. And while many users had a telltale twitch, Lisa Jordan had them all: pulling on her earlobe, twirling her hair, rubbing her hands. Vernie had felt an urge to lean over, pat her shoulder, and murmur, "There, there, calm down, calm down, everything's going to be fine . . ."

As for Miss Jordan's mental focus during that first interview, her assistant would bring her back to reality from time to time with a tap on her wrist and a few quiet words. And for a brief interval the conversation would be between three people once again.

As it turned out, Laverne had eventually been hired by the efficient young assistant dressed from head to foot in black Prada. The sleek, cool-as-a-cucumber brunette liked that Laverne had worked long term for one of the major Hollywood producers, who everyone in the industry knew partook of recreational drugs with considerable frequency. She particularly liked that no public gossip had ever surfaced about the producer's family.

Miss Ingram had made a generous offer, and Vernie had accepted the substantial retainer, with the understanding that she would only work occasionally. At her age, semiretirement held great appeal, a fact Miss Ingram was aware of when she'd approached Vernie in the first place.

Miss Ingram had also said in an undertone as she escorted Vernie from the room, "Miss Jordan is entering treatment again next week. She'll be more herself next time you see her."

And Miss Ingram had been right for several months afterward.

But opportunities for relapse were plentiful in the drug-chic world Lisa Jordan inhabited. And only the strong were able to resist temptation.

In the four years since Vernie had entered Lisa Jordan's employ, she'd become a surrogate mother of sorts to the messed-up young beauty whose own mother was on husband and face-lift number five. And counting.

She'd also become a friend and playmate to Jordi on her infrequent visits. As well as her protector. When Lisa was too spaced out, she kept Jordi as far away from her mother as possible.

It wasn't that Lisa Jordan hadn't tried to beat the drugs. She'd been through rehab three times. Hopefully, the fourth time would be the charm.

Meanwhile, Laverne had a vulnerable child in her care. The first chance she had once they landed, she was going to call Jordi's father.

This perpetual, traveling party with rich-as-they-may-be hoodlums was no place for a young girl like Jordi.

Eight

WHILE JOHNNY RAN OVER THE FLIGHT PLAN with his pilots upon their arrival at the private airstrip, Nicky decided to forgo calling her family. Her mother would have a thousand questions she'd prefer not answering—ditto for her sister. She did call her project manager, though, since he'd be running things while she was gone. After giving him a quick once-over on her immediate plans, she said, "I'll call you from Paris tomorrow, and we can discuss whatever construction crises have come up in my absence. I shouldn't be gone long."

"I hope like hell not," Buddy Mack grumbled. "We're up to our ears, babe."

She'd tried to break him of that "babe" habit when he'd first started working for her, but it was a lost cause. And since he was the best project manager on the north coast, he more than made up for a few "babes" with his on-time or under-deadline wraps on their tree houses. He was invaluable to her bottom line. "It's sort of an emergency, or I wouldn't be going," she explained.

"I'll tell that to the client who wants her kid's tree house ready for his birthday. I'm sure she'll understand, even though she doesn't understand anything but 'I want it yesterday.' "

"Sorry, Buddy."

"Don't sweat it. If it's an emergency, it's an emergency."

"Thanks."

"No problem. Call me tomorrow pronto, though. I can't do this alone."

"I will. First thing." But it took her a few moments to reconcile her controlling impulses. She was in charge because she liked it. Maybe needed it. Not that she was going to ask a therapist the reason why. She might not like the answer.

"Ready?"

Johnny had come up and was looking at her expectantly. "All set," she said. There was no point in elaborating. Her business was way down on his list of priorities at the moment.

And she didn't blame him.

JOHNNY'S BOMBARDIER G5000 LIFTED OFF THE TARmac shortly after four. Handing Nicky over to a steward who looked like he'd stepped from the pages of *GQ*, he excused himself and walked forward to sit with the pilots.

After being offered a menu and wine list fit for royalty, Nicky was shown to a private sitting room cum bedroom that dramatically demonstrated the opulent taste of some world-class decorator. She'd never seen the inside of a private plane—let alone such luxury. It was fucking impressive—from the hand-rubbed walnut paneling to the malachite handles on the doors, not to mention the coral pongee quilt on the divan that had been embroidered by a small village, from the look of the intricate design. Or if only one person had been involved, it had taken him or her a lifetime to complete.

She turned down the offer of champagne, figuring she'd better have her wits about her if she was involved in a possible international kidnapping. But she didn't turn down the plate of hors d'oeuvres that arrived a few moments later. Really, it was a mouth-watering sight: prawns bigger than she'd ever seen, spiced whole pecans—and you know how hard it is to get them out of the shell without breaking them into bits, rumaki that was so delicately crisp she could tell just by looking at it that it was going to taste like heaven, pretty little crudités made in all those flower and animal shapes that you only see in Asian recipe books, a Brie so rich it was oozing calories as it sat on its little lace doily, and the pièce de résistance to any woman with taste buds—a tray of truffles decorated with gold leaf, coconut, crushed pistachios, and for those with edgy appetites, chili peppers.

Having been raised in northern Minnesota, she wasn't sufficiently edgy to have a totally sophisticated palate, and the chili pepper truffles were one of the few items left untouched when she finally pushed the tray away and collapsed in a beige linen chair.

Could she turn on the TV, she wondered, or would the pilot go into a tailspin should an electronic device be activated? She was never quite sure, having been suitably intimidated by numerous flight attendants over the years. There seemed to be stark danger in turning on a switch while in the air.

Surveying her other entertainment options, her gaze

fell on a rack of magazines and books. Finding it delightful that she wasn't buckled in as she would have been on a commercial flight, she perused the books—all serious nonfiction—helped herself to several magazines instead, debated calling for a cup of tea, and decided against it—not wishing to appear too forward.

After all, Johnny Patrick was concerned for his daughter's safety.

This wasn't the time to be even remotely demanding.

Two magazines later, she was thinking about getting a drink of water from the bathroom to assuage her thirst, when the door opened and she was dazzled by the smile that had graced hundreds of tabloids under various titillating headlines having to do with women and sex.

"Care for some coffee or tea?" He indicated a tray he was carrying with a dip of his gorgeous head.

"I'm about to become a believer in extrasensory perception," she said, smiling. His good looks were even more striking at close quarters. Maybe it was just that she'd not seen that dazzling smile up close and personal, or maybe that old canard about movie and rock stars being America's royalty was true.

"So I guessed right."

Her stomach lurched at his remark, considering her mind was currently consumed with thoughts having to do with his outrageous physical beauty, their proximity, and various other completely shameful possibilities.

STOP! she commanded herself. It was just plain *WRONG* to be thinking of anything but his daughter's possible peril at a time like this.

"Tea or coffee?" He shoved the decimated hors d'oeuvre plate aside to make room on the table for the tray.

"Tea, please." There. That was better. An appropriately businesslike tone to match her purified state of mind. *Remember why you're here,* she cautioned herself. Because you speak French and Jordi likes you. Not for any other reasons. And more pertinently in terms of possible humiliation, remember how many women have been dogging Johnny Patrick's heels for the past decade or more.

He's not looking for a relationship at thirty-five thousand feet. He wouldn't be even if the circumstances were more normal.

Which they weren't.

They were so far from normal, this entire, surreal scenario was more like fiction than reality.

For a second she considered pinching herself—just to make certain.

But he was handing her a cup of tea, and she didn't want to spill it. Nor could she surreptitiously pinch herself when he was no more than two feet away. Get a grip. Like seriously.

Pouring himself a cup of coffee, he sat down across from her, drank half of it down in one long draft, and said with a long, drawn-out sigh, "Now we just have to wait."

"How many hours?"

"The pilots are pushing it, and we have more speed than the Gulfstream G450 my ex is in, but even then"— he shrugged—"we won't land for another ten hours. So you might want to sleep." He nodded at the museum quality artwork covering the divan. "Feel free."

While she was trying to refrain from thinking inappropriate thoughts involving Johnny Patrick, she found a ready reply to allusions about beds to be damnably difficult. As her brain discarded all the unsuitable, generally salacious comments that kept popping up, she pretended to drink her tea and look—if not thoughtful and serene—at least not half-witted. "Maybe later," she managed to say.

"So tell me about your family," Johnny said, smiling.

"Since we'll be together for a while. I know a little about your grandmother and the long ago Quebec connection, but how about your mom, dad, brothers, sisters? Are you from a small town, big town? Do you like cats—dogs, et cetera?"

It would have helped her regain her composure if he hadn't been leaning forward with his elbows on his knees so that the width of his shoulders under his Sierra Club T-shirt looked enormous and the muscles in his shoulders and arms were like practically bulging. Nor did it help that his heavy-lidded gaze was framed by dark lashes so long any woman would weep with envy. She forced her brain to function by sheer will. "My mom and dad, a brother and sister live in Black Duck, Minnesota. I may have mentioned that before. Did I say, population six hundred ninety-five?" There was something about being alone with the killer-face and rippled-body Johnny Patrick that was making her feel an attraction she'd rather not feel.

Considering the reason she was here.

And about a thousand other reasons that made any relationship between them—other than business—about as unlikely as marriage domesticating Russell Crowe.

"Did you have a school in a town that size?"

Jerked back to reality, she quickly rewound Johnny's question and abruptly thought—how did he know? "Are you from a small town?" she blurted out. The consolidation of Black Duck and Bemidji schools during junior high had been one of the major traumas of her life.

"Yep. Population seven thousand—a mill town in northern California that's seen better days. There was always talk of closing down the high school and busing us over the hill to Ukiah."

"So your small-town roots kept you in the Bay area instead of L.A."

"More or less." He didn't say the drug scene in L.A. had almost taken him down when he first started out in the music business. Berkeley gave him the distance he needed to maintain a normal life.

She felt more of a rapport with him from that point, their small-town backgrounds overcoming some of the showbiz dazzle that had been rattling her since she'd boarded the opulent private jet. Although, being alone with Johnny Patrick in this tiny little space was definitely a factor, too.

But she found herself relaxing as they compared small-town memories and exchanged brief histories of their families—he had a mom and dad who lived in Napa now, a brother in Colorado.

"We get together on the holidays," he said. "At my place or in Napa—in the ski season we're more apt to go to my brother's place in Denver. He has kids; they're younger than Jordi, but they all get along. How about you? Do you go home on the holidays?"

"Pretty much. My folks and brother and sister operate a tree farm, so Christmas is a big deal. Once the trees are shipped in early November, everyone relaxes and starts baking. The whole family cooks, and Thanksgiving and Christmas are one gargantuan feast."

"You cook, too?"

" 'Course. I make candy."

His brows rose. "No kidding."

She smiled. "It was a matter of taking what was left on the seasonal menu. Not that making candy is oppressive in any way. But my dad makes the sausage and smokes the bacon, my mom handles the Scandinavian coffee breads and lutefisk, my older sister opted for the Christmas cookies before I was big enough to complain, and my brother makes the best egg rolls and scalloped potatoes in three counties. And actually, it helps to have an engineering degree when it comes to candy making. It's a very precise art. The rest of my family are biologists and wing it more than I do."

"So you're odd man out."

"Like the houses I build," she quipped. "Tell me, are you in step with your family?"

He laughed. "Not really. My dad worked in a mill and listened to baseball on the radio, not music. My mom's a librarian, retired now, and her idea of music is hymns. My brother's a math teacher. But no one ever gave me any grief for taking the route I did. Even when things were sort of rocky." Those days when he was partying so hard he forgot what day it was, for instance.

"How did you get your own label?"

"Probably the way you started your own business. I just went for it." He grinned. "I had a garage band that was pretty damned good, for starters."

"How did you know they were good?"

He slumped back in his chair and gave her that practiced smile—the one he could turn on and off effortlessly. "It's a gut feeling. Believe me, a music degree from Berkeley isn't the key, although I don't discount it. But mostly, I learned by trial and error."

"When did bodyguards enter your life?" So maybe it wasn't a good segue, but those guys were intimidating.

His eyes widened for an almost imperceptible moment, and then he smiled. "They bother you?"

"Well, sort of."

"Barry and Cole are just along for backup."

"That's what I was afraid of."

"You're not in any danger."

She frowned. "Then what does backup mean?"

"Just general assistance," he calmly said, apparently picking up on the bristle in her tone. "Like sometimes they help me out when I go to some red carpet thing; they get me through the crowds. Or if I'm out clubbing, which I rarely do these days, they help keep . . ." He hesitated.

"The women away?"

His lids lowered fractionally, and for a brief moment he considered lying before he decided against it. "Yeah . . . sometimes." And then he got back to the subject at hand. "I don't have Barry and Cole around much—occasionally for outside work. Or for times like this. A little extra muscle never hurts."

"They're on your payroll, though." She could tell the men were comfortable with each other.

"I have lots of people on my payroll. Look, I'm sorry they make you nervous, but I'm not exactly sure where I'm going to find Jordi, or with whom. I'm playing defense and bringing them along. I hope it's not too much of a problem for you. But you're perfectly safe; you have my word."

This probably wasn't the time to argue about their varying definitions of safety. Bottom line, he had to consider his daughter's safety. "Sorry I brought it up," she murmured. "I'm good with the program." What could she say? Let me out at thirty-five thousand feet?

"With luck, we'll pick up Jordi within a few hours and head right back. I'm figuring on a short trip."

But his expression had changed when Jordi came into the conversation; he was clearly distressed. "Here I am being difficult about your bodyguards and you're worried sick about your daughter," Nicky said, feeling guilty as hell. "I'm really sorry."

"Forget it." He tried to smile but didn't quite manage a credible one. "I keep telling myself there should be some crew on board who'll keep an eye on Jordi—that she's okay and not frightened. But I don't know . . ."

"I'm sure she's fine. Jordi's such a sociable child. She can get along with anyone." Platitudes all, but gritty reality wasn't an option.

"Here's hoping." His current mood wasn't upbeat, though. Lisa had screwed up so many times he wasn't relying on her to act like a grown-up today. "Look," he said, "I'm going to check our course time with the pilots." He came to his feet. "Thanks for the conversation," he said, both polite and oddly detached.

"You're welcome. I wish I could do more."

"You can do some fast talking for me once we get to Paris and start looking for Jordi." He paused at the door. "You know, be diplomatic and pushy at the same time."

"I'll do my best." This wasn't the time to say she wasn't sure she was adept at either one.

"Sleep if you can." He opened the door. "I'll wake you before we land."

She hadn't realized she was tired, but only moments later, she was in bed and sleeping.

Being on show for so long must have been fatiguing.

MEANWHILE, JOHNNY CHECKED ON THE PILOTS, chatted briefly with Barry and Cole, and put in a last call to Lisa's assistant, grimacing as she gave him the same answer she had the last time he had spoken with her. As far as she knew, Lisa was on her way to Paris. From there, she didn't have a clue.

He and Mandy Ingram had a strained but working relationship. Her loyalty was to Lisa, of course, but she knew as well as he did who took care of Lisa when she needed help. When the drugs took over or a boyfriend was making unreasonable demands, ex-husband he might be, but he was the one who was always called on to do the heavy lifting, should it be required.

But nothing was required right now.

Because everything was in fucking limbo—including his daughter's whereabouts.

Swearing softly and then not so softly, he began pacing.

Nine

IT WAS MIDMORNING, BRIGHT AND SUNNY, when they landed in Paris. Two black Mercedes sedans were waiting on the tarmac, the uniformed drivers striding toward them as they exited the plane.

Handing their carry-ons to one of the drivers, Johnny said to Nicky, "We'll take the second car. I'll be there in a minute."

After a brief conversation with his bodyguards, Johnny joined Nicky in the backseat. He was assuming—more . . . hoping—that his ex had booked her usual suite at the Ritz; he'd had his secretary arrange for rooms across the street. "Hotel Castille, Rue de Cambon," he said to the driver and a moment later the car slowly picked up speed.

*   *   *

THE LOW THROATY PURR OF THE ENGINE WAS oddly soothing, Nicky thought. Or maybe it was the silken luxury of the dark interior and the quiet obsequiousness of those in attendance, she decided. Everything was unruffled and frictionless in the world of the über-rich.

Kidnapped daughters aside, of course.

"Did you sleep?" she asked, as though she had the right, as though the dark circles under his eyes weren't answer enough.

"A little," he lied. "You?"

It was such an obvious effort at politeness, she felt an immediate surge of sympathy. "Have you heard from your daughter?"

"I had a message from her nanny, but the transmission was garbled. It sounded as though they'd landed. Thankfully Vernie's with Jordi; she'll look out for her. Or as much as she can with my twisted ex in charge."

"You like the nanny. That's a plus."

"Yeah—she's a rock. But those men with Lisa"—his jaw clenched—"that's another story." He blew out a breath. "We'll check out the Ritz first. My ex usually stays there."

"Maybe it won't be long then till Jordi is back with you," Nicky said, soothingly, hoping she was right. The man slouched low in the seat beside her didn't in the least resemble the public sex-and-drugs-and-rock-and-roll icon.

He just looked weary and disheartened.

And incredibly worried.

FIFTY MINUTES LATER, AS THE CAR PULLED UP outside a discreet hotel entrance on a quiet Parisian street, Johnny turned to her, his hand on the door latch. "If Lisa is at the Ritz, we shouldn't have much trouble.

The staff there knows how to kiss ass." He nodded at the Castille entrance. "Do you want to go to your room first, or are you okay with going to the Ritz right now?"

He was unbelievably polite, considering the state of his nerves. "Let's do the Ritz first," she said.

He was out of the car and helping her from the back-seat when his bodyguards, who'd jumped from the lead car before it had come to a complete stop, reached them. Then flanked by muscle, they crossed the street and entered the back door of the Ritz.

The one Princess Diana walked out of that fateful night, Nicky couldn't help but think.

She sent up a small prayer that their excursion would end more fortuitously.

Ten

THEIR INITIAL RECEPTION WENT WELL.

The staff at the front desk greeted Johnny like the celebrity he was, showering him with smiles and affability like he was a long lost friend. He'd racked up considerable time there during his marriage, and seven thousand bucks a night for the Coco Chanel suite his ex favored got you that kind of toadying.

"Would you tell Miss Jordan I'm on my way up," he said first chance he had in the midst of the effusive hospitality, playing his spurious she's-expecting-me card.

Everyone's expression froze.

He immediately turned to Nicky, knowing a degree of tact and sublety was called for now. "At least Lisa's here," he said in an undertone, feeling a great wave of relief wash over him. "Explain to them—very politely—that I just want to talk to her. She may have told them not to let me up, or maybe they're remembering the screaming matches Lisa and I have had here in the past. Make sure they understand I have no intention of making trouble. They'll understand it better in French."

Feeling like a mediator at the UN, Nicky chose her words carefully, apologizing up front for her antiquated accent. She presented Johnny's case with great tact, promising them that Mr. Patrick would only speak to Miss Jordan if she wished to see him. She suggested they call Miss Jordan to clear the visit.

As she quickly recapped her comments for Johnny, he added a bargaining chip he'd been holding in reserve. "Have them tell Lisa I brought her a present from Uncle Yogi. She'll know what that means."

After Nicky relayed the added message, the manager stepped into a back room to make the call. He was smiling a few moments later when he reappeared. "Miss Jordan will see you, Monsieur Patrick," he said, a collective relief evident on every staff member's face.

"Thank you," Johnny said, pleasantly. "The Chanel suite?"

Numerous heads bobbed in reply.

"Merci," Johnny said, employing one of the few French words he knew, and lightly touching Nicky's arm, he guided her away.

As the desk staff watched Johnny walk off, the manager understood a potentially contentious scene had been averted. Fortunately Miss Jordan had greeted the news of her ex-husband's appearance with cordiality. Not that the staff weren't trained to diffuse volatile situations and smooth feathers. But it wasn't always easy with those in the flamboyant world of entertainment.

The last time Mr. and Mrs. Patrick had been in residence, the hot-tempered Miss Jordan had attacked her husband in the lobby.

The tempestuous scene had been impossible to ignore.

Like watching a train wreck.

Lisa Jordan's ethereal slenderness had been barely concealed by a flimsy red chiffon dress so short the color of her thong wasn't in question. Screaming at the top of her lungs, swearing at her husband for apparently being ill-mannered enough to drag her back to the hotel before she was ready to leave the club, she had pummeled him mercilessly, her long blond hair swirling around her bare shoulders with each wild swinging blow.

Johnny Patrick had kept backing up toward the elevators, warding her off with gentlemanly grace, only grabbing her wrist once when she tried to rake his face with her nails.

On reaching the elevators, he'd dragged her inside and had been heard to say before the doors shut, "You're taking the fucking fun out of life, babe."

Unaware of the special memories of those at the front desk, Johnny was calculating whether or not to go up alone. Did he need Nicky for any more translation? Would bringing bodyguards send the wrong signal? How stupid would it be to go up alone?

"I'll go first," Barry said, interrupting Johnny's reflections.

"You think so? I'm not sure." They were nearing the elevators.

"I'll be sure for both of us. Cole"—Barry nodded at his companion—"take the lady."

Nicky found herself inches away from a man who represented either protection or danger—with the scales definitely tipping toward danger in her estimation.

Johnny blew out a breath. He'd never quite accepted the idea that he needed bodyguards. "Crap," he muttered.

"Everything will go a whole lot smoother," Barry said, holding the elevator door open. "You can go back

to your small-town persona once we're out of here."
They'd had this argument before. Many times.

"So I should listen to the professionals," Johnny
muttered.

"That's what you pay me for, boss." He smiled.
"When are you gonna get with the program?"

"Never. How about that?"

"In the meantime . . ." Grinning, Barry waved
Johnny into the elevator.

Barry knew a helluva lot more than Johnny did about
Lisa's companions. He'd filled Johnny in on some of the
sordid details over and above the dossier information.
Fortunately, Yuri and Raf were essentially rich losers,
their fathers' illegal activities run by men more clever
than they. Yuri and Raf only played at being tough.

"Okay, I'm listening," Johnny muttered, acceding to
his bodyguard. He ushered Nicky into the elevator, and
they were joined by Cole and Barry, who waved off a
man trying to get on. "Just a word of warning," Johnny
said to Nicky as the elevator began to rise. "Ignore Lisa.
She's into drama—not a surprise considering her line of
work, but you know what I mean. She can have a mouth
on her. Don't take it personally."

"Got it," Nicky said, although she'd take it real personally if she got caught up in a gunfight. A shame there
was no way to say that tactfully.

When the elevator doors opened with a soft whoosh,
the four passengers exited and moved down a sumptuous corridor papered in gold silk damask, carpeted with
museum-quality carpets, lit by gilt and crystal sconces.

Even the luxurious surroundings couldn't mitigate
Nicky's fear.

Her Cowardly Lion psyche was unimpressed by
damask and gold.

And it didn't help that two very large bodyguards,

sitting on chairs on either side of a door she was guessing was the Chanel suite, came to their feet and glowered at them as they approached.

Johnny seemed not to notice their menacing posture. *Maybe I've seen too many kung fu films,* Nicky thought. Men like those at the door scared the shit out of her.

Johnny, however, only smiled as he reached them. "Would you let Miss Jordan know Uncle Yogi's present has arrived," he said, smooth as silk. "I believe she's waiting for it."

Nothing.

"Try French," he said to Nicky.

Half of nothing. One man replied in extremely rough French, "Name—give me."

Nicky spoke very slowly, giving Johnny's full name, pointing to Johnny, then saying Miss Jordan wanted to see him and pointing at the suite door.

The man who knew the rudimentary French spoke rapidly to his companion in his native language. Nicky guessed it was one of the guttural -stan dialects although she'd never heard them—or was it Chechen? Twenty-four-hour global news definitely made the outbacks of the world a little more recognizable.

The man turned back and growled, *"Attendre*—Wait."

As he disappeared inside, the other guard stood before the door in one of those you'll-have-to-go-through-me poses.

Nicky shot a nervous glance at Johnny.

He smiled. "Everything's copacetic. Relax."

This wasn't the time to explain to him that she wasn't about to relax no matter how much he smiled. The man in front of the door was carrying, and the bulge under his arm was a real deterrent to relaxing.

As they waited, the silence in the corridor was humming with tension, Nicky thought, although no one else appeared to be disturbed.

Her heart was pounding in her chest. Her palms were sweaty. She could hear Cole breathing beside her. Any moment she expected someone to pull out a gun and start shooting.

When the door suddenly opened, Nicky choked back a shriek. Just barely.

Although the glamorous woman in the doorway was no doubt used to shrieking fans. Maybe Nicky could have passed herself off as a fan.

"Well, well, if it isn't my favorite messenger of good cheer," Lisa Jordan murmured in a low, throaty contralto, pushing the kung fu/Chechen/Kazakstan guard aside with a brush of her finger, her gaze focused exclusively on Johnny. "You brought something for me all the way from your old stomping grounds." She smiled her movie-star smile—the one with all the perfect white teeth. "How sweet."

"That's me, babe," Johnny said, smiling. "Sweet as hell."

"And who do we have here?" Lisa pointed at Nicky, her perfect brows arched high, velvety malice in every syllable.

"My translator. Nicky Lesdaux, my ex, Lisa Jordan."

"So you're his translator." Lisa's smile was snide. "Is that what you call them now?" she said, turning back to Johnny.

"Don't start," Johnny warned, "or your candy man might go home." His ex had always viewed every woman he knew as a rival. There was no point in dragging Nicky into *that* conversation.

"You can't fault a girl for being curious," Lisa purred, offering Johnny her sexy kitten look, all violet eyes and pouting mouth.

Johnny's gaze narrowed. "Play that game with someone else, sweetheart. I'm immune. Now," he said, "are you going to invite us in, or what?"

"Uh-uh, darling—there's no *us*. But since you come bearing gifts, *you're* more than welcome."

Turning to his small entourage, Johnny said, "I'll catch you later. Say in the lobby?"

"You sure?" Cole said.

"Might not be a good idea," Barry agreed.

"Give me an hour," Johnny murmured so low the sound barely left his mouth.

Nicky knew what that meant. *Come and get me if I don't return.* The lobby was sounding better by the second.

"I won't be long," Johnny said in a normal tone of voice, nodding to his bodyguards.

"What a shame," Lisa murmured in a sexy undertone. "When you used to take such a nice *long* time . . ."

"Sounds as though you have company," Johnny said, acknowledging audible conversation from inside the suite. "And you know me. I never perform well in front of a crowd."

"Liar."

He wasn't going there no matter what. "Do you want this present from Yogi, or don't you?" he said, patting his jeans pocket.

Lisa made a small moue. "You're being troublesome, darling," she pouted, tossing back her platinum hair with a practiced gesture. "But of course I want it. I wouldn't have invited you up if I didn't."

Turning, she entered the suite, and Johnny followed without a backward glance.

The door shut behind them.

The two kung fu look-alikes took up their respective positions.

Barry looked at Cole, Cole looked at Barry.

"I'm going downstairs," Nicky said, feeling as though she'd just escaped some nameless danger.

By the time she reached the elevators, Barry was there to push the button.

As they entered the elevator, Nicky said, "Johnny was married to her for quite a while, wasn't he?" Was she fishing, or simply making an observation? Or wondering out loud how anyone could have been married to Lisa Jordan for more than a day.

"Longer than he wanted," Barry muttered.

"He stayed for Jordi," Cole said.

"Have you been with Johnny long?"

"Yeah," they grunted in unison.

Definitely not the chatty types Nicky decided, as the silence lengthened.

But certainly polite. They escorted her to a chair in the lobby, asked her if she wanted anything. When she shook her head, Barry said, "We're going back up. You'll be safe here."

She didn't argue.

She was happy as a clam to wait downstairs.

Eleven

TWO MEN AND A WOMAN WERE LOUNGING in oversize chairs as Johnny and his ex walked into a sitting room resplendent in Louis Quatorze decor. The dark-haired woman smiled and waved. "Hi, Johnny. Haven't seen you for a while."

"Long time, Chantel. You're lookin' good."

The two men didn't greet him, but he recognized them from the dossier report. The Russian and the Colombian. Dressed in Armani. They looked half in the bag—no surprise there. Chantel was floating, too, but what else did he expect in this den of iniquity from which he hoped to extract his daughter.

"If you'll excuse us," Lisa said. "Johnny and I have some business to discuss." She smiled at Johnny. "We have to decide on Jordi's private school."

"Long way to come for that," the Russian muttered, but he was too out of it to move.

"I was in the neighborhood," Johnny said, blandly. And he didn't believe in private schools, but no reason to bring that up. "After you," he murmured, waving his ex before him.

She brought him into a small faux library, although the books looked real enough. Just unread.

Shutting the door behind him, he leaned back against it.

"So, let's have it, darling," Lisa ordered, dropping into a languid pose on a tapestry covered sofa. "Don't stand there. You know how I love Yogi's special botany experiments."

"He sends you his best," Johnny offered, pulling a small bag from his pocket.

"He's a sweetie. We used to have such fun with him, didn't we?"

"A couple lifetimes ago."

She wrinkled her flawless nose. "You've gotten dull."

"You're edgy enough for both of us," Johnny replied. "Someone has to mind the store."

"Let's not have that old argument," she murmured.

"Whatever you want, babe." He wasn't here to argue; he was here to get his daughter.

"What-*ever*?"

Her smile was meant to be tantalizing, and it might have been to someone else. But sex with his ex was definitely not on the schedule. "Let's keep it simple. Especially with your friends out there for company," he said, pushing away from the door.

She shrugged. "They wouldn't even notice."

"Vernie could show up," he said, moving toward a desk near the window overlooking the Place Vendome— a familiar desk. He'd rolled a few here in the past, and he set about doing it again.

"It sounds to me like you're making excuses." She

did her little pouty number again. "Don't you like me anymore?"

Johnny glanced up from his task and smiled. "I like you just fine, but this place is practically Grand Central, so let's just cool it." He was going to politely dance backward from any action with his ex until doomsday. After a quick lick, he ran his finger down the length of the paper to seal it and walked toward the sofa. "Let me know what you think of Yogi's newest hybrid," he said, taking a seat beside her and offering her the spliff. "He said it's his best since that hot summer you were filming up there."

Lisa Jordan was the kind of woman who never had enough of anything—drugs, clothes, adulation, money—and Yogi's special blend was right up there in the category of things she couldn't get enough of. Fortunately, Johnny had what she wanted. Which was the entire point of this tête-à-tête.

Her eyes were half-lidded when she handed the spliff back to Johnny, and lolling against the sofa cushions, she softly sighed. "Darling Yogi has put his chemistry degree to excellent use," she whispered. "Give him my compliments when you see him."

"Will do." Johnny pretended to inhale and handed it back to her. Not that his ex was in any shape to notice pretense. She hadn't been exactly straight when he'd walked in, as evidenced by those three outside, who were communing big time with their inner selves.

"Does Yogi ever come down to L.A.?" she murmured, turning her head and blearily meeting Johnny's gaze.

"Not often. When the surf's up—sometimes."

"Does he still have his dreadlocks?"

"Oh, yeah."

"Blond dreadlocks." She giggled. "I suppose it goes with the territory."

"Not necessarily. There's the business types up there now, too. The biggest cash crop in California has a certain appeal to the financial wizards. But Yogi's still the old school, back-to-the-earth farmer." He smiled. "Organic."

"Perfect," she breathed, as though it mattered if her drugs were organic or not.

He talked old times, while she zoned out, making sure he only mentioned the good times, not the rest.

"It seems like yesterday when we were in Bali lying in the sun," she murmured, reaching over to touch his cheek. "You were sexy as hell."

He had to consciously resist drawing away, his memories of Bali slightly darker than hers. Not that she'd remember much, considering she'd been intent on getting high every day. "Yeah, time flies doesn't it?" he said in lieu of the less palatable truth.

"Does it ever." Her eyes opened wide for a fraction of a second. "Can you believe Jordi is nine?"

Finally, he thought, and he didn't have to bring up the subject. "They grow up fast," he said, keeping his voice neutral as hell. "She's a good kid."

"She has your smile." Lisa lazily traced the contours of his mouth with her fingertip.

"And your good looks," Johnny returned, gently placing her hand back down in her lap.

"Speaking of smiles—there's Vernie who never smiles," she grumbled. "I know Jordi adores her, but I don't think Vernie likes *me* very much."

"It's just her way." His voice was soothing. "Vernie's a tad starchy. She believes in rules."

Lisa snorted. "Rules. Fuck 'em."

No shit. But maybe it didn't hurt to have a couple when you were trying to raise a kid, he thought. "Did I mention, Jordi has a swim meet coming up in a couple of days?" Johnny lied, deciding to go for it. "She'd like to go, I know. Are you staying here long?"

His ex fluttered her fingers. "Who knows."

"I could bring Jordi back with me if it would save you a trip." He held his breath.

Lisa was silent so long Johnny thought she might have gone comatose. He was just about to check her pulse, when she said, "Why don't you ask her?"

"Why don't we both ask her?" He wasn't going to be able to take Jordi from the suite without Lisa's express approval. Not with those two pretty boys outside.

"Just go and ask her yourself. I'm too lazy." Her lashes drifted downward.

"You want a pick-me-up?" He needed her on her feet and semicoherent.

Her eyes snapped open.

Some things never change, he decided.

She pushed up into a seated position. "What do you have?"

"A little of this, a little of that. Take your pick." Sliding his hand into his pocket, he pulled out a handful of colorful pills. He'd come prepared. Whatever it took to get his daughter back, he'd figured.

She picked one of her favorites, and from that point on, he knew he was home free.

What was still nerve-racking, however, was having to casually sit there until Lisa would agree to go and see Jordi. He kept glancing at his watch, feeling as though a time bomb was ticking, and every second lost could change the course of things.

"Make sure you take Vernie with you, too," Lisa declared. "She's such an annoying old bitch."

"Not a problem. I'll take her off your hands." Christ, he felt like a CIA agent duping some rube. He would have preferred playing it straight, but that would have gotten him nowhere fast. "Vernie likes to do lunch. We'll go to Bouchet's."

"You *are* a darling when you want to be." She patted his hand, or meant to and missed.

"I could say the same about you." He didn't completely discount the years they'd been together. Everything hadn't been wrapped in black crepe. In the early years they'd been in the same party groove.

"All Jordi does is play video games," Lisa muttered, coming to her feet. "She must have learned that from you."

"Nah." Johnny steadied his ex. "It's just the younger generation."

Minutes later, they were finally moving down the hallway toward Jordi's room, Lisa's lethargy shifting into the mindless chatter that was a by-product of her happy pill.

Twelve

THERE WAS NO POINT IN ALARMING JORDI, Johnny decided as they made their way to her bedroom. He'd just say he happened to be in Paris if she asked.

Opening the door, Johnny quickly scanned the opulent room, his gaze coming to rest on his daughter seated before the TV playing a video game.

"See—what did I say?" Lisa pronounced, flipping an exasperated wave at Jordi. "It's always the same."

A wave of profound relief washed over Johnny, his world back on track.

"Hey, baby girl," he said, careful to keep his voice bland. "What's goin' on?"

Jordi turned and burst into a wide smile. "Daddy! Vernie said you might come! Check out this game. It's sweet."

He liked that his daughter was immune to the major

aggravation raising his hackles, that the vicissitudes of a journey halfway across the world apparently hadn't disturbed her. "Why don't I check it out later," he said with the utmost restraint. "Your mom said it's okay if you come home with me now."

"Let me grab my game disk. Hey, Vernie, we're going home," Jordi added with a glance at her nanny.

Vernie didn't so much as blink, but she gathered up her knitting and came to her feet. "I'll get our things," she said, holding Johnny's gaze for a pregnant moment.

He stood beside Lisa, who kept up a running commentary about the uselessness of video games, while Vernie quickly pulled together the few items they had with them. Jordi just nodded her head as her mother talked. "I know, Mom. Right, Mom. I won't forget," she said, like children do without really listening. Johnny was agreeable as hell, not uttering a discouraging word, only saying at the last when Vernie swept by them and walked from the room, "I guess we're all set, then."

Vernie had disappeared by the time they reached the sitting room, the sound of the outside door slamming a clue to her whereabouts.

Escorting Lisa to a chair, Johnny bent low and murmured, "I left Yogi's stuff in the library. I'll tell him you said hi."

"Maybe I'll drive up and see him sometime. You know, for old-time's sake."

Or some superior stash, Johnny thought, but this close to escape there was no way he was opting for the truth. "Yogi'll show you a good time. Guaranteed," he said, and stood upright. "Good to see you again."

"You're not staying?" Chantel murmured, her gaze half-lidded, apparently unaware of her male companions' inhospitable scowls.

Johnny smiled. "Maybe next time."

Neither of the men acknowledged Johnny nor did he them—male testosterone nevertheless perfuming the air. Or for those rich, young strung-out scions of the drug cartel who never did anything even remotely dangerous, perhaps it was only their expensive cologne scenting the air.

"Say good-bye to your mother," Johnny prompted Jordi, who was playing her PSP game as she waited for her parents to finish their business.

She looked up, her thumbs suspended over the keys. "Bye, Mom. See ya. Thanks for everything," she added politely.

"Good-bye darling." Lisa smiled and waggled her fingers.

Jordi went back to playing.

Lisa rolled her eyes. "She's absolutely addicted to those games. Can't you do something, Johnny?"

Speaking of addictions, he wanted to say, but said instead, "Jordi plays videos more when she's on the road."

"I doubt that. You should think about enrolling Jordi in some acting classes—maybe mime or puppetry at her age. I'm serious, Johnny. She needs to be weaned from those horrid games."

"Good idea," Johnny replied. "First thing we get back." Or right after he had his head examined. Another actress in the family he didn't need.

"Daaaaddd!" Jordi protested, stopping her play long enough to give her father an appalled look. Adult conversation was not completely unheard, apparently.

"Come on, Jordi, we'll talk about it later," Johnny said. "See you, Lisa." This was not a fight he cared to have right now.

He ushered his daughter out of the suite with lightning speed, something he'd been geared up for from the onset. Although finesse was always useful and in this case, thanks to Yogi's product and some polite conversation, Lisa was left in a relatively calm state.

Vernie was waiting for them in the hallway, staring down the guards with such hauteur Johnny felt a brief moment of sympathy for the men. "Thank God you came," she said. "The food was not up to its usual standards," she added with a meaningful glance for Johnny as they moved toward the elevators.

Johnny smiled at her euphemistic allusion. "I'm sorry to hear that. We'll have to see that your menu improves."

"Along with everything else," she significantly declared.

"Not a problem."

"Vernie doesn't get along with Mom," Jordi said, glancing up from her video game long enough to give her dad a how-dumb-do-you-think-I-am look. "Everyone knows that. Are we going to the video arcade?"

So much for adult subtlety.

Children really were sponges.

"Sure, kid, we'll go to the arcade whenever you want," Johnny said, swinging his daughter up in his arms and giving her a big hug.

"You're squeezing me too tight," Jordi complained, wiggling in his grasp. "But thanks, Dad, for coming," she added, freeing her arms enough to put her game on pause. "Mom's friends are so boring, aren't they, Vernie?"

"I'd use another word," Vernie said with a sniff. "Thank your father for coming such a long way to get you."

"I already did."

"We're good, Vernie." Johnny winked at her over Jordi's head. "Real good."

It felt heavenly to hold his daughter again.

It felt like a major disaster had been averted.

Or like maybe he'd just won ten Grammys and an

Oscar for best musical score all in one night. Okay, so that wasn't possible, but he was definitely feeling fine.

And once he had Jordi safely back in California, everything would be perfect.

Barry and Cole were waiting at the elevator—out of sight, but watching—and they entered the elevator behind Johnny without a word. They stopped to get Nicky in the lobby, Jordi acknowledging her with the same casualness with which she'd greeted her father.

Jordi kept up a steady chatter about the video arcade that was just down the street, as the small party exited the Ritz.

Half-listening, Johnny thanked whatever gods and saints in heaven had contributed to the successful conclusion of his pursuit.

But first chance he had, he was calling his lawyer.

He wanted to make sure this didn't happen again.

Thirteen

WHILE VERNIE SETTLED INTO THEIR SUITE AT the Hotel Castille, Johnny and Jordi showed Nicky to her room. But before Nicky had even checked to see that her carry-on had been brought up, Jordi said, "You gotta come with us to this video arcade. Dad's taking me, right now. You are, right?" Her gaze swung from her father to Nicky. "You play, doncha?"

"A little."

"Feel free to refuse." Johnny smiled. "This might not be your idea of fun in Paris."

He was obviously giving her a way out, Nicky thought. Now that he had his daughter back, she'd probably be in the way. "Thanks for the invite, but maybe next time," Nicky said.

"Daddy, Nicky *has* to come! It's funner with more people. We can play Mortal Kombat or Tekken together. I *love* those games."

He grinned. "It looks like I'm getting some static here. Look, come along," he offered. "I'll give you combat pay."

"You don't have to pay me. I *like* arcades."

"See, Daddy! Nicky *wants* to come!"

"Well, then. Are we ready?"

He really shouldn't smile at her like that. She wasn't used to that melting smile. He must be walking on air now that Jordi was back. That's all it was. No point in taking it too personally. "I'm ready," Nicky said, pleased to hear her voice sounding more or less normal.

"It's not very far. We can walk," Johnny said.

As it turned out, she and Johnny walked while Jordi skipped and hopped down the street, leading the parade.

"I'm glad everything went smoothly," Nicky remarked. "Jordi seems in good spirits—no trauma apparently."

"She's completely unfazed as usual. I can't take credit for it, though; she's always taken everything in stride. She never even cried much as a baby."

"Maybe her life's been good. You know that old joke about the little girl who didn't speak until she was six. When her astonished parents asked her why, she said, *Everything's been pretty good until now.*"

Johnny smiled faintly. "That would put my therapist at ease—if I had one."

"I thought every celebrity had one."

"I'm not a celebrity."

Okaaaay. And she wasn't addicted to chocolate. But rather than rain on this very nice parade, she said, "Well, Jordi's a sweetheart, and that's a fact."

"Thanks."

My God, he really meant it. Johnny Patrick as proud father didn't hit the headlines, but it was as real as his glitz and glamour image.

He paused briefly at a waste receptacle, pulled out a

handful of pills from his pocket and tossed them away. "Those were my backup," he said to her assessing gaze. "I didn't know what Lisa might want," he said, resuming his pace, "so I came prepared."

"A colorful mix," she said, in lieu of asking, *Does your ex really take all those different drugs?*

"Yeah, well . . . it's over. Mission accomplished. And now I have a big favor to ask you," he added, without warning. "Feel free to say no."

As if he took no for an answer, she thought, having seen him in action the last twenty-four hours. "What is it?" She tried to disguise her wariness, but failed.

"Seriously, you can refuse."

"Seriously, you can't be serious."

He grinned. "Am I that threatening?"

"Let's just say if it was a match between you and a bulldozer, I wouldn't bet on the bulldozer."

"Then maybe I'll just *tell* you instead of ask," he wisecracked.

"Now you've done it." She grinned. "For sure it's a no, now."

"You could bill me for your time. How would that be for a compromise?"

"I'm already billing you for my time."

His smile was candy sweet. "In that case, maybe you could just up your charges. The thing is—I wouldn't mind catching my breath after pulling an all-nighter to get here. If your schedule in any way allows"—his smile turned even sweeter, if that were humanly possible—"maybe we could take a day to chill, wind down—whatever—before we head back."

His request was benign enough, and she did *love* Paris. "You could use some sleep I suppose." She was mostly a pushover when it came to accommodating people anyway. That's what came from being the baby in the family.

"Yeah, probably. Although, I'm not complaining. It was worth the long flight to have Jordi safe. What do you think?"

"Sure, why not," she said, knowing Buddy was going to scream his head off—but what the hell—she'd deal with it. She was in Paris, after all. "I'll take advantage of the art scene while we're here, run through a few of my favorite museums and galleries, stuff like that."

"Sounds good. Jordi and I'll just hang out."

Whether he was being polite or preferred the no-fraternization policy between the boss and the hired help, she couldn't tell. But she didn't need company to enjoy Paris. In a way, maybe gypsy fate had taken a hand and given her a short break; her schedule had been nonstop lately. She could use some time off. She'd give Buddy a call when she got back to the hotel, square away another day in the world of tree house construction and then play tourist tomorrow.

NICKY WAS SURPRISED TO FIND THE ARCADE WAS über-upscale; she'd never seen so many kids in designer clothes. The claw machine didn't have the usual shiny plastic jewelry and cheap stuffed animals, the soda machine was filled with politically correct juices and fancy bottled water. Even the video games were posh—embellished with walnut veneers and leather seats and wiped down constantly by a staff in crisp white shirts and black slacks. The lights overhead were colorful, Italian handblown glass—Murano, no doubt—while the plush carpet was devoid of the usual sticky gum-spots and soda stains.

This was one swanky place.

She didn't take more than a second to register the opulence and decide Lyle's in Black Duck, with its linoleum floors and duct-taped machines, was way down on the list when it came to decor.

Jordi was frantically waving them over to a machine.

Her dad played her first, and Jordi beat him big-time at Off Road Rally. Or maybe he just let her win. Whatever. Jordi was having a ball.

When Nicky took her turn, she realized that Johnny might not have let his daughter win after all. It required serious focusing just to keep from being put down in the first round of Tekken. For maybe ten minutes she eluded defeat, before her samurai eventually succumbed to a fatal blow.

The kid was *really* good.

Jordi ran off next to try her luck with the claw machine, giving Nicky and Johnny an opportunity to adjourn to the wine/coffee bar with the other parents and child minders.

"Jordi's one super-coordinated kid," Nicky said, smiling, while Johnny ordered them each a glass of wine. "I think she's ready for the world tour."

"Sometimes I think she's too damned ready for everything." He smiled wryly. "But then I'm not in charge of the world."

"Kids are growing up faster than they did in my day." Nicky shrugged. "Of course, Black Duck is way off the fast track."

"It's not as though Fort Bragg is exactly the center of the cultural universe, either," he said with a grin. Lifting the wine glass the waiter had set before him, he said, "To the prospect of more-sheltered childhoods. And thanks again for your help."

Nicky raised her glass. "I didn't do much."

"You talked the manager of the Ritz into that phone call. That was important."

She smiled. "To obliging managers, then."

They each took a sip in a companionable silence.

"This is really good," Nicky said, indicating her glass with a nod. "Is it something special?"

"Sort of. My friend owns the vineyard."

Her friends owned economy cars and affordable houses. Maybe an occasional sailboat. He was way out of her league.

But then he suddenly touched her hand and gave her an intimate smile—like friend to friend. "I just want to say again how much I appreciated your company last night. I was stressed to the max. It helped that you were there—you know . . . like a sympathetic ear."

At his touch, her pulse spiked into the stratosphere for no rational reason; she found it impossible to speak for a second, even though she told herself he was just being polite. "No problem," she finally choked out, wondering if every woman was dazzled by that intimate smile.

He grinned. "You didn't sign on for this extra duty when you agreed to build Jordi's tree house. I'd like to get you something in appreciation. Like Hermès? Or Chanel? Maybe some of that perfume by JAR. They're all close by."

"God, no. That's not necessary."

His brows rose. The women he knew didn't turn down expensive gifts. "Are you sure? We could have some things brought up to your hotel room. Those JAR scents, in particular, are supposed to be something special."

"Please, no. I don't need anything, and I'd be intimi-dated as hell to have someone from Hermès come to my room." She waved a finger downward. "Take note of my clothes. I'm not a Hermès kind of person, or Chanel or

anything like that. But thanks—you know . . . for the offer. I'll be more than happy just to see some of the new
exhibits tomorrow. The Louvre has an Ingres show and
one on Bernini's drawings, or maybe the Turner exhibit
would be—"

She was grateful the bartender came over just then,
curtailing what was turning out to be a rambling, convo-
luted, gauche explanation of why she couldn't take his
gifts.

The bartender set a bottle of wine on the marble bar
top with a flourish. "Compliments of your friend," he
said, motioning toward a table in the corner.

As Nicky followed his gesture, her mouth dropped
open. Sean Penn was smiling and giving them a finger-
gun wave.

"You know *Sean Penn*!" she whispered, not sure if
she should pretend she didn't see him or stare.

"Yeah. We go way back." Johnny returned the wave,
then turned back to Nicky as though nothing unusual
had happened. "Are you hungry?" he asked. "They have
good hors d'oeuvres here."

"No, no, I'm fine." She was still trying to digest the
fact that *Sean Penn* was maybe thirty feet away having a
drink while his kids were playing video games. In her
everyday world—rich clients aside—she never saw actual celebrities.

"I'm going to have something. I forgot to eat."
Johnny ordered an assortment of hors d'oeuvres, along
with some pastries, and while Jordi proceeded to pillage
the claw machine, he ate and Nicky tried real hard not
to keep looking at Sean Penn. She loved every movie he
was ever in.

But of course, ultimately, she ate, too. Everyone
knows there's no such thing as bad French food. Even
the crepes in the street stands were to die for.

Johnny asked her about the tree house as they ate. She was grateful. Unlike couturier houses and A-list movie stars, tree houses brought her back down to earth. She proceeded to describe the next stage in Jordi's treehouse—her hands moving rapidly as she talked, her concepts rendered with lifelike clarity. She didn't do designer-speak or express herself in esoteric terms. She talked about plumbing, lighting, exterior finishes, about satisfying Jordi's wishes and her own in the bargain.

Johnny found himself charmed. Even though they'd talked last night and he'd seen her a few times at home, he'd never sensed this enormous warmth in her. She was completely different from his usual companions; nice different. He asked her more about Minnesota, wondering if he'd missed something in her background to explain why he was feeling this special rapport. "Does a place like Lake Wobegon truly exist?" he teased. "Where the men are all strong, the women good-looking, and the children above average?"

She laughed. "Of course and add to that—we have the biggest mosquitoes known to man and winter temperatures you Californians couldn't endure. But most of the people are really friendly and nice, and the countryside is lush green in the summer unlike the Bay area. There's lakes everywhere—ten thousand plus. I have a cabin on one of those lakes up north—on an island." She smiled. "No mosquitoes on an island. And no bears."

"Whoa. Bears?"

"Wolves even. They aren't endangered anymore thanks to the wolf project started years ago in Ely by one man with a vision. And the eagles are coming back, too, with the help of the local raptor programs. There's a nest on the lakeshore across from me."

"It sounds like real wilderness. I have a cabin in Tahoe, but the area is getting to be condo city."

"I only have loons in my neck of the woods. There's not a condo in sight, nor likely to be any. It's too far from everywhere. My favorite spot is my screened porch. It's suspended over the lake with a diving board off one corner, so you can dive in for your morning swim."

"Sounds nice. Do you get there often?"

"Not as much as I'd like. How about Tahoe?"

He shook his head. "Hardly ever. Business gets in the way."

"Tell me about it. I'm working five crews and still having trouble keeping up."

"And now I've dragged you away."

"Hey—extenuating circumstances. Anyone would have said yes."

He wasn't so sure about that. "So how's Buddy doing?"

He remembered her manager's name; the man paid attention. "Buddy'll survive," she said. "He bitches, I listen, he bitches some more, and then we get on with our lives. I told him I'd be home soon."

"Day after tomorrow. After you check out the museums, maybe we could meet for a late lunch. Jordi tends to sleep in. I'll check out some toy stores with her, you could catch your exhibits, and we could compare notes over lunch."

"I'd like that."

"Good," he said, figuring a couple glasses of wine had probably precipitated his invitation for lunch. He hadn't intended to ask. He preferred noninvolvement— his mantra of late. Maybe her refreshing lack of artifice inspired him to disregard normal procedures. She was like a breath of fresh air in his climate-controlled, synthetic world of make believe. Even her clothes were without pretense. Slacks and a T-shirt. *No name* slacks and a T-shirt. And he knew the difference—labels were de rigueur in his flash and dazzle business.

The first bars of "Vertigo" echoed from his pocket, interrupting his useless speculation, and flipping open the cell phone, he frowned slightly. "Excuse me," he muttered and turned away to take the call.

"Yes, I said I would," he murmured, a faint irritation in his voice. "I promise, okay? Yeah, really. Look, Lisa, how about I give you a call when Jordi's signed up."

Nicky was trying not to listen, but it was impossible at close range. She could hear his ex's voice, although her actual words weren't decipherable. But she was going on about something at great length. That much was clear.

"We're both on the same page," Johnny said, taut and controlled. "There's nothing to argue about. I'm with you all the way. Can we talk about this later?" As the monologue continued, the muscles of his jaw clenched and unclenched, his nostrils flared, and he finally said, tight-lipped, "Look, I'm hanging up. I'll talk to you later."

Shutting the phone with a snap, he slipped it into his jacket pocket, turned back, and grimaced faintly. "Sorry. My ex is on some roll, but I doubt she'll remember anything tomorrow."

"All's well with Jordi, though, right?"

Exhaling softly, he shot a glance toward the claw machine and smiled. "Yeah, life's good." He met Nicky's gaze once again. "So—where were we?"

"Lunch tomorrow." She shouldn't have said that. She should have said something innocuous and let him remember himself. But she found herself really wanting to go.

He looked surprised for a moment, like she might have said, *My gown for the Oscars is ready to be picked up.* Then he collected himself. "Lunch—right. We'll go to Dominique Bouchet's restaurant. Jordi likes the desserts, I like the wine list, and the chef is a friend of mine."

Oh, shit, he hadn't remembered. Not that she was so

obliging that she'd let him off the hook. It must be the Paris air. Or else she was acting like a fifteen-year-old, dazzled by his drop-dead good looks. Either way, lunch sounded good. "You have lots of personal friends," she said, repressing any guilt she might have with only a minor qualm.

"It goes with the territory. Not that I'm complaining. I could be working in the Georgia-Pacific mill in Bragg." He grinned. "If it were still running."

Fourteen

"HERE, HAVE A LITTLE MORE. IT'LL MELLOW you out."

"The man is a total ass," Lisa Jordan muttered, taking the small glass pipe from Chantel. "He hung up on me."

The pretty, waiflike woman ran her fingers through her short, black curls and smiled faintly. "He's not an ass, and you know it. He's beautiful as sin and hardly ever gives you any grief. Plus, he brought you this fine weed."

"He's still irritating."

"Aren't they all at times? Look how Yuri sulked when you said you were going to let Johnny come in."

Lisa shrugged, her lightly tanned shoulders lifting slightly. "But Yuri came around when I told him he could go to my next premiere with me. He likes to party and have a good time."

"And he also doesn't mind being part of the international *cinema* scene," Chantel murmured.

"So that gives me leverage," Lisa purred. "I *like* having leverage."

"Johnny never played that game—or did he?"

"Are you kidding? He abhors the limelight. Although," Lisa said with a small sigh, "he used to be ready for anything—anytime, anywhere." She wrinkled her nose. "After Jordi was born, he turned into a damned Boy Scout overnight. Booooooriiing."

"But nice boring, you have to admit. Speaking of really boring, though, what did you think of that little side trip to that museum in the Marais after we got here? The place looked more like some old lady's apartment to me."

"It was some family thing Yuri had to do." Lisa slowly exhaled a mouthful of smoke. "Did you see how hot he was about that old jewelry?"

"I don't know why *we* had to see it."

"He was proud of it for some reason; I think it was Russian and some empress's." Lisa did a little palms-up gesture. "Whatever—it turned him on."

"Like those stops at the chocolate stores."

"That was for his father. Yuri has some—like—shopping list of special chocolates he has to bring down to Nice when we go."

"Speaking of Nice. We're going to need some new bikinis for Yuri's yacht."

Lisa set the pipe down, stretched languidly, and studied her manicured fingernails for a moment. "No problem. There's tons of shops in Nice. I'm not sure I like this color. What do you think?" She held her hand out for Chantel to look at.

The women were dressed casually in pastel slacks and little matching barely there tops. Both women af-

fected an ultrafeminine style that accented their ethereal, delicate beauty.

"Try that pink sparkle we saw at Chanel—what was
it called—Stargazer Pink?"

"Or maybe the glossy melon . . ."

"You know, I was thinking—"

"You like the pink."

"No, I was going to say it worked out well that
Johnny took Jordi back home. She wouldn't have had
much to do while we were partying. And if we're enjoying Yuri and Raf's pharmaceuticals, you wouldn't have
had time to spend with her anyway. Plus, you don't like
that nanny around with her constant sour expression."

The pale perfection of the film critics' favorite face
took on a studied reflection. "I suppose you're right."
Lisa sighed. "You *are* right. Not that I'm going to tell
my ex that, prick that he is."

Chantel smiled. "And why should you? So, let's try
some of those chocolates Yuri bought. I'm getting the
munchies."

"I don't eat chocolate."

"More for me, then."

"Be my guest. I'm going to help myself to one of
those strawberry tarts"—Lisa waved at a pastry tray that
had been brought up by room service—"and then I'm
going to help myself to some of those black pearls Yuri
has in his luggage." She flashed a set of dazzling white
teeth, thanks to Beverly Hills's finest dentist. "Yuri
won't miss a few; there must be hundreds there. And
they can't be too valuable, or he would have put them in
the safe with all that other stuff."

Chantel's azure eyes narrowed. "I wouldn't take any.
He might have counted them."

Lisa made a small moue, like she had so effectively
in *Whisper of Life* the year it won the Palme d'Or. "I'm

sure Yuri can afford to give me one or two. Or if he takes issue"—she half-lifted her slender hand in a negligent gesture—"I'll offer to pay for them."

"I wouldn't mess with *anything* of his. The man has a temper."

Lisa marginally lowered her delicately colored lashes. "Trust me—I can handle Yuri."

WHILE THE TWO LADIES WERE INDULGING IN chocolates, pastries, and some quality cannabis, Yuri and Raf were seated opposite two men in the back room of a dingy warehouse on a largely uninhabited cul-de-sac in Montmartre. The rude graffiti on the boarded-up structure deterred the curious, as did the barbed wire on the wrought iron fence surrounding the property, while the faded sign in Cyrillic characters above the shabby main door lent an air of neglect or possibly risk to those passing by.

Yuri lounged in his chair with the jeunesse dorée indolence of a wealthy young man, his hands resting lightly on the arms of an Alexander I Empire–style cathedra that looked wildly out of place in the room. Although if one looked beneath the dust sheets on scattered furniture surrounding the scarred table separating the men, one would have found that more than one item would have borne museum serial numbers. "You have the sketchbook?" he drawled in French, immune to the cold gaze of the heavyset man opposite him who looked like a Bulgarian weight lifter.

"The money first." An unwavering stare.

Yuri slowly surveyed the man's shaved head, no neck, and muscled arms that could probably bench press a horse, then shrugged and turned to Rafael. "Show him the money."

Rafael's lesser rank was the result of their respective father's relative status in the hierarchy of global crime. Yuri's father had prospered in the new Russia, but then everyone who had connections had, organized crime included. Raf came from a South American cartel of lesser scope, their business solely drug-related. Although both families were becoming immeasurably richer since the collapse of the Taliban. Opium production in Afghanistan was at an all-time high.

In fact, everyone was at this warehouse today because one of the largest drug-transit dealers in Uzbekistan had a penchant for art—particularly Picasso. The stolen sketchbook in the Bulgarian's hands was rumored to be from Picasso's early period and would serve as payment for a shipment of opium being relayed to Europe. The sketchbook had been targeted and stolen from a private collection—its worth estimated at five million dollars. Not that the petty thieves with the sketchbook understood its value.

"The money is all here," Raf said, lifting a small briefcase onto the table and opening it. "Two hundred fifty thousand euros." Euros had become the currency of choice for drug deals since the dollar's recent decline.

The Bulgarian's cohort quickly thumbed through the packets of bills, then snapped the briefcase shut and set it in his lap.

"Here. It's not much—mostly scribbles," the weight lifter said, his French heavily accented and rough.

Yuri drew the small sketchbook closer and flipped through a few pages before shutting it. "My father appreciates your fast service." He stood and nodded at Raf, who came to his feet as well. "If our client has any other requests, we'll call you."

Neither young man looked back as they left the

room. They didn't have to. Their families wielded enormous authority in the criminal world, and their guards were stationed outside the door.

Not that Yuri and Raf were involved in any of the more unsavory aspects of their fathers' businesses. They only served as couriers from time to time on low-level assignments.

When dangerous missions arose, professionals were employed—ruthless men without the benefit of Ivy League educations or consanguinity to those at the top.

It was left to Yuri and Raf, heirs to a business that had taken on global proportions and with it the requisite accountants and international bankers, to simply enjoy the hedonistic lifestyle of the über-rich.

Fifteen

AFTER SEVERAL GLASSES OF WINE, JOHNNY was ready to crash by the time they returned to the hotel. Not that he was about to admit it, but Vernie had seen enough children fighting sleep in her day to recognize the symptoms. Taking charge with the authority of three decades of putting unwilling tots to bed, she said, "You take a short nap, Mr. Johnny, and Jordi and I will see that Miss Nicky is entertained." Jordi had wheedled and coaxed Nicky to come back to their suite and play video games.

"Maybe I should go," Nicky said, feeling way out of place in this family scene, cognizant of the fact that Jordi, not Johnny, had been begging her to come back to their suite with them.

"You *have* to stay," Jordi implored. "Tell her, Daddy. Tell her to play Project Gotham with me."

"I'll play with you." Johnny smiled at Nicky. "You're off the hook."

See, Nicky thought, really feeling like a fifth wheel now. It hadn't been a double invitation.

"Not so fast," Vernie warned, her eyes half-narrowed. "*You're* taking a nap, Mr. Johnny, and that's that."

"Uh-oh, Daddy—you're in trouble now," Jordi said, her glance flicking from her dad to her nanny. "Vernie's giving you the evil eye."

"*No* arguments, Mr. Johnny." Drawing herself up to her considerable height, Vernie pointed toward one of the bedrooms. "Go. We'll manage fine without you. We three girls will have a chat over tea."

"Tea with *scones*?" Jordi cried.

"And your favorite—clotted cream," Vernie said, smiling as Jordi hopped up and down. "Lots of Brits stay here," she explained to Nicky. "So the scones are excellent. You must have some with us."

"YES, YES, YES!" Jordi exclaimed. "You don't have to play video games. Tell her, Dad. She doesn't *have* to play."

Johnny met Nicky's gaze, a gleam of amusement in his eyes. "It's up to you. I have no clout, as you can see."

Vernie snorted. "As if. But you can barely keep your eyes open. Now skedaddle."

Johnny grinned. "I'm only giving in because I can't replace you on short notice."

"You can't replace me at all," Vernie said, bluntly.

"Mommie says she has to put up with Vernie because she's ir-re-place-able," Jordi piped up.

Vernie lifted one brow. "I rest my case."

Having grown up in an area of the world devoid of nannies or even the concept of nannies, Nicky hadn't realized the degree of authority they wielded. She was thinking maybe she'd better stay for a scone or she might be put to bed without her supper.

"Enjoy the scones," Johnny said to Nicky, as though reading her mind. "I'll see you all later."

The door to his bedroom shut a moment later, and Jordi nudged Nicky's hand. "Can you play cribbage?"

"Sure can."

"Yesss! Hey, Vernie, Nicky plays cribbage!"

Vernie smiled. "This is our lucky day. And whenever you get tired, feel free to leave," she added, turning to Nicky. "Mr. Johnny said you slept on the plane, or I wouldn't have coaxed you to stay."

"I *did* sleep—rather well."

"Mr. Johnny has a nice plane. Now, you two girls go set up the cribbage board, and I'll fix the tea."

The nanny had said "nice plane" casually, like most people would say, You have a nice lawn, or maybe a nice couch. Was she outside her normal venue or what? Ooooh yeah.

On the other hand, private jets and five-star hotels aside, these people had the same problems as everyone else—albeit in more posh surroundings. But they fought just the same (this rushed trip to Paris a case in point) and probably cried as hard, and happiness wasn't guaranteed them any more than it was to those who lived in Black Duck.

Okay, so she was trying to maintain her perspective, find some balance in this rarefied world of nonstop sycophancy and personal bodyguards—not become overwhelmed by the sheer economics of all this affluence.

"What color pegs do you want?" Jordi called out from across the room.

"Green." So much for seeking enlightenment; the mundane always had a habit of butting in.

"That's *my* favorite!"

"Yellow then," Nicky said, moving toward the table where Jordi was setting up the game.

"Perfect, cause Vernie doesn't like yellow," Jordi muttered, arranging the pegs into three different piles.

Nicky had learned to play cribbage from her grandmother, who was not only a great cribbage player but could also win against God himself at gin rummy. Nicky could hold her own in both those games, which came in handy a short time later, when she came up against Vernie, who liked to play for blood when confronted with a worthy opponent.

It felt like old-home week for Nicky, since her grandma didn't like to lose, either. Having honed her skills against cutthroat competition, Nicky enjoyed the game, although wouldn't you know it, Jordi, novice that she was, won in the end.

The young girl was all smiles, as the two women exchanged conspiratorial glances.

"Another scone?" Vernie asked, offering the cake plate to Nicky.

"I shouldn't, but what the heck," she said, reaching for one. "They're really good."

"A woman needs a little flesh on her bones; those models look like they'd blow away in a good wind."

The reference might have been about women like Lisa Jordan, Nicky reflected, although she herself wouldn't blow away even in a typhoon. But having nary a single anorexic bone in her body, she piled on the clotted cream and strawberry jam and ate another deliciously flaky scone with great relish.

While Nicky was tending to her scone, Vernie had taken a moment to slip in a DVD and Jordi was currently enthralled in the adventures of a sci-fi heroine dressed in skintight silver-studded leather to match her platinum hair.

"Jordi could use a little downtime," Vernie murmured, flicking a glance toward the young girl. "Her sleep was interrupted last night." She rolled her eyes. "The party never stopped."

"Johnny was so worried, I doubt he slept at all. Jordi's mother had never taken her out of the country before, I guess."

"And she won't again." Vernie nodded at the closed bedroom door. "He's pretty grim about this. Not that it shows now," she added, softly, "but he was furious when he showed up at the Ritz. I could tell."

"It's always hard when parents can't agree."

Vernie snorted. "There's no agreeing with a drug addict. Once they're on a roll, you might as well just get out of their way."

While Jordi watched her movie, Vernie and Nicky visited, or more aptly, Nicky answered Vernie's questions. How had she met Johnny? Did she have a boyfriend? A smile when Nicky had said no. Where was her family? Did she see them much? Was she close to her siblings?

And after hearing that Vernie had little family of her own, only an elderly aunt who lived in Aberdeen, Nicky understood her curiosity. If you come from a large, extended family, solitude and personal space sometimes trump family ties. On the other hand, a person like Vernie—more or less alone in the world—might tend to value family more.

But after having been raised by a mother and grandmother who talked your ear off, Nicky was perfectly comfortable with a chatty woman who asked personal questions.

Jordi fell asleep before the platinum-haired heroine had killed off more than three bad guys. Although that might have been influenced by something about the lack of dialogue that dulled one's brain sensors. Background soundtrack or not, two cups of tea or not, Nicky was having trouble keeping her own eyes open.

Not that she'd actually had a full night's sleep last night.

Not that it wouldn't be heavenly to shut her eyes for *just* a minute.

Or maybe *just* a second . . .

VERNIE SMILED FAINTLY AS NICKY'S EYELIDS closed, her head lolled back, and she gently dozed off.

After finishing her tea, Vernie gazed at her sleeping charges with a satisfied smile, and rising from her chair, she covered Jordi with one of the numerous throws in the richly appointed room. Then moving to the couch where Nicky was half-sitting, half-lying, she gently eased her down, slipped a pillow under her head, and covered her, too. After thirty years of practice, she could shift a sleeping person without them so much as fluttering an eyelash.

Then taking a chair that would give her a view of the two sleepers as well as the closed bedroom door, she sat down. Picking up her knitting—all the rage again—she proceeded to add several inches to the argyle sweater she was making for Jordi.

Sixteen

AN HOUR LATER, THE DOOR TO THE BED-room opened.

Meeting Johnny's gaze, Vernie put her finger to her lips, nodded at the two sleeping figures, and motioned him toward the kitchen.

"Everyone was tired," she said, following him into the small kitchen and shutting the door.

"Including you, I'll bet," he said with a smile. "Why don't I take over now and watch the two sleeping beauties. You rest for a while."

"Since we're going out for dinner tonight, I'm going to take you up on your offer."

Johnny grinned. Vernie never missed a meal, particularly one prepared by a world-class chef, although she was also known to drive ten miles for a good Coney Island hot dog. "Then, hop to it, babe. We have reservations for eight."

"At Le Troquet?"

"Where else? It's your favorite."

She arched one brow. "That's why you have all the women after you. You know how to charm. Speaking of which, you should think about charming that lovely Miss Nicky. She's actually normal—with a regular family—unlike most of your other female acquaintances. And you're not getting any younger. You don't want to be still dating bimbos when you're pushing fifty."

"First, I won't be pushing fifty for more than a decade. And second, I'll consider your advice when and if I ever have the inclination to settle down again."

"You should think of Jordi. Maybe she'd like a woman in the house who is normal."

"Are you saying you're not?"

She pointed her finger at him. "You know very well what I mean. I'm not around all the time. Jordi might like to be part of a family again."

He put up his hand. "Stop already. I'm way past the white picket fence fantasy. Jordi and I manage just fine the way we are."

Vernie knew when she'd said enough. One didn't survive in the world of high-powered Hollywood employers without understanding the virtue of silence. "I'll be taking my nap, then. And you're a real good father. It's just that Nicky seems—I don't know—different . . . in a nice way," Vernie couldn't resist adding with a wink.

Johnny smiled. "It's obvious she's nice. But I've got too much going on right now to deal with any one woman."

"Maybe once your ex is settled or at least stable."

He snorted. "You're a dreamer if you're waiting for that. But so long as Lisa doesn't put Jordi in danger again,

I'm good. We're outa here in a day, and after that Lisa can go to hell any way she pleases. Now, go take your nap."

"Yes, sir."

He chuckled. "You must want something."

"Just *think* about taking her out."

"Nicky?"

"Yes."

"No. And as far as 'taking someone out,' I haven't done that since high school. Furthermore, how stupid would it be for me to start something with Nicky when she's building Jordi's tree house. She's gonna be around for at least a month. Think how awkward that would be. Most of my relationships are measured in hours."

"You're going to end up old and alone."

"No, I won't. I've got Jordi."

Seventeen

JOHNNY FOUND A COMFORTABLE CHAIR IN the sitting room, put on his headphones, and listened to some new tracks he'd been working on in his studio before he so precipitously left the Bay Area. Taking notes from time to time, he fine-tuned the sound, the rhythm, the lyrics—some of the words were questionable even to his ultraliberated sensibilities.

The sleepers slept on—both in his line of vision. So he took notice when Nicky stirred. Eyes shut, she rolled over on her back and kicked off the cashmere throw Vernie had tossed over her. Mumbling something unintelligible, she threw her arms over her head like children did in sleep, and let out a soft sigh.

That particular pose lifted her breasts high. The plump mounds provocatively on show and the shapely woman stretched out on his sofa suddenly took center stage in his brain. His focus on music faded away, short-circuited by one helluva good view. Jeez, he'd never really noticed her great tits before—the brevity of their acquaintance and recent events no doubt to blame.

Although, now that he had—those were world-class. Not that silicon didn't offer every woman equal-opportunity tits, but the possibility of checking hers out suddenly crossed his mind.

Not that Vernie would approve. Nicky was normal, she'd said—as in nice normal. As in off-limits for ultra-casual sex normal.

He pursed his lips and softly sighed. Vernie was right.

Nicole Lesdaux from Black Duck, Minnesota, was normal as apple pie—an all-American girl.

Not his type—*at all.*

So why was he looking?

He didn't have an answer. And before he could rationalize a suitable one, she abruptly stretched, arching her back languidly, like a cat in the sun. As if that wasn't a full-fledged ripe-for-sex image, a moment later, she began moving her hips in a highly suggestive rhythm—half-smiling all the while, as though enjoying a pleasurable dream.

No way was *that* frigging apple pie, the drift of her hips erotic as hell, as were those spectacular upthrust breasts, their lush fullness barely covered by the light T-shirt stretched over them. Not to mention, the imprint of her nipples was searing his eyeballs. She must be having one helluva good dream with nipples that hard.

Shifting in his chair to accommodate his rising erection, unconsciously reverting to type, he swiftly sized her up from head to foot, his gaze finally coming to rest on target. The tantalizing juncture of her thighs offered a riveting view of her mons in that horizontal pose. Gap chinos never looked so good.

Forcibly wrenching his gaze away a second later, he reminded himself not to deliberately look for trouble. Sex with Nicky Lesdaux would compromise Jordi's tree house—sure as hell.

Especially transient sex.

So seriously, she was off-limits—as in *no way, no how.*

Grappling with his rare need for restraint—sexual temperance an oxymoron in his world—he blew out a breath. A vehement, deeply frustrated one.

Nicky's lashes lifted at the sound, her eyes flaring wide at the sight of Johnny staring at her. Still half-asleep, she scanned the room, trying to come to grips with her unfamiliar surroundings, struggling to make sense of what she saw. Paris—that was it—Johnny Patrick's hotel suite, Vernie and Jordi; she must have fallen asleep. Oh, Christ, how gauche was that? She opened her mouth to apologize.

Johnny silenced her with an upraised hand, then pointed at his sleeping daughter.

Having cleared away the traffic jam in her mind, all she wanted to do was escape as fast as she could. Falling asleep in Johnny's suite was so juvenile or worse—like maybe some groupie attempt to hit on him? Quickly rising from the couch, she waved and moved toward the door, hoping he didn't think she'd intruded purposely. Women were always trying to inveigle their way into Johnny's life, she suspected. The last thing she wanted was for him to think she was hustling him.

Au contraire.

Johnny was too busy dealing with his own indecision.

Should he or shouldn't he give chase? he was wondering.

Where exactly did prudence rank in the grand scheme of things?

Or more particularly in terms of tree house construction?

Or let's be honest—in terms of *his* life?

She was almost to the door. It was *crunch* time.

What the hell. He came to his feet.

Call it lack of restraint.

Or maybe innate male behavior.

Or more likely, a long-standing habit of instant gratification.

Pulling off his headphones, he quickly dropped them and his notes on a side table and caught up to Nicky just as she stepped out into the hall. "Wait," he said, catching her hand to bring her to a halt. Easing the door shut behind him, he drew her around. "I'd like you to come to dinner with us tonight." How was that for benign? It was only dinner. No ulterior motive. Or so he told himself. He might have even half meant it.

They were standing very close in the empty corridor.

Too close, Nicky thought.

Not close enough, he was thinking when he shouldn't be thinking anything of the kind. He let her hand drop. "How about it?"

"Sure," she whispered, trying to find breath to speak when he was looking at her like that, when his last question was open to interpretation.

"Dinner—right?"

Now that was less ambivalent. But she found herself nodding yes anyway, her words caught in her throat with his heated gaze triggering desires she'd been trying real hard to suppress.

"Perfect."

His smile was boyish and sweet. Like on that *People* cover of the sexiest man alive. Soooo damnably sweet she could no longer resist, and rising on tiptoe she impulsively kissed him.

He tensed.

Shit, shit, shit. Was she a complete imbecile or what? "Sorry," she muttered, dropping back on her heels, flushing red with embarrassment. As if women throwing themselves at him was anything new; she was probably the ten-thousandth this week.

After a millisecond, he smiled again. "No problem," he said. "I've been wanting to do the same thing."

"Really?" she said.

He grinned, her breathless disbelief apple-pie charming. "Yeah." Cupping her shoulders, he bent low so his mouth was only a hair's breadth from hers. "Really." His mouth touched hers, curtailing any further speculation she might have apropos of the vast differences in their lives, the warmth of his lips ultra-light, as though he liked to take his time.

She shouldn't have melted against him so willingly. She should have shown more restraint. Yeah, right. When this might be her only chance to kiss the sexiest man alive, she wasn't about to play coy. Actually, she didn't know how to play coy. Call her impulsive. It was true.

He didn't seem to mind. She was glad about that. In fact, he pulled her closer so the imprint of his you-know-what was hot against her stomach, and even if she'd wanted to play coy, it was pretty much out of the question after that. He was *hung*. Perhaps one of the criteria no one ever talked about in the judging of the sexiest man alive.

The pressure of his mouth intensified infinitesimally, and he added just enough tongue to make her think of soft beds and warm bodies as he leisurely savored her like maybe she was a Baskin-Robbins flavor of the month. He knew what he was doing, she thought as he backed her against the wall and leaned in to her. He knew how to make a woman hot and bothered in seconds flat.

The feeling was definitely mutual, but in the interest of keeping Vernie happy, he curtailed his carnal impulses, cutting the kiss short before it was too late. Lifting his head, he let go of her hips. "So what about coming to dinner?" he said, giving himself Boy Scout points for his honorable behavior.

As if she could refuse now, she thought, her ideas about coming not confined exclusively to dinner.

"I have to get back; I'm babysitting," he explained, figuring that was as good an excuse as any. He lifted his hand in the direction of the door, as though she'd never kissed him, nor he, her—as though he didn't have a hard-on and she hadn't felt the world momentarily skid off track.

He probably knew no woman of sound mind would say no. Although, if she was rational, she'd refuse—because all things considered, his kiss suggested something more than dinner. Probably something like a one-night stand.

The question was: Did she care to add her name to the very long list of Johnny Patrick's one-night stands? "I'd love to have dinner with you," she heard herself saying.

So much for self-control. Then, as though in presage of what was sure to follow this potential one-night stand, Johnny instantly took a step back.

"Sounds good. We'll pick you up at seven-thirty." Turning, he walked away, entered his suite, and shut the door.

Left standing in the corridor, Nicky allowed her heartbeat to resume its normal rhythm, while reminding herself that one-night stands weren't exactly a *complete* novelty for her. She didn't have to get all bent out of shape about sex. Sex was sex was sex, after all. And on the bright side, this particular occasion might very well rate a sumptuous spread in her fantasy diary of amorous memories.

Although, female that she was, her next, immediate thought was—WHAT would she wear? She hadn't thought she'd be going out for dinner in Paris. Okay, duh . . . she might have considered the possibility. So she wasn't perfect. Hadn't her mother always called her flighty when it came to long-range plans? In this case, she might have to admit her mother had been right because aside from slacks and T-shirts, she had *nothing* to wear. And celebrity-type people always ate at celebrity-type restaurants.

Eeeek and double eeeek.

This called for some quick thinking and quicker shopping. And not Hermès or Chanel shopping. Although how she would find economy shopping in this city of high and higher fashion was anyone's guess. Also, sometimes she forgot to pay her personal bills—like on time . . . if she was busy, which was always. She hoped her cards hadn't been canceled. They always reinstated them, because she actually had money now, but this wouldn't be a real opportune time to have to argue with some credit card company over the phone from a shop in Paris. Had she brought her debit card? There should be money in her account; her secretary did an automatic deposit for her each week. Worse thought, though . . . did she even have her wallet? She tended to be a little disorganized.

No wallet. No purse. Shit.

She'd had her purse at the arcade—which meant it was probably in Johnny's suite.

So knock on the door and ask for it. Really, he was only an ordinary man.

Right. And Black Duck, Minnesota, is the same as Paris.

Then again, she couldn't have built a company single-handed if she was faint of heart.

She knocked, and when he came to the door, she whispered, "My purse," and waved vaguely as though she was sure it was there. Luckily it was. Or she would have been wearing Gap chinos and a T-shirt for dinner.

With another wave, she left, the door closed whisper soft behind her, and after checking her purse for her debit card—eureka—she raced down the hall to the elevator.

Something demure but sexy would be perfect, she thought.

A dress that said class but wasn't above a suggestion of receptivity in the right circumstances. In her case, that meant anywhere within a mile of Johnny Patrick should he crook a finger in her direction. Although maybe she should play hard to get. Not that she'd given him that impression five minutes ago.

But a woman could always change her mind, couldn't she?

It was really just a question of moral fortitude—whatever that meant.

On the other hand, she was in France—the land of amour.

Maybe she should just lie back—literally and figuratively—and give in to the prevailing culture.

Eighteen

HE DIDN'T SAY, WOW, WHEN HE CAME TO pick her up for dinner, but she saw it in his eyes and decided the much-too-expensive dress she'd bought was worth every euro.

But he did say, "You look good in green," which she already knew, because she had green eyes, and this dress matched them exactly.

"Thanks, you look good in"—she was going to say *anything*, but censored herself—"that shade of blue." His shirt made the gray of his eyes look less cool. Or maybe it was his smile that did that.

"I'm told the color's called gentian."

Nicky flicked a hand over the front of her short, flirty dress. "Pistachio."

"Definitely good enough to eat," he murmured, holding her gaze.

Jordi came racing up, defusing the rising heat that

seemed to have reached flash point in mere seconds. "Daddy! Daddy! Look at me! Vernie says I look like a princess!"

Johnny spun around and did a dramatic double take that evoked a giggle from his daughter. "At your service, princess," he said, sweeping her a bow. "And is this the queen?" he asked, smiling at Vernie, who had dressed for the occasion.

"I prefer empress."

Nicky wasn't sure she didn't mean it. Vernie looked serious, and she was wearing real jewelry along with an evening purse that hung from one of those distinctive Chanel chains.

Johnny grinned. "Empress sounds fine to me, Vernie. You run the show better than anyone I know."

"Years of practice, young man," Vernie replied with a wink. "Just remember to remind me of my two-martini limit. You forgot last time."

"With good reason," Johnny drolly noted. "No way I'm going to cross you after two martinis."

"I'll do it," Jordi piped up. "I'm not scared."

Vernie smiled. "I'm counting on you, then, sweetie. Especially if we're going to get up early and go to that café that serves those strawberry crepes you like. I need my rest." She tapped her wristwatch and glanced at Johnny. "We'd better go. You know how long it takes to eat in France. Come along, Jordi, we'll lead the way."

"Vernie keeps everyone in line," Johnny murmured with a smile, as he and Nicky fell in behind. "She's good for Jordi. I'm a little too lax about rules."

On the few occasions Nicky had seen Jordi with her dad, there had been no rules in evidence. Johnny was the archetype of doting dads. "Rules or not, Jordi seems to like Vernie."

"Oh, yeah. They're buds. Vernie comes to stay with

us from time to time, so Jordi doesn't just see her at Lisa's."

"You're a lucky guy."

He shot her a look.

"What? I meant finding a nanny you like. Don't look at me like that. It was a perfectly innocuous remark." Her gaze narrowed. "You're superstitious."

"Let's just say I don't like to tempt fate. When it comes to luck, I've had more than my share."

"And you don't want me to hex you."

He shrugged. "I suppose. Life's too unpredictable."

She wanted to say, the kind of life he'd led was more unpredictable than most, what with traveling around the world constantly, and paparazzi going through your garbage on a regular basis, not to mention your love life being splashed across the pages of every tabloid on the planet. "It can be, can't it?" she politely said instead, because he was taking her out to a real nice place for dinner and their heated kiss a short time ago was likely to lead to maybe another kiss or two later tonight. And she was currently feeling as though Jordi wasn't the only princess in the crowd. Right now, she was empathizing with Cinderella big-time.

Nineteen

DINNER WAS EVERYTHING IT SHOULD BE AT A Michelin three-star restaurant that catered to presidents and rock stars and moguls. The chef was one of the famous super-chefs who had said a short time ago, "I have nothing more to prove. I no longer want to be bothered by restaurant guide books. I just want to please myself and my customers," and he'd opened a restaurant without the glamorous trappings, but with the same perfectly executed meals. He knew Johnny personally; their rapport when he came over to their table was that of two men who moved in the same celebrity circles.

For Nicky, the culture shock of such a sophisticated menu was mitigated by Vernie's down-to-earth conversation and Jordi's comments about icky foie gras that she was no way going to eat, and when could she have some of that chocolate cake she'd had last time they

were here. For those who could afford it, the homey little bistro was just another neighborhood café, with the
exception of the limos and bodyguards outside.

Nicky had to admit, the people-watching practically
gave her whiplash. There was a table of generals from
some South American country, the glitter of their medals
blinding, their consumption of champagne prodigious.
A discreet corner table held an older married movie
star of considerable fame and a young-enough-to-be-
his-granddaughter ingenue playing kissy-face over their
coffee and port. *Get a room,* Nicky was thinking. Then
there was the table of Brits, most of whom had been in
the news lately as diplomats trying to deal with the Ira-
nians and their nuclear ambitions. Cable news was really a remarkable font of information. It seemed as
though she knew them personally. The Parisians who
had come to dine were quiet and refined, taking their
time over each course, discussing wines with a nuanced
expertise (she could hear the ones behind her) and in
general trying to ignore the tourists.

She ate too much, but how could one refuse such
beautiful food? The fact that the menu didn't have any
prices made her a little nervous, but Jordi was ordering
one of everything, and Johnny didn't seem to mind, so
she figured she could order a couple extra things, too.
Like two desserts because it was impossible to narrow
the list down to any less.

Jordi forgot to stop Vernie from having a third martini, although Johnny and Nicky exchanged a look as
she ordered it.

He mouthed, *no way,* and grinned.

Nicky smiled back and then kept her eyes on her
dessert. *She* sure as hell wasn't going to make any
waves.

They ate faster than most, thanks to Vernie, who

didn't brook leisurely meals, and after coffee and some excellent port, they returned to their limo, which was waiting outside. Johnny's bodyguards had been dispensed with, now that his crisis with Lisa was over. Ensconced in the luxurious backseat, Nicky listened as Jordi, seated on her father's lap, pointed out all the monuments of note on their return to the hotel.

The only monument from her childhood in Black Duck was the twenty-foot-long fiberglass Muskie wearing a saddle at the Conoco station. Not that it wasn't impressive to anyone under the age of twelve. She must have ridden it a million times. It just didn't ring with the same cultural resonance as the Eiffel Tower or the Arc de Triomphe or Cleopatra's Needle, which had been stolen from Egypt by Napoleon. (Jordi even knew that. Such were the hands-on history lessons of children of wealth.)

As Nicky was musing about the vast gulf that separated her childhood from Jordi's, and not entirely sure whether she was envious or not, the car came to a stop in front of the hotel. No time for a therapist now. Not that they ever told you anything anyway. They just took your money and nodded their heads at appropriate times. And she knew of what she spoke, since she'd paid for four sessions—with borrowed money from her sister—in the aftermath of Theo's flight.

Johnny leaned over and murmured, "Let me get these two to sleep"—he nodded at Vernie, who was dozing across from them—"and we can go somewhere for a nightcap."

"Vernie said I can watch a movie before I go to sleep," Jordi proclaimed, tugging on her father's shirt collar.

"Not a problem, baby." Meeting Nicky's gaze above his daughter's head, he mouthed, *Wait for me.*

She smiled and nodded. Maybe she should have played hard to get. Maybe if she'd not been utterly infatuated, she might have.

He gave her a dazzling smile that warmed her clear down to her toes in their new, peony pink stilettos. And as he helped her out of the limo and escorted them through the hotel lobby, the phrase *walking on air* would have been an apt and fitting description for Nicky's mood.

They parted at the door to her room, everyone waving at everyone else, and she surreptitiously watched them through her half-closed door as they traveled the several yards farther to their suite at the end of the corridor.

CAN YOU BELIEVE IT????? a little voice inside her head was screaming.

JOHNNY PATRICK—THE ONE AND ONLY SEXIEST MAN ALIVE!!!

COMING TO SEE ME!!!!!

As the trio disappeared from sight, she shut her door, leaned back against it, and trembled. Which would never do.

She had to remain calm, or she'd embarrass herself completely.

"He's just another man, for God's sake," she told herself, speaking out loud and slowly in an effort to compose herself.

ARE YOU KIDDING? that little voice hysterically exclaimed.

He's just another man, like the Pope is just another German, or Lincoln was just another lawyer, or Bill Clinton was just another devotee of Krispy Kremes, or—you get the picture.

And what was really freaking her out, besides Johnny's celebrity, was the fact that she'd *forgotten* to buy some really sexy lingerie. She'd been in such a rush to find a dress and shoes and get back to the hotel in time that she'd totally forgotten she only had unbelievably plain cotton underwear! Fuck.

Maybe she could pretend she never wore underwear.

Maybe she'd just go without.

Ee-eew. If they went for a nightcap like he'd said, she'd probably end up getting all hot and bothered, and she'd leave a stain on the back of her skirt. That would be fucking embarrassing. She'd have to walk out of the bar backwards. Even in a nice hotel like this, she didn't suppose the concierge could find her some sexy silk undies at this time of night. Such a request might be outside the realm of their duties.

So she'd apologize for her cotton underwear, or maybe she'd act like a mature adult and say nothing at all.

In the end, she decided to do nothing. It was just easier.

Let him figure it out for himself.

And knowing his record with women, he'd probably seen it all, from thongs to chastity belts. There actually had been that story that everyone had denied about him and that nun in Italy. Even the Vatican had weighed in.

Now, that was notoriety.

After something like that, how could she possibly do anything wrong? So screw it. She was going to see what the minibar had in the way of drinks. She could use one.

Twenty

SHE OPENED ONE OF THOSE TEENY, TINY bottles of champagne that probably cost a fortune and drank it in two gulps. Luckily she wasn't paying for the minibar. And on that note, she took out the other teeny, tiny bottle and sipped it more leisurely. In three gulps.

She needed them for tranquilizers. Okay?

Although she supposed that was the oldest excuse in the book—like I need a drink to calm myself down or make my very bad day better, or some other lame reason for overimbibing.

But in her case, it was true. A tranquilizer was crucial.

Because she didn't get a chance to be with Johnny Patrick or a Johnny Patrick type every day of the week—or, honestly . . . *ever*.

Champagne or not, though, she was still wired. Needing distraction, she flicked on the TV and ended up watching *Sky News* because it was the only channel besides CNN in English. Even better, they were airing a program on Scottish architecture. Was this her lucky night—in more ways than one—or what? She *loved* Scottish architecture.

After raiding the minifridge a couple more times—chocolate was her comfort food when she was stressed—she was eating the last truffle from the pretty box tied with a blue ribbon when she practically leaped from her chair at the knock.

Could it be that she needed a really heavy-duty pharmaceutical-grade tranquilizer to calm her?

Better planning would be her mantra in the future. Bereft of that pharmaceutical option at the moment, however, her only choice was to at least give an appearance of calm. She smiled pleasantly but not effusively as she opened the door, holding her hands behind her back to hide their tremor. "Jordi must be sleeping." Oh, Christ, was that a vacuous remark, or what?

He seemed not to notice. "Yep. Fast asleep. Vernie, too." He smiled. "I'm free for the night."

He shouldn't have said that "free for the night" line in that soft, husky tone. It was an instant trigger for a flood of highly creative, salacious images to inundate her mind. All of which she resolutely tried to ignore. But a couple of the better ones wouldn't disappear—like the one with Johnny's powerful, nude body poised over hers just before—*STOP! GET A GRIP!*

Oh, shit—he must have said something. He was looking at her expectantly.

"Sorry, I was thinking about the great dinner we had," she lied, the bedroom scene in her head resisting her best efforts to dismiss it.

"I was just asking if you wanted to go somewhere for a drink?"

He was leaning against the doorjamb looking sexy as hell, and his cool, wolfish eyes were asking something else entirely. That look suddenly brought her to one of those forks in the road—you know . . . where one made moral choices (the increasingly compelling nature of the bedroom scene in her head putting her at a disadvantage).

Where questions of virtue had to be addressed. (Ditto, above.)

On the other hand this wasn't the nineteenth century, women were liberated what with birth control and credible professions and salaries. Thank God for a voice of reason. Although, liberated or not, she still wasn't completely off the hook—morality wise.

What the hell, she decided, if she had to worry about virtue, he might as well, too. "It's up to you," she said, throwing the ball back into his court.

"Then I'll come in."

The man had no trouble making decisions. "Be my guest," she said, waving him in, giving herself points for handling things with her usual evasion. So it was a bad habit. She'd deal with it tomorrow.

As he eased past, he leaned over and lightly brushed her lips with his.

Was that one of those casual European hellos, or was that an actual kiss? she wondered. Her body apparently preferred the kiss option, because it instantly began revving up—every little cell sending out heated, passionate messages of anticipation.

"Mind if I order a cognac?" he asked, moving toward the phone on the desk in the sitting room.

It was a question that obviously didn't require an answer. It also suggested he wasn't in a big hurry, which meant she would be wise to discipline her sexual synapses to show a tad more restraint. "I'll have one, too," she said, like she drank cognac every day, like she drank it at all. Like she might actually have sexual restraint.

Tossing her a smile over his shoulder, he punched the room service button and ordered a bottle.

While she was debating where to sit and what to say, as well as seriously trying to curb her restive desires with his kiss still tingling on her lips, he sat down on the couch, leaned back, and spread his arms along the top in a relaxed pose. "This is the first time I've been able to kick back since we took off from San Francisco. Come on over." He patted the back of the seat. "Sit down. Talk to me."

He'd been here before, she was guessing. That was definitely not the hard sell.

She didn't have to worry about resisting a sex fiend from the looks of it. In her current mood, she wasn't sure that was entirely good. Although, a man like Johnny probably didn't have to come on too strong. All he had to do was sit back and wait.

She should probably attempt an equal maturity and not fling herself at him like some groupie. Which meant stanching her baser impulses.

"What movie did Jordi watch?" she asked, sitting down, leaving a comfortable space between them, pleased to hear herself sound calm as a cucumber. Maybe she could play hard to get, too.

"She started watching *Fantastic Four* for the umpteenth time. But she fell asleep pretty fast." He smiled faintly. "She was worn out."

"After three martinis, I don't suppose Vernie put up any fuss about going to bed, either." Nicky wasn't sure how long she could remain calm when the heat from his body was bombarding her senses. Smile politely and think good thoughts, her voice of reason suggested, loosely paraphrasing the advice Queen Victoria had given her daughter on her marriage—"Lie back and think of England."

"Vernie was out before Jordi." He offered her a sympathetic look. "You must be tired, too."

"I'm okay," she managed to say. "I slept last night."

"I didn't, but I'm too psyched about having Jordi back to be tired."

Was that a hidden clue; was he saying he was good for all night? Did that mean he wouldn't take offense if she jumped him? "It's great how everything worked out with Jordi," she said, feeling the weight of virtue on her shoulders as she responded responsibly.

"The understatement of the century," he murmured. "Getting her away from Lisa's crowd was a relief. Those guys my ex knows have fathers who launder more money than Enron ever did."

The thought of actual criminal activity was mega-sobering. "They don't sound like nice characters," she said, a jolt of apprehension partially mitigating her lust.

"No shit. They're way the hell out of Lisa's league. But she likes the drugs, and they have them by the truckload."

Funny how actual fear could raise havoc with sexual desire. "These guys aren't run-of-the-mill street dealers, are they?" she asked, nervous now.

He shook his head. "This is big-time worldwide traffic."

"Jesus." Her heart did a nervous pit-a-pat. "Like in the movies."

"Unfortunately, it's not the movies," he said, ultra-calm, like they were talking about the weather. "No way do you want to fuck with these people."

"No kidding?" She could feel the hairs rise on the back of her neck. "Maybe we should find another hotel. Or another country. Black Duck didn't prepare me for stuff like this."

"We're out of here soon. It's not a problem anyway."

She must have seen too many movies about drugs that had bad endings. "You're way more cavalier about this than I am."

"In my business I run into big money that isn't always on the up and up. People like that are always looking for legitimate investments. They like the glitz and glamour of the entertainment world; they can get rid of some money legitimately and also rub shoulders with—" He glanced up at the knock on the door. "Excuse me," he said, coming to his feet. "The cognac's here."

Or maybe drug dealers with guns, Nicky thought, the knock on the door ultradiscreet like maybe it was some cunning artifice, and seconds from now she'd be blown away by an automatic weapon with a silencer.

But as Nicky was bracing herself against the worst-case scenario playing in her head, Johnny opened the door to a young waiter with a dusty bottle of cognac. After politely *bon soir*ing them, he set about opening the bottle and pouring them each a glass of an obviously very old liquor.

Johnny handed the man a large bill, then glanced at Nicky. "Tell him we appreciate the quick service."

She did, the man told her to tell Johnny how much he liked his record label, and after a few minutes more of translating a conversation about specific artists the waiter favored along with a ton of effusive praise for Johnny, the man left.

"I suppose you get that a lot. Adulation."

"More than I need, that's for sure," he said, sitting down again and handing her a cognac. "I'm only the producer. I don't make the music. Cheers." He lifted his glass. "This is usually good."

It was, in a slightly fruity, high-octane way. Her previously heated senses revived, her close proximity to a man who no doubt featured in thousands of women's dreams was not without its potent effect. And since no killers had materialized, her morbid fears had been dispelled. Also, he smelled *divine*, not something she usually noticed— then again, maybe the men she dated didn't buy their cologne in the same high-end shops as Johnny Patrick.

She found herself thinking she'd like to lick him all over he smelled so good, the fragrance kind of vanilla-ee with a hint of—really . . . she had to say chocolate. Was that possible? If she hadn't had wine at dinner, two *small* bottles of champagne, and now cognac, she might not have said, "Is that chocolate I smell in your cologne, or am I crazy?"

"Dunno," he said like a guy would. "I get it at a shop in San Francisco. It's French, though. I forget the name."

"I *adore* chocolate." Oops, that was open to a possible subtext, and she'd warned herself about openly drooling over him. "I mean I eat it all the time. Oh, shit," she muttered, flushing pink at his smirk. "Strike those last inanities. I just like your cologne, that's all."

"Don't get bent out of shape. I like a helluva lot more than your perfume, or I wouldn't be here."

That was nice. Succinct, yet sweet. "So this isn't any port in a storm."

"No storm here, babe. I know what I'm doing."

"It's good one of us does. *I'm* not so sure."

His brows rose. "Of?"

She blew out a breath. "Celebrity types like you." Her anxieties about assassins giving way to more basic, everyday doubts.

He grinned. "That's all bullshit. I'm as ordinary as the next guy."

"Puleese."

"Okay, so I know a few more people than you."

"A-list people who are all infinitely familiar with the red carpets of the world."

"What's that got to do with this?" His dark gaze was suddenly intense. "Seriously?"

She held his gaze for a moment, then melted under his boyish smile, which appeared like sunshine after the rain and effectively obliterated the red carpets of the world in one fell swoop. He looked like a kid from some small California town.

"So can we dispense with the celebrity shit?" he murmured.

"Yeah, I guess." It was incredible how he could transform himself with that fucking sweet smile.

"And we're not going to get hung up on anything more than having a good time?"

"I guess."

He laughed. "You're gonna give me a complex."

She grinned. "Maybe it's about time someone did."

"So, you're gonna take me on?"

"I was thinking about it."

"Not as long as I've been thinking about it."

"Betcha."

"Since I first saw you," he said smoothly, not an amateur with women.

"Okay . . . we're even. You looked damned nice in that Speedo."

"Jordi liked you right off, too." That at least was true—as for him . . . maybe he *had* noticed her and just didn't let it register.

His daughter was that important to him. Christ, she felt like crying or at least breaking into one of those songs from a family movie like *The Sound of Music*. "So are we done with this cognac?"

"Are you asking?"

"I guess I am." Shit, she wasn't going to.

"I'm glad. Being a gentleman is really fucking hard."

His gratifying candor along with his smile went a long way toward assuaging her moment of guilt. Setting his glass down, he took hers and placed it next to his. "You can still change your mind," he said, pulling her to her feet. "But five minutes from now," he added with a grin, "I can't give any guarantees."

"Back at you. I've been restraining my carnal impulses. Be forewarned."

"Nice," he murmured, drawing her in to his body. "An assertive woman. I like that."

"Not as much as I like this," she whispered, moving her hips against his blatant erection. "You'd better have protection."

"No problem."

"We're good then."

"One small caveat."

Uh-oh, here's where he'll say, *I need you to sign a release. No stories to the tabloids.* "What?" She leaned back a little to meet his gaze.

"I just don't want this to screw up Jordi's tree house."

"This one-night stand, you mean."

He wasn't sure of her tone of voice, but he *was* sure about what he needed from her long term. "I just don't want you to be pissed later and shelve our deal."

"So you piss off a lot of women?"

That ambiguous tone again, but he answered honestly because there was no point in not. "Once in a while," he said.

She put her hands on his chest and pushed him away.

Fuck, he thought. He'd blown it.

"Sex is sex in my world. Tree houses are tree houses"— she smiled—"and never the twain shall meet. How's that?"

"You made my day, babe." He pulled her back.

"Just so long as you make my night, honey, everything will be kick-ass."

He grinned. "Now I'm feeling the pressure."

"You mean the tabloids have been wrong—you can't satisfy five women in one night?"

"I didn't say that."

"Arrogant man."

He smiled. "It ain't braggin' if you can do it."

"Now I *am* looking forward to the night."

"Kidding aside," he said softly, "so am I."

He led her into the bedroom like he'd been there before, but she wasn't about to quiz him on his understanding of the hotel floor plans when she had better things to do. Her libido was focused on short-term goals in the form of instant gratification.

And who wouldn't be with the quintessential stud Johnny Patrick—of five women in one night fame—drawing her toward the bed. Not to mention, he was so handsome, you could practically come just looking at him. A shallow assessment, perhaps, but true. Which brought her senses all aquiver, her pleasure centers revving up for action and "AN-TI-CI-P-A-A-TION" singing big-time in her brain.

"Sit for a minute," he said, lifting her up on the canopied bed. "I'll open the curtains. We're high enough up to see the Eiffel Tower from here."

She felt like saying that she didn't know if she had a minute—if she could actually put two words together in a coherent sentence.

He seemed not to notice—women bereft of speech perhaps a given in his life. "You'll like the view," he said.

She smiled and nodded, although the view she was looking at right now was more than fine, thank you. One could willingly drown in those sexy eyes, his smile was capable of melting the polar ice cap, while his hard, muscled body . . . "Could the view wait," she said on a suffocated breath.

A quick, flickering assessment, then a flash of a smile. "Not a problem," he murmured, reaching down to push her skirt up over her thighs. "You need some instant gratification, right?" It was a question that didn't require an answer, because he'd already slipped his middle finger under the crotch of her panties and was running his finger down her silky wet cleft. "Ummm, nice . . ."

Hard-up, impatient, she shivered at the sexually explicit male appreciation in his rough/soft tone.

"You wouldn't have lasted if we'd gone for a drink." Sliding his finger up her vagina, he whispered against her mouth, "How about we get you off?" As he kissed her, he added a second finger to the first, then with slightly more difficulty, a third. "Hey, hey, relax," he soothed, gently pushing her down on her back with his other hand. "We're gonna take this slow and easy . . ."

He didn't really expect a reply, with her eyes going shut and her hips arching up into his hand. Although if he needed a go-ahead, her soft, breathy moan was as good a one as he'd heard.

And he'd heard a bunch.

Oh-oh-oh-oh-God!! In the grip of a feverish delirium, a hot, seething rapture flooded her senses as Johnny's slender fingers moved inside her with a right-on-target, done-this-before *incredible* sensitivity. Delicately stroking and massaging, he forced his way in re-e-al-ly slowly, pressing gently on that little rough spot on the roof of her vagina both coming and going— over and over again, retracing his route with the kind of virtuoso concentration and expertise that was going to take her over the edge real, real, *real* soon.

Especially when his thumb was on her clit at the

same time, his doing-the-tango combination a sure winner.

"A pussy this wet is gonna last for hours," he whispered, a smile underlying his low, husky tone.

Okay—that did it. Not that she had much farther to go—but the thought of hours in bed with Johnny Patrick's great hands and hard cock, not to mention his sweet fuck-me talk—was all she needed to push . . . her . . . *overthebrink!*

Her climax kicked off with a tiny, shimmering tremor that rippled outward from her hot, throbbing core in ever-widening circles, quickly picking up speed and intensity until it reached the outer limits of sensation where it detonated with such explosive force, her shrill orgasmic scream startled even a man who thought he'd heard it all.

Holy shit, he thought, his ears ringing. This little tree-house architect was one fucking hot number.

Not only did she come in literally seconds.

He was pretty damned sure she wasn't faking it.

Although, even if she was, he figured *he* was gonna have a *real* interesting night.

MOMENTS LATER, NICKY'S LASHES SLOWLY LIFTED. "Wow, thanks," she murmured, her green eyes an emerald brilliance in the lamplight. "My very, *very* happy pussy thanks you as well."

"Don't mention it," Johnny replied with a grin, easing his fingers out. "My pleasure." He gestured toward the windows. "How about the Eiffel Tower now that you've come down a notch and can check out the view?" Call him sentimental, but Paris *was* the Eiffel Tower.

She smiled a lazy, self-absorbed smile. "Sure. Break time."

He quirked a brow. "Am I on the clock?"

"Sorry, my mistake. I didn't mean to press you. Although with a hard-on like yours"—her gaze rested on his crotch—"I'm guessing your clock and mine might be on the same time."

"You don't mind asking for it, do you?"

"I didn't know you were looking for shy."

Christ, he must be too used to accommodating women. His smile instantly appeared—ingratiating, apologetic even. "I'm not," he said, moving to open the curtains. "Forgive me—it must be jet lag screwing up my brain."

"There's nothing to forgive. I probably speak my mind more than I should, but I figure you're more apt to get what you want that way," she finished on a teasing note.

"I'll see what I can do," he said, reaching for the drapery cord, "about you getting what you want." Sex was sex was sex, he reminded himself. "Now, check this out," he added with a smile of translucent charm. Pulling on the cord, he drew the draperies aside, and there was the Eiffel Tower all lit up like a Christmas tree.

"Ohhh—it's absolutely *gorgeous*!" Nicky exclaimed, sitting up to take in the glorious sight. The soaring tower was outlined in white lights against the dark sky, stars twinkling in a halo around it, the most dramatic symbol of Paris smack-dab in the center of her bedroom window. "Did you know this room had this view?" she murmured, awestruck, experiencing one of those pinch-me moments again.

"I thought you'd like it."

It wasn't precisely an answer, but she wasn't inclined to grill him after their recent exchange about her asking for sex. "I sure do like it," she said, this fairy-tale setting doing a real number on her reality-based perceptions.

"You really know how to charm a lady, Mr. Patrick. What else do you have in your bag of tricks?"

He laughed. "A couple things you might like."

"If you don't mind my saying, there's one in particular that has my attention," she pointed out, half lifting her hand in his direction.

"Want me back on the clock, boss?" If she liked to take charge, he was more than willing—until he wasn't. Which wasn't right now.

"That would be ever-so-sweet."

"I didn't think you were looking for sweet," he said, kicking off his shoes.

"Maybe one person's sweet is another person's—"

"Head-banging sex?" he finished with a grin, unbuttoning his shirt.

"I was thinking more along the lines of non-head-banging sex," she offered, slipping off her sling-back heels. "Less bruises and more finesse."

"You like finesse?"

She nodded. "Although, you definitely have it. Virtuoso fingers and all."

"Glad we could be of service," he casually remarked as he stripped off his shirt.

She immediately lost her train of thought at the sight of his well-chiseled male torso. The man was ripped—every muscle clearly defined, abs like rock, biceps that brought Olympic weight lifters to mind. "You must work out," she said in lieu of openly drooling.

"Occasionally," he said, unbuckling his belt.

She was definitely having second thoughts about taking off her dress after looking at Johnny Patrick. The last time she'd worked out was in college gym class. Maybe it might be wise to turn off the lights.

"Need help with that dress?" He let his slacks slide to the floor.

"Ah—" A thousand excuses raced through her mind.

He looked up from stripping off his boxers, his gaze amused. "You, indecisive? Am I hearing right?"

One glance at his enormous, upthrust erection tempered any impulse she might have to quibble over lights or dresses on or off. All she wanted was that rock-hard cock inside her—NOW. Sliding off the bed, she turned her back to him. "Unzip me."

"Yes, ma'am," he drawled, figuring she must crack the whip at work. But he wasn't above acquiescing since there were obvious advantages. "And then what?"

"Then if you'd be a dear and let me feel this"—reaching behind her, she ran her fingers down his cock—"as soon as possible."

"Any place special you want to feel it," he murmured, pulling her zipper down.

The roguish pitch to his voice struck her with apprehension. Rock stars were famous for kinky sex, and she wasn't so sure his kinky and hers were the same. "I prefer the usual if you don't mind."

"What's usual?"

Oh God, he *did* want something else. She swung around, holding her dress against her chest. "Just for the record," she said, not sure she wasn't screwing herself royally, but unwilling to be *that* obliging, "I don't like anal sex. And I'm not giving you a blow job right this minute."

"Okay, that narrows things down," he remarked, looking entertained.

"I hope that's not a problem." She tried to use her most diplomatic tone, wanting what she wanted as she did.

He tried to keep from smiling. "I don't know."

If he was toying with her, which appeared likely, she wasn't sure she was ready to play his game. He probably had women submitting to his every wish 24/7. Bottom line though, she was really selfish when it came to orgasms. "When do you think you might know?" she murmured, needing to come again—quickly.

His mouth twitched. "You sound anxious."

"I *adore* a perceptive man," she breathed, smiling faintly. "And *anxious* is a thousand degrees too tame a word for what I'm feeling right now."

"If the party's starting again"—he glanced down at his cock, then up again and grinned—"count us in."

"I'd love to . . . seeing how my party started five minutes ago—right after I came last time."

His brows flickered. "So you're into multiple orgasms."

"If at all possible." She smiled. "Although really good chocolate comes in at a close second. And a combination of the two is right up there approaching nirvana."

"If I'd known, I could have called room service and had them send up chocolate," he drawled.

"Right now—as in I can't wait—I'd much prefer *that*." She pointed at his gorgeous erection. "If you don't think me"—her grin was intentionally flippant, her tone ultrasweet—"too brazen."

Fucking her had been on his agenda since he'd knocked on her door, so flippant or not, they were on the same page. "It would be a real pleasure," he whispered, lifting her arms up.

After pulling her dress over her head and tossing it on a chair, he turned back and went motionless.

Christ!—she was wearing white cotton underwear—*plain cotton* . . . without a single lace ruffle or even a hint of embroidery. Junior high Bible camp, and all the horniness that went with being fourteen and spying on the girls' cabins with his friends hit him with a flashback to the past. Hit his prick with the same lecherous sentimentality. He must have seen too much La Perla of late, that this simple, white underwear was taking on

porn status and making him horny as hell. Fucking A.
He was getting off just looking at it.

And his resident French translator filled out those bra
cups real fine, her large breasts straining the cotton knit
fabric to the max, while her delectable cunt was wetting
those pure white panties.

Suddenly he was on the same speeding freight train
as she was.

Deftly unhooking her bra, he slipped the straps down
her arms, watching her breasts quiver as they were re-
leased from bondage. "Great tits," he whispered, his
voice soft with lechery, his gaze shifting downward.
"And I like what's under these sexy panties, too," he
added, slipping a finger under the waistband.

"Don't tease," she pouted, clearly embarrassed.
"They're all I have."

"No way I'm teasing, babe. They're turning me on. I
remember panties like these."

"Meaning?" A pettish little sound.

He looked up. "Good memories, babe. That's all I
meant." He figured he'd better not ask her if he could
take them off with his teeth or she might freak, but it
was definitely a thought. Man, it'd been a long time.

Vernie'd been right about apple-pie nice.

She was sugar sweet.

Although more importantly, she had a hot little
pussy, white panties and all.

"I'm real happy you came with me to Paris," he said,
sliding her panties off like a gentleman.

"Me, too." She stepped out of them. "And at the risk
of pressuring you, I'll be even happier when I come
again."

Lifting her up on the bed, he gave her a quick kiss.
"Be right back."

She panicked for a second, thinking she might have

offended him—until she saw he was only taking a condom from his pants. Actually several condoms, she was pleased to see. Call her greedy, but she was, thanks to his handsome studliness and utter beauty. Although, let's face it, his huge dick had the most to do with her current attraction for him. She was literally aching with longing, she wanted him so badly, every nerve in her body was primed for pleasure.

Sliding higher on the bed, she spread her legs.

He smiled at the sight, availability always high on his list of qualities in a woman. Although, he had to admit, Nicky Lesdaux wasn't in the usual category of women he fucked. Nor did this night fall under the heading of business as usual in terms of the casual sex he preferred.

Not that he was about to analyze the differences.

Especially now when he was seconds away from sinking his cock into that tight little cunt.

He ripped open a foil packet.

She watched as he deftly rolled the condom down his erection without a single wasted motion. He'd done this before, she decided, not that she'd thought otherwise. But it made her feel a bit like a tyro in contrast. A feeling, however, quickly replaced by a more powerful sexual craving, one that had held her in its grip from the moment he'd walked into her hotel room.

"Hey," she whispered a second later, as he positioned himself between her legs. "Thanks for your understanding about impatience and—"

"We're both there, babe," he whispered back, swiftly guiding his cock into place. "Although, I'm warning you"—his grin flashed—"I'm on a fucking hair trigger."

Her eyes sparkled. "Wanna race?"

He laughed. "Oh, yeah." He pressed forward with a controlled thrust he'd learned long ago. He was large, most women were not, and penetration required a certain restraint in gauging speed and depth in order not to do any damage.

Meeting with a familiar resistance, he took it even slower. When he would have much preferred ramming speed. But he had plans for the night; no point in ruining a good thing.

As her ready-to-party, hotter-than-hot, and wetter-than-wet cunt was slowly invaded by one world-class dick, Nicky decided it was actually possible to *die* of pleasure. She was going to simply *expire* of pure, unadulterated rapture and do it with a smile on her face.

"Can you take a little more?"

She wiggled her hips in reply, and he forced his way in a small distance deeper while she held her breath, waited for the next wave of ecstasy to break over her, and when it did, she moaned in gratitude and heartfelt appreciation.

Then he started over again, her vagina slowly yielding, and by cautious degrees, between soft kisses and whispered endearments, he crammed her full, stretched her, filled her with both cock and exquisite longing, forced her legs wider to accommodate his hard, rigid length.

Until, at last, she was firmly impaled, he was buried to the hilt, and they were both gasping for breath.

Sexed up and horny, frenzied and overwrought, neither was sure whether to preserve the dizzying pleasure—to sustain the wild, seething sensation as long as possible—or feverishly move on.

Less disciplined, Nicky went off the deep end first.

Even as her orgasm commenced, Johnny debated his options.

She liked multiple orgasms.

He could give her this one and wait for her next one.

If he was made of stone—maybe he could.

Or if this was his usual casual sexual encounter.

Or if he hadn't felt like coming for the last twenty minutes.

"I'm takin' your wave, babe," he whispered.

With superhuman effort, she levered her lashes marginally upward and gave him the sweetest I-can't-talk-right-now smile.

He was impressed. She'd really struggled to respond.

There was something memorable about the effort she'd taken to please him and gratification as well in the strange delight—maybe even happiness—he felt in fucking her. He was probably flipping out; maybe having Jordi back brought with it this rare enchantment. Or maybe Nicky Lesdaux *was* different from all the rest.

Whatever. But he came that time like he'd never come before. That much he knew. And as he lay braced on his elbows afterward trying to catch his breath, he was already making plans to fuck her again. And if this meant he was going ape-shit—screw it. He was having a helluva good time.

He held her afterward, after the condom had been disposed of and he'd dug up a couple towels, after he'd gotten himself a cognac to try and dispel his strange mood. After she'd lay inert for so long he was beginning to worry.

He held her close, her head on his chest, the scent of her perfume tickling his nostrils, and they counted the lights on the Eiffel Tower like children might. Like he'd done years ago, the first time he'd come here on the school trip funded by cookie sales and car washes.

"This is about as close to heaven as it gets," she whispered, arching up to kiss his strong jaw.

"Amen to that," he whispered back. "I think I've entered your nirvana."

"Nice, hey?"

"Yeah, nice."

And then they lay in companionable silence, both feeling as though they'd crossed some inexplicable line.

He was the first to shake away the outré feeling. He didn't really believe in nirvana other than as a possible lapse of judgment for carnal reasons. "I was thinking," he said.

"Let me guess." Her voice held a smile.

"You get three chances."

"Do I get a prize if I guess right?"

"Sure do."

She laughed. "You're ready for sex. I'm ready for sex. We're both ready for sex."

He pulled her up on his chest, brushed the curls away from her face with his palms and found himself momentarily nonplused by a curious sense of longing. Nonsexual.

She looked at him searchingly. "What?"

He gave his head a shake, as though it were possible to dislodge the odd feeling with so small a gesture. "Nothing."

"I'll bet you're tired." She gently touched his cheek. "You haven't slept at all."

"Nah, I'm good." He smiled. "So tell me what you like best—sex-wise." Keep it casual. Keep it about fucking. Don't go off track.

"Really?"

"Sure."

"You probably wouldn't like to do it."

Now he was intrigued. "Sure I would. Give me a hint."

"Make me do something."

"Like what?"

"Like I have to do something you tell me."

"Like S&M?"

"God, no. Like you won't fuck me unless I kiss you or—"

He grinned. "Kiss me where?"

She sat up, straddling his hips. "Forget it. I shouldn't have even said anything. But you asked and"—she shrugged—"I don't know . . . you make me feel really sexy, that's all."

"More than usual?"

"Yeah, as if your ego needs bolstering. A whole lot sexier if you must know, okay? Now you can add another notch to your belt and forget my name in a couple days. Not that I expect you to remember my name." She blushed. "Jeez, why don't I shut up while I'm ahead?"

He was looking up at her, thinking she was about the cutest thing he'd seen in a long time. Starlets and groupies and little rich girls looking for something to break the boredom didn't hold a candle to this candid, sometimes outspoken, always honest lady from some small town in Garrison Keillor land. "Talk all you want. And just for the record, you're pretty unforgettable. Now, if you want me to make you do something, how about we try something like a man and a maid."

"Really, you don't mind? That story makes me *so* hot."

"You know that, do you?" he said gruffly.

"What? You're getting huffy about me having sex? This from a man who can't remember how many women he's fucked?"

"So sue me. I'm not in the mood to picture you having sex with some guy, okay? It screws up my concentration."

"Then I'll have to pretend you're a virgin, too, or maybe I won't be able to come again."

"You're lookin' for trouble, babe."

She grinned. "Promises, promises."

"I'll promise you this," he growled, lifting her up as though she were weightless, rolling her under him and plunging inside her without waiting for a condom or her okay or directions from her for any game. "I'm gonna fuck your brains out. And you'd better be on the pill cause I'm not stopping."

"Maybe I am, and maybe I'm not." She held his gaze. "What are you gonna do about it?"

"Screw you until I can't screw anymore."

"I'm not sure I like that."

"Too bad." He didn't break his rhythm.

"What if I told you to stop."

She was beginning to pant, so he figured he was home free on that one. "I wouldn't," he said.

"I could make you."

He laughed.

"Hey!"

"How about you make me stop doing this," he murmured, easing first one leg, then her other over his shoulders, holding her hips in a harsh grip and pounding into her.

Oh, jeez, oh, God, he wasn't playing, he really was doing whatever he wanted to do, and she was getting so turned on she was going to come like—RIGHT NOW!!

He half smiled and slowed down enough for her to feel the entire shimmering wave, and once her orgasm had died away, he picked up the pace and started all over again.

"No, no, not yet," she whispered at first, for a brief, fleeting few seconds, but he knew better, and before long, she was panting and gasping and clutching at him as though he was her lifeline in a hurricane. And that time they came together.

He didn't even wait to wipe up; his cock had a mind of its own. It surged upward again, higher, larger, as though her hot, slick cunt had bewitched it. He really took his time that go-around, all his nerves on high alert, every sensation seemingly magnified, a kind of revelatory intensity of sensation bombarding his brain.

"Can you feel that?" he hissed, sliding in until he hit bottom.

"Oh, God, oh, God . . ."

Her cheeks were flushed, her eyes shut, her words no more than a whisper, so he figured she was feeling it just fine.

Like him.

In fact, his head was going to blow off this time.

Or as near to it as the human body would allow.

It must be the scent of Paris in the air.

Or the lights of the Eiffel Tower out there.

Because this was a kind of raw lust he'd never felt before.

"Don't stop," she breathed. "Please . . ."

He couldn't. She didn't have to worry.

He couldn't stop if he wanted to.

THAT FIRST TEAR SLIDING FROM UNDER HER CLOSED lids finally made him stop—brought him back to reality. Filled him with guilt. Gathering her in his arms, he sat up, held her close, and apologized over and over again. Until her eyes fluttered open and she whispered, "I wanted you just as badly. You're just stronger, that's all. You can last longer."

"I should call a doctor." He was stricken with remorse. He'd gone crazy. There was no other word for it.

She smiled faintly. "Give me a minute to rest."

"No way," he muttered. "We're done." Christ, he might have really hurt her.

"Maybe we can talk about it." Her smile was pure sunshine. "I have this insatiable craving, you see. I figure you're too good looking, and that's why I'm out of control."

"Whatever," he said, not willing to agree. Although

his own feelings were as inexplicable. He thought maybe having Jordi back was the reason, or being dead tired. Maybe they were both just in some peculiar, quirky, tie-me-up, tie-me-down place, and in the cold light of day, they'd be back to normal. "We'll talk about it later," he added, needing time to deal with the shit going on in his head.

"When later?"

Her voice was a seductive whisper, her green-eyed gaze provocative as hell. "Not for a while," he said. The last thing he needed were headlines about some lady ending up in the hospital because of him.

"Five minutes?" she pleaded.

He blew out a breath, inhaled deeply, and tried to think rationally. "We'll talk about it in half an hour."

"Okay," she said.

A smile slowly formed on her damned kissable mouth, and he was suddenly shaken to the core. He wasn't going to be able to say no. Whether in five minutes or half an hour or tomorrow, he fucking wanted her.

Twenty-one

"I GOTTA GO. SOMETIMES JORDI WAKES UP early."

The soft sound was warm against her ear, the voice deliciously familiar, the words a first for her in terms of male excuses. They tended to be more like, I have to go to work, or school, or once, walk my dog. Not that she'd had tons of morning-after excuses, but she'd had her moments. She'd even heard the one about having to catch an early flight, although that had been understandable. She'd met the guy on a layover in Miami. But having to get up for a child? Johnny had the perfect alibi for a quick retreat.

"Ummmm," she mumbled, not up to any conversation that would be patently false. Anyway, she was still half-asleep after a very, *very* lovely night of flame-hot sex. And seriously, still all aglow from Johnny's exceedingly pleasurable attentions. There was no way was she going to say anything to put him on the spot.

"I'll meet you back here at noon for lunch."

Dropping a light kiss on her cheek, he walked away.

Yeesss! So it wasn't just a wham, bam night of steamy sex. Lifting her lashes marginally, she watched him leave with the kind of adoring gaze predicated by a night of unbelievably fabulous orgasms. He'd dressed so quietly she'd not even heard him. But then he'd probably had plenty of practice at quick getaways. Not that she was going to complain when she'd benefitted so exquisitely from his expertise. The man was good at what he did—there was no doubt about it. And she wasn't talking about his music.

And now she'd see him at lunch!

She fell back to sleep with a smile on her face.

HOURS LATER, SHE CAME AWAKE WITH A START. Quickly glancing at the bedside clock, her eyes flared wide. OHMYGOD!!! IT WAS ELEVEN-THIRTY!!

Which meant she had only a half hour to shower, dress, and make herself presentable for lunch. The time wouldn't normally be an issue, were she in other than her current milieu—i.e., in the presence of a man who consorted with the great beauties of the world. A bit more makeup and attention to detail than usual was *definitely* called for. Or if the world had been a more perfect place, her own hairdresser and design consultant on call. Or even better—enough time to go out and buy something *decent* to wear.

Damn. If only she'd brought a better wardrobe.

If only she actually *possessed* a better wardrobe.

Unfortunately, her closet was a disaster zone of

leftover-from-college grunge, the requisite black suit, and mostly Gap—because the store was conveniently close to her house.

Aaaagh . . .

WHEN THE KNOCK ON THE DOOR SOUNDED PRE-cisely at noon, Nicky shouted, "Just a minute," sprayed another spritz of perfume around her neck and shoulders and shook her damp curls into place. Wrinkling her nose at her Gap-clad reflection in the mirror, she grabbed her jacket (okay, that was nice because she had a very talented friend who designed in leather) and purse (ditto there). But she was pretty near to marching into Chanel first chance she had and recklessly spending a month's salary on a decent outfit.

When she opened the door, Johnny surveyed her with a quick head-to-toe look. "You look nice and clean," he said in a low, sexy, highly insinuating drawl that went a long way toward saving her a bundle at Chanel. "How were the museums?" he added with a much-too-knowing grin.

She grinned back. "Very educational."

"Liar."

"So, I was tired. You, apparently, never sleep."

He winked. "I had better things to do last night."

"Did you actually go to the toy stores this morning?"

"Yep."

Of course he wouldn't disappoint his daughter. What was she thinking? "Did you buy them out?"

"Yep. Including something for you."

"No kidding?"

"No kidding."

"What did you get?" She couldn't help herself. She loved presents, and one from a toy store couldn't be expensive like the Chanel or Hermès he'd tried to give her. She could enjoy this one.

"You have to wait."

"Why?"

"Because."

"That's no reason."

"Because I'll show it to you tonight, then."

He'd said *tonight*, as in he was having sex with her tonight. Her vagina quivered in anticipation. She could feel the melting sensation send little waves of warm pleasure throughout her body. Taking issue, however, with his way too arrogant presumption that there was no need to ask her if she wanted sex with him tonight, she took a stand for female independence. "What if I were to say no?"

A flicker of surprise flashed in his eyes. "Then I'd try to change your mind," he smoothly replied, his gaze once again neutral.

"What if you couldn't?"

"Then I'd try harder." He didn't say this was a pointless conversation because he had no intention of irritating her. He leaned in closer. "I'd try really, really *hard*," he whispered.

Oh, God, oh, God . . . she remembered how hard he'd been, how resilient and indefatigable. How lusciously *large*. "Okay, so maybe tonight's good," she said, in a suffocated tone. "Damn you."

"I feel the same way, so we're even." He knew what she was damning as well as he knew that he shouldn't get involved with her in any way, shape, or form. She was building a tree house for Jordi. The construction would take weeks. He wasn't good with long-term relationships or *any* relationships, for that matter. He could be getting himself into one helluva mess.

"So we're making trouble for each other."

He blew out a breath. "Probably." His mouth quirked in a rueful smile. "But screw it."

She half-smiled. "Is that an invitation or a casual statement?"

He laughed. "If we had time"—he glanced up and down the hallway—"it would definitely be an invitation."

"I'd be happy to take a rain check."

"Ask me why I'm not surprised."

"Now why would I do that?"

Her voice had taken on a tiny edge. Oops. Dipping his head, he brushed her lips in a conciliatory kiss and eased her back a step so they were both inside her room. "You've been on my mind—like constantly." He shut the door. "So, if you want a rain check right now, I'll change our reservation. How's that?" He ran his finger lightly over the severe line of her brow.

"No, no, don't . . . really, I shouldn't be so—"

"Hot for sex?"

She gave him a look.

He laughed. "We're both hot for the same thing—okay? Although, just for the record, Vernie scares the shit out of me, and she and Jordi are waiting downstairs." His grin was boyish and sweet. He kissed her again, a butterfly kiss. "Why don't I make good on this later?" he whispered, lifting his mouth from hers. "I promise you'll like it."

Who was she kidding? Sex with him was awesome. No way was she gonna be difficult about when and where. "I *am* hungry," she said, planning on collecting her reward for Miss Congeniality later tonight.

He crooked his arm and grinned. "Then we'd better see that you're fed."

Carnal images from last night having to do with eating you-know-what suddenly surfaced, and her temperature racheted up big-time. Followed by a jolt of lust that rippled up her vagina, leaving her breathless. For an unnerving second, she debated the embarrassing ramifications that might ensue should she actually touch his outstretched arm. Not that she had a choice; he was expectantly *waiting*.

So with due warning to all her senses and sensibilities to *behave,* she gingerly placed her palm on his arm—and found that instead of behaving, SEX, NOW, NOW, NOW, was being instantly communicated to every susceptible nerve in her body. She should have known better. The impact of his physical beauty and animal magnetism up close and personal was irresistible.

It took every ounce of willpower she possessed to keep from pleading, *Please, please, can we have a quickie?"*

"Fucking A you turn me on," he murmured, as though reading her mind, or perhaps under the spell of the same prurient fairy dust. Dragging her into his body, he slid his hands down her back and held her hard against his rising erection. "I've been missing you something *fierce.*"

"I'm feeling out of control—insatiable," she whispered, twining her arms around his waist.

"Christ, I could fuck you right here and now." He grimaced, his nostrils flaring wide. "You're screwing with my head, babe."

"I don't like this mindless obsession any better than you," she muttered. "Maybe we're bad for each other," she suggested with that minor portion of her brain not entirely overwhelmed by lust.

"Uh-uh. No way." He might question his abnormal cravings for this woman, but not the inevitability of his fucking her again. *That* he was going to do. "It's just going to be a *long* day for both of us," he said with a sigh. Letting his hands drop, he took a step backward. "So I'd better keep my distance. Restraint's never been my strong suit."

To which all the tabloids would agree with full-color photos to prove it. In an effort to keep her face off the cover of *The Star* and save her family from embarrassment, Nicky said, "Maybe I shouldn't go for lunch."

"Hey. You're coming for lunch," he growled, all strong, virile male.

"Hey," she shot back, a tremor in her voice. "Tone down the macho shit. You're turning me on. Okay?"

He spun away, needing to get a grip on his raging lust. Slamming his palms against the wall, he hung there, head down, breathing hard.

Nicky shuddered, so incredibly aroused she wasn't sure she wouldn't come standing right there.

The air reeked with sexual need.

Like, the more you get, the more you want.

An almost uncontrollable craving hung in the balance.

Abruptly pushing away from the wall, constraint evident in every muscle in his body, Johnny said, "I'm good now. Under control"—he smiled tightly—"more or less. But don't touch me, don't look at me, don't even pass me the bread at lunch, or I might carry you off to the nearest dark hallway and fuck you senseless."

Nicky smiled faintly. "I'm so horny, I'm not sure I'd take issue. Look"—she held out her hand—"I'm shaking. Did you slip me some ecstasy when I wasn't looking?"

"I wish—because this drug-free, permanent hard-on I have for you is *freaking* me out."

She shouldn't have felt so gratified. She should have taken his comment at simple face value—as in he was unhappy with the intensity of his lust. But there it was—the difference between men and woman. She *adored* be-

ing wanted *that* badly while he was jumpy as hell over
wanting her too much.

Mars and Venus.

Immutably at odds.

Twenty-two

OVER LUNCH JOHNNY WAS ULTRACAUTIOUS not to make eye contact and Nicky was more than willing to comply. She was operating on the edge of reason anyway. The littlest thing—like a look or a smile—could push her over, and there she'd be making a fool of herself in some posh Paris restaurant.

Johnny limited his conversation to Jordi and Vernie, while Nicky participated in the general discussion only when it was absolutely necessary. It was safer if she kept her gaze elsewhere. Since the restaurant overlooked a garden and the people-watching was world-class, it was easy enough to use those distractions to keep her from shamelessly lusting after a man who should be *only* a client to her.

It also helped, distraction-wise, that Jordi chattered on nonstop, her relationship with her dad warm and unconstrained. The man was charming on every level—damn him. Father. Lover. Client. It wasn't fair that he was so divinely perfect in *every* way—including his mastery of the *Kama Sutra*. It made it real difficult to consider giving up sex with him—when, of course, she should.

For the sake of her business.

The potential for problems down the road was inevitable with a man like Johnny who never stayed with a woman much longer than it took for a rose to wilt.

If she had any sense at all she'd keep things strictly business.

On the other hand, she could be Zen about this entire episode—like live in the present and go with the flow. Definitely a more satisfying option.

The words *Nice* and *villa* jolted her out of her internal debate, and she began to listen to the conversation taking place. They were discussing a trip to the south of France. The playground for the rich and famous had such cachet—Cannes, Nice, Juan les Pins, Fitzgerald, Picasso, yachts the size of football fields . . .

Jordi, apparently, liked their villa in Nice because she had friends there. Vernie liked the climate and shopping. Johnny liked the seclusion. They all liked the private beach.

How great would it be to have a private beach on the Mediterranean, Nicky thought. Not that she would ever be in that tax bracket. In fact, not too long ago, she'd been wondering how to make her house payment. And in her business, she never lost sight of the fact that six-figure tree houses were luxury items. If the economy soured, those purchases would be the first to go.

But even such sobering thoughts couldn't dispel her current good cheer. A night of highly erotic, orgasmic pleasure left one feeling as though the world might in fact be one of endless pleasure. Like the tantalizing dessert that was being placed before her. The mouthwatering

scent of chocolate wafted into the air, the steaming con-
fection oozing sweet decadence and calories.

Not that she cared about calories at the moment.
She'd burned off enough calories last night to allow her
a full cart of pastries.

As Nicky was putting spoon to dessert, Johnny's
phone rang, but she barely noticed, so overwhelmed
were her senses by succulent chocolate.

She heard Johnny say, "Excuse me," but only glanced
up in passing as he left the table. She was intent on her
first delicious taste of a dessert that could pass for a flamboyant Easter hat. But she'd also been seriously ignoring
Johnny during lunch in order to keep desire at bay, and
continuing down that path seemed an expedient exercise.

So it was a bolt from the blue when she felt a hand
slip under her arm and lift her to her feet before she was
half done with her dessert.

"Vernie, if you'll take Jordi back to the hotel when
you've finished," Johnny said, taking the spoon from
Nicky's hand and dropping it on the table. "I just received
a business call I have to handle, and I need Nicky to trans-
late for me. This fellow doesn't speak English very well."

But my *dessert*, Nicky silently protested, eyeing the
chocolate pastry with longing.

"We might stop at the arcade on our way back,"
Vernie declared.

"I'd rather you didn't until I return." Johnny's voice
was mild, but he held Vernie's gaze for a charged moment. "When you're finished here, Barry will take you
back to the hotel."

Vernie nodded; if Johnnie had called Barry to come
for them, she wasn't about to ask questions. "We'll
work on that fairy tale Jordi's been writing instead."

"I'm on page ten already, Dad. Vernie helps me with
the spelling, but otherwise it's all my stuff."

"She has your creative talent," Vernie said, smiling at Johnny. "It's a fascinating story."

Jordi jabbed her finger at her father. "But you can't read it till it's all done."

"Whatever you say, sweetie. This shouldn't take long. I'll be back soon."

With a wave, he began leading Nicky from the restaurant, when a male voice called out, "Hey, Surfer Man!"

She could feel Johnny's grasp tighten, but his smile was in place as he turned to the nearby table. "Hey, yourself, Mikey. Small world."

"We're here for the races. What about you?"

"Hi, Jill." Johnny nodded at the woman seated beside Mikey in the banquette. "Just a visit for me. This is Nicky Lesdaux. Nicky, Mikey and Jill Chambers. We all went to high school together."

Mike did a thumbs-up. "Championship football team our senior year, right?"

"Thanks to you. Mikey was our quarterback," Johnny explained to Nicky.

"If ol' sticky fingers hadn't caught every one of my passes, we never would have made it. So how're things goin' for you?"

"Can't complain," Johnny said. "You know, mostly workin' hard. How's the law firm?"

"We're keeping our heads above water. You have to come back, and we'll hit the waves on Casper Beach."

"Jeez, I haven't surfed in years."

"I go out with my kids." Mikey smiled. "You know, maintain the skill set—or at least try."

"Christ, it sounds good. I'll give you a call. I have an appointment, or I'd stay and chat. Great to see you both."

As they moved toward the door, Johnny said, "Mikey and I used to watch the weather forecasts and wait for the big waves. It's not world-class surfing up there, but damned fun." He blew out a breath. "Christ, life fucking changes. That was Lisa on the phone, and she's in some goddamned mess. I had to call Barry and Cole. Not that they had to come far," Johnny grumbled. "They were parked across the street."

Personally, Nicky was glad they'd ignored Johnny's orders to stay at the hotel. Talk of drug cartels and money laundering made her nervous. "They just worry about you, that's all," she said.

"I guess," he muttered, as they stepped outside. "If you'll excuse me for a minute," he said, walking toward the Mercedes that was sitting at the curb. The passenger-side window rolled down, and he leaned forward and started talking fast.

His voice was low, so Nicky couldn't hear what he was saying, but she could tell he was pissed. His tone was brusque, his dark brows were set in a scowl, and then he said loudly enough for anyone to hear, "Fucking Lisa. She's nothing but trouble."

Moments later, Barry accompanied Johnny back. As he went inside the restaurant, Johnny took Nicky's arm. "We're taking the car. Barry, Vernie, and Jordi will go back in a cab." Helping Nicky into the Mercedes a moment later, he took his seat beside her. Cole gave them a nod from up front beside the driver, and the car pulled away from the curb and eased into traffic.

Cole half turned. "Where to, boss?"

"Lisa was in hysterics as usual, but near as I can tell, we have two choices. She was whispering—apparently she's on her boyfriend's shit list for taking something of his—so she didn't make a lot of sense. But she needs rescuing; that much I figured out." He smiled tightly. "Sound familiar?"

"Been there, done that, boss. The woman is in constant crisis mode."

"Affirmative there, but this time, she might be in over her head. These guys she's with are loser hoodlums, but their daddies aren't above sending out a hit squad or two."

"Not to worry. We brought along extra firepower. Yours is under my seat."

"New stuff," the driver added in a distinct Bronx accent. "Prime stuff."

"So where to first?" Cole asked.

"A shop in the fifteenth arrondissement." Johnny gave the address.

Extra firepower? Had she heard right? "Did he say extra firepower?" Nicky murmured, hitting Johnny on the arm just to make sure he was paying attention.

"You won't be in any danger," Johnny replied, intent on unzipping a small duffel bag he'd pulled out from under Cole's seat.

"Then why do you need WEAPONS?" she gasped. Cars with guns in bags under the seats were way the hell outside her normal operating zone.

"Relax." Johnny glanced up and gave her a reassuring smile. "It's just insurance." He sat up, a deadly looking handgun held lightly in his grasp.

It didn't help her peace of mind when he slipped out the clip, checked it, and shoved it back into place. It really, really didn't help when he bent over again and pulled out another smaller handgun.

"This is nice. Is it custom?" The weapon shone in his palm with a jewel-like, poisonous gleam.

"Beretta's newest model," the driver noted. "I couldn't pass it up."

"Who could? It's a beauty."

In her world, beauty was defined in terms of nonlethal objects. She was truly out of her element. In fact, she was so far outside anything remotely recognizable that she felt as though she might melt into a puddle of fear where she sat. Like now—this second.

"Hey," Johnny whispered, as though he was psychic. "It's okay. Don't freak. We're going to two chocolate shops, there'll be lots of people around, you couldn't be safer."

"If it's so safe, why does your ex need rescuing?"

"She probably doesn't. She probably just thinks she does." And that might even be true, although Lisa's boyfriends—zoned out or not—gave him pause. But he wasn't going into any detail about possible risks because he needed Nicky to ask questions once they reached the shops. She had plenty of protection between the three of them anyway. And it was broad daylight.

Dropping the smaller handgun into his jacket pocket, he shoved the other one back under Cole's seat. Then, he took Nicky's hand and held it the rest of the way to their first stop, making casual conversation as though the subject of guns and hit men had never come up. He even made her laugh once or twice before they reached their destination.

Unfortunately, at the sight of the dingy neighborhood, low-rent government office buildings across the street, and the battered white door before which they eventually stood—unmarked and without a handle or bell to ring—Nicky's apprehension returned.

"Are you sure you're at the right place?" she whispered. It didn't look like a chocolate shop to her. There was no sign, no windows, not a clue that anything existed behind the crusty facade.

"We'll find out," Johnny said and banged his fist on the peeling paint.

The door opened a few inches, and the whiff of warm, fresh chocolate practically knocked them over.

At least the chocolate part was right, Nicky thought, feeling a modicum less anxious.

After she asked for the owner by name, a few moments later, a slender, young man with a shock of black hair appeared from behind one of two gleaming stainless-steel machines that were spreading chocolate in a thin coating over every imaginable filling. Trays of delicate chocolates were everywhere.

The sight of so many bonbons reminded Nicky of the *I Love Lucy* episode where Lucy and Ethel were working on the candy conveyor belt and stuffing chocolates into their mouths and pockets as fast as they could. Definitely a thought, she reflected, her fingers unconsciously flexing, her saliva glands ramping up into overdrive.

She even forgot about possible danger for a moment with her senses assailed by such a largesse of chocolate.

As the man approached, Johnny broke into Nicky's blissful reverie by saying, "Ask him if a woman or two women and two men were here recently? One would have been blond. He might even know Lisa from the movies. They were coming here for some special chocolate order."

Nicky tamped down the sudden fear that reasserted itself at Johnny's words and quickly translated his queries.

"Non, non." The shop owner shook his head and proceeded to explain in a torrent of French.

Johnny glanced from one to the other until the man finished. "Lisa was here?" Her name had come up several times.

"They were all here, but he told them he couldn't fill their order," Nicky interpreted. "He has more customers than he needs. And he didn't like the men's attitude. He's an artist, he says, not a shopkeeper, and he grew up in the rough part of town, so he can't be intimidated. He told them to take their business elsewhere. Actually, he told them to shove it."

Johnny's brows rose. "Brave man," he murmured. "But just in case they show up again, ask him to give me a call." Johnny handed the man his card.

Another rapid-fire conversation in which the Frenchman sneered a reply even Johnny could understand. Then with a beaming smile and the words *U2*—clear in any language—he proceeded to hug Johnny and kiss him on both cheeks.

Whisking a large red box from a nearby shelf filled with red boxes, the chocolatier handed it to Johnny with a sweeping bow. Glancing at Nicky, he spoke again in rapid French.

"The chocolates are for you. He's making these for some prince, but he wants you to have this box. Or take them all if you want, he says." Nicky grinned. "He thinks you're real special."

Johnny took the offered box, smiling. "Thank him and tell him we appreciate his information. Then cut it short. We have to go, babe. ASAP."

Shortly after, they were being escorted out of the factory by one of only eleven chocolate specialists in recent years to have received the MOF (Meilleur Ouvrier de France—those most honored chefs and pâtissiers). They were also extended an effusive invitation to come back any time.

After more kissing of cheeks all around, they were finally back in the Mercedes.

"Dalloyau next," Johnny instructed the driver. "And Lisa better be there," he grimly said. Because if she wasn't, he was out of options—and maybe patience, too. Who knew if this wild-goose chase was even for real?

Twenty-three

IN THE COURSE OF THEIR DRIVE TO DAL-
loyau, Nicky tried very hard not to give in to her
weakness for chocolate. Especially at a time like
this. They were on a serious rescue mission, not to mention she'd almost freaked out only minutes before. Her
cravings should have been irrelevant. It was probably
disrespectful to even consider them at a time like this.
But then they got stuck in traffic, and everyone started
swearing. As if she wasn't stressed enough, what with
guns and hit squads.

Take a deep breath. Focus. Think of ocean waves
washing the shore.

Yeah, right.

"Would you mind?" Nicky blurted out, pointing to
the red box lying on the floor between them.

She got one of those blank looks like she might
have if she'd asked when the rocket to the moon was

lifting off. And then joy of joys, her question seemed to register.

"Sure. Go for it," Johnny said.

Then he was off in some other dimension again, his gaze on the snarl of cars surrounding them in the traffic circle. Every driver was honking his horn and making lewd gestures, as if the din and acting out would unravel the gridlock.

Not that Nicky minded everyone's serious mind-set on the traffic. It allowed her an opportunity to open the box and offer obeisance to distinguished chocolate unheeded by those less discerning of its wonder. Plucking out a small round bonbon, she popped it into her mouth, letting her taste buds absorb the matchless flavor of chocolate nurtured by loving hands from plantation to finished product. Ohmygod, it had a coconut center. That made it almost as good as sex. Really. She'd given this considerable thought over the years. So stress wasn't her only excuse for eating chocolate. She had a boatload of reasons. The motto CHOCOLATE ISN'T JUST FOR BREAKFAST was prominently displayed on her fridge.

By the time the Mercedes broke free and was moving again, she'd sampled three exquisite chocolates and was luxuriating in gustatory bliss. "Want one?" She offered the box to Johnny in one of those automatic gestures.

He glanced over, frowned, opened his mouth, shut it, then apparently deciding to be polite, smiled. "Not right now, but thanks."

Oops. Clearly, he was distracted. As if she didn't know. "Sorry," she murmured. "You must be really worried."

He looked at her for a second like she'd grown another head. "Worried? Hell no. I'm fucking pissed. Do you know how many times Lisa's done this to me? How many times we've had to deal with her real or make-believe disasters? Ask Cole—he knows—hey, cut over two blocks to the left, Vinnie," Johnny said, sharply, leaning forward and concentrating on the road. "We'll make better time."

If she'd been perhaps slightly clueless before, she no longer was, having been bluntly apprized of the current state of affairs between the former Mr. and Mrs. Patrick.

And truth be told, she was feeling considerably better for having broached the subject. Johnny and his ex-wife would not be reconciling any time soon. Not that she should be concerned one way or the other. And she wasn't—truly; she was firmly based in reality.

Vinnie had taken a sharp turn to the left, then a right, and they were driving down a street with very little traffic. Vinnie was pushing the speed limit enough that—in the interest of surviving to finish the box of chocolates—Nicky grabbed hold of a conveniently placed hand bar and sent up a prayer to whatever saint was in charge of traffic accidents. The Mercedes ran three red lights, taking numerous corners on squealing tires, until Vinnie brought the car to a hard braking stop perpendicular to the curb. In a no parking zone. Ten feet from the entrance to a classy looking shop with a display of pastries in the windows so spectacular they didn't look real.

Maybe they just dusted off the plaster of Paris facsimiles from time to time, she was thinking as Vinnie opened her door and helped her from the car. After almost bumping into a Maserati, Nicky noticed several other upscale cars in the no parking zone. Big money had its privileges, apparently.

After being whisked through the door of Dalloyau's, Johnny came to a stop just inside the entrance. He surveyed the room while Nicky took in the dazzling sight of every delicacy known to man. Not just pastries lined the display cases, but gorgeous, pretty-as-a-picture, take-out food for royalty.

Indeed, the customers all reeked of status.

She did a quick check of shoes, the ultimate sign of wealth.

Sure enough. Not a Payless shoe in the store.

Before she could move up to estimating wardrobes, she was being nudged forward.

"Lisa's not here," Johnny muttered. "We'll check upstairs."

The curved staircase was paneled in some exotic wood and illuminated with muted cornice lighting, the room at the top of the stairs filled with ladies who lunch, a schoolgirl or so with her father (one would hope), and a smattering of tourists distinguished by their guide books and camera bags.

"Wait here."

She didn't mind Johnny's brusque command, since it offered her the opportunity to examine the desserts everyone had ordered. The diners weren't just eating desserts, of course, but the colorful confections were an obvious draw at Dalloyau.

Before she had time to decide which she'd like best, Johnny and Cole returned, looking displeased.

"Nothing," Johnny said in the essentially shorthand speech he'd adopted since they'd left the chocolate factory. "Fuck."

Figuring that was an expletive rather than a question, she didn't reply as they moved to retrace their steps.

"What now, boss?" Cole asked as they stood at the bottom of the stairs.

"Good question."

"Would you mind if I did a little shopping while you two decide what to do?" Nicky interjected—real politely though—just in case they were inclined to say no. "It'll just take a second," she added with a smile for good measure.

Cole looked at Johnny.

Johnny frowned at her. "I need you to ask someone here a few questions."

That didn't sound like a yes. Too bad. Then again, everything looked like it was at least ten thousand calories, so maybe God was telling her something. "Ask what?"

"Has Lisa been here? With anyone? And when." Clipped, curt, all business.

Which didn't promise time for any shopping, she gloomily decided. After a swift glance around, Nicky figured the woman wearing a suit and name tag in the back where all the boxes of chocolates were displayed looked managerial. Unlike the shopgirls behind the counters.

Approaching her, Nicky smiled, prefacing her queries with an apology for her accent. The French always liked when you spoke French, even if it was the antiquated version of French-Canadian still spoken in her grandmother's part of northern Minnesota. The woman turned out to be more than amiable.

Yes, Lisa Jordan had been here. Obviously, this manager knew her celebrities. But the men who had come in with Miss Jordan, she said, had offended her. She referred to them with a vulgarity, then added with a shrug, "But what can you do. They're regular customers."

In better humor, however, she went on to describe Miss Jordan's exquisite coral-colored Chanel ensemble as well as her friend's and not wishing to offend, Nicky listened at some length to the runway-type descriptions. It was true. Haute couture *was* in every French person's genes.

When the description finally wound down, Nicky

thanked the manager for the information and returned to Johnny. "Your ex was here," she explained. "They all were—just a short time ago. The women walked out first while the men made some purchases. The men were crude, but good customers, so they're tolerated, it seems."

Johnny grunted.

Whether in affirmation or dissent was unclear.

"Back to the Ritz, then?" Cole's brows rose in query. "I don't suppose it would be wise to call your ex's cell phone?"

"Probably not. She sounded frightened." Johnny shrugged. "Whether it was true or not, who the hell knows." He turned to Nicky. "Buy something if you want." He pulled some large bills out of his pants pocket and held them out. "We'll wait a few minutes."

He didn't smile. His voice was without expression. Should she or shouldn't she?

It was a short-lived debate, surrounded as she was by beautiful, succulent delicacies beyond the imagination. Or at least the imagination of anyone from Black Duck.

"Thanks, but I have money." Then understanding she was on sufferance, she rushed through the store making her selections. She couldn't eat them right now, what with their crisis and the fact that she'd just eaten lunch and some chocolates, but clearly she wasn't going to be back here anytime soon. One had to take advantage of a rare opportunity like this.

Literally five minutes later, carrying three little boxes, she joined Johnny, who was waiting at the door.

Gentleman that he was, he took the boxes from her and even managed to open the door with his hands full. But his mouth was set in a firm line, his brows drawn together in a scowl.

She felt a twinge of guilt for her selfishness.

Until she reminded herself that she'd asked. He could have said no.

She was really excellent at rationalizing.

"I'd say the Ritz is our best bet," Cole noted as they walked toward the car.

"No doubt," Johnny muttered. "And I'm in the mood to pistol whip someone about now."

Jeez. Was it her? Nicky shot him a look.

"If Lisa is at the Ritz with those guys, I'm pissed off enough to set them straight. They're fucking wusses anyway."

No pistol whipping for her, thank you, Nicky noted, although she would prefer being somewhere distant if any serious disputes took place.

"Sounds like a plan, boss."

"Where do you want these?" Johnny asked as they reached the car, half lifting the boxes in Nicky's direction.

Close enough to inhale the sumptuous aromas, Nicky wished to say, but not with that scowl on his face. "I don't care. Wherever."

"Hey, Vinnie, open the trunk!"

Some people apparently didn't appreciate the gustatory pleasures of life as much as other people, she thought, but didn't dare protest as her little savories were placed in the trunk.

The mood in the car was dark as they pulled out of the no parking zone in front of Dalloyau. Even without a word being spoken, an inhospitable air of ruthless purpose permeated the car. Or maybe it was *because* no one spoke.

Scrunching into a corner of the backseat, Nicky tried not to breathe too loudly. It was that quiet.

They hadn't traveled very far when Vinnie rapped out, "There they are. By the Elysée Palace. Beside that guard with the Uzi."

"Yesss." Johnny breathed, victory and satisfaction in

that sibilant utterance. "Pull over at the corner. Slowly. I don't want any sort of scene."

The residence of the president of France was on the posh Rue de Faubourg St.-Honoré where all the fine shops were located. When Paris had been smaller, the palace had once been home to notable women—Mme. Pompadour, Napoleon's sister, Empress Josephine. Just as Dalloyau had been their little local market of choice.

And now another notable woman was in the neighborhood, standing only yards away from the soldiers on guard before the Elysees Palace. The stunning Lisa Jordan in her dazzling Chanel ensemble and a dark-haired woman of equal beauty were admiring the facade like tourists.

"She's with Chantel."

"Who else?" Cole affirmed. "Sisters in addiction."

"Do you see any punks in the vicinity?"

"That limo down the block might be theirs."

Johnny smiled. "You have to give the ladies credit. They picked a pretty unassailable position."

At which precise moment, Johnny's cell phone rang.

He glanced at the number and grinned as he flipped open the phone. "I'm looking at you, babe." There was a smile in his voice. "Stay put. We're coming to get you."

Johnny and Cole were out of the car in a flash, striding toward the women like heroes in a movie, Nicky thought, finding the scene mildly disturbing. There he was, being gracious and obliging to his ex, going to her rescue like some selfless defender of the weak and oppressed. Maybe Johnny didn't really know if he liked his ex or not. Maybe he was still enamored of her after all. Although, it was none of her business whether Johnny Patrick was happy to see his ex or not. She had absolutely no right to feel an ounce of possessiveness after sleeping with him once. Probably half the women in the world had as much right as she, according to the tabloids.

Cautioning herself to act like a mature adult, Nicky warned herself against feeling the littlest smidgen of jealousy. She'd be crazy to even consider the notion. A one-night stand did not a relationship make. Period. End of story. Really. Do not go there, she sternly admonished her wavering psyche.

Chantel joined Cole in the front seat, while Johnny offered a helping hand to Lisa as she stepped into the back. Nicky moved over as far as she could on the broad seat, shifted her purse closer to her feet, picked up the box of chocolates from the floor, put it in her lap, and took pains to put a smile on her face as Lisa sat down beside her. Nicky even kept her smile in place when Lisa sharply elbowed her in the ribs and shoved her even closer to the window.

As Johnny shut the door behind him and the car pulled away from the curb, Lisa fidgeted with her purse on the floor. Sitting up a moment later, she held a cigarette and lighter in her hand. With the detached air of a female grandee speaking to a servant, she pointed the cigarette at Nicky. "I see you're still around. You must be *very, very special.*"

In an apparent attempt to shift the conversation to one less fraught with contention, Johnny stepped in and explained that in addition to serving as his translator, Nicky had designed a fantastic tree house for Jordi. "It's going to be a real beauty."

"You're kidding." A silvery little movie-star laugh rang through the car. "Tree houses? Is that like building birdhouses?"

"They're a little bigger," Nicky replied, feeling totally mature as she ignored Lisa's pettiness with a completely Zen-like generosity of spirit. There was no way building tree houses was inferior to playing make-believe on the silver screen anyway. But a second later, it took every ounce of discipline she possessed to keep from snapping something uncivil when Lisa Jordan cast her violet gaze on Nicky and purred, "Just because Johnny sleeps with you doesn't mean a thing. He sleeps with everyone, don't you, darling," the goddess of Hollywood added. The smile she turned on her ex-husband was sweetly understanding.

"Christ, Lisa, can it. Sorry," Johnny muttered, leaning forward to glance past his ex and offer Nicky a rueful smile.

"You can make it up to her tonight. He'll make it up to you tonight, Mickey," Lisa Jordan said, her voice soft with malice, the glance she turned on Nicky ice cold. "He's very *good* at making up."

"Just a reminder, Lisa, we saved your ass. So kindly shut the fuck up," Johnny growled. "And don't smoke in the car."

"My, my, aren't we touchy." She leaned over and dropped the cigarette and lighter back into her purse. "I meant it as a compliment, darling," she went on, sitting up once again. "You're *excellent* in bed."

"Jeez, Lisa, take it easy," Chantel murmured over her shoulder. "Johnny's right about saving us, and I for one am grateful. Although, if you hadn't taken those black pearls we wouldn't *be* in trouble. I *told* you not to take them, but no, you could handle Yuri, you said."

"What black pearls?" Johnny demanded, his gaze laser sharp.

Lisa glared at the back of her friend's head, then shrugged dismissively. "Yuri had so many pearls, I never thought he'd notice," she airily replied. "They weren't even in the safe. But thanks to Chantel here who caves at the smallest pressure, he found out I took them."

"Excuse *me*," Chantel drawled. "I call a threat to dump us in the middle of the Mediterranean more than a little pressure."

Lisa snorted. "They wouldn't have."

"Is that why you called me? Because you thought they wouldn't?" Johnny observed with delicate sarcasm.

"No. That's not why I called you," Lisa replied, huffily. "I just wanted to get out of town."

"Wise choice," Chantel shot back.

"Screw you."

"Okay, ladies, cut the useless recriminations. Let's talk about something more productive," Johnny interposed, not about to listen to an endless blame game. "I'll send you home in my jet so you don't have to deal with any possible problems with your friends. But I'd suggest in the future you steer clear of men who operate outside the law. That way you can both live long and productive lives."

"I don't need any lectures from you," Lisa said. "Not when you've always done whatever you've pleased."

"You need something from me right now, or you'd still be standing in front of the Elysée cooling your heels," Johnny said, curtly. "So don't give me any shit. I'm sending you home before you get into any more trouble." He leaned toward the front seat. "We're going to the airport, Vinnie."

"I need my clothes from the Ritz first," Lisa snapped.

If looks could kill, everyone in the limo would be wasted, Nicky thought. With the exception of one blond, fuming movie star. Although every little exchange that had transpired since Lisa Jordan had entered the car allowed Nicky to better understand Johnny's feelings for his ex. He might be willing to rescue her—out of some sense of duty or for old-time's sake, or maybe because he was a nice guy. But it wasn't for love.

"I'll have your clothes sent to you," Johnny said, brusquely. "Cole, call the Ritz and tell them to pack up the ladies' clothes ASAP and send them to Lisa's place in the States. Yuri was in that limo across the street, right?" He gave Lisa a hard, searching look.

"Yes," Chantel quickly answered, sensible of their perilous position, even if her friend was in denial.

"Okay. That means there's time to get your things out of the hotel, even if they drive there directly. Which I doubt." Yuri was a spoiled brat. He'd go somewhere to sulk—preferably where he could get high and find women to console him.

Even if Nicky was irritated about Miss High and Mighty's nastiness to her, the scenario unfolding in the limo was fascinating to watch. It was like being in the front row at a play. Only this time the performance was for real. One sullen little movie star who apparently lived in a fantasy world made possible by her looks and celebrity, rescued from the big, bad villains by her ex-husband.

And she doesn't even thank him.

What the hell had he ever seen in Lisa Jordan? Why had he married her? Was she missing something? Or was Johnny Patrick like every other man in the world—dazzled by a sexy, gorgeous goddess of the silver screen?

It gave Nicky food for thought on the largely silent drive to the airport. It presented various possibilities to consider about who, what, when, where, and why these two very different people had married. Mostly, it made her wonder how stupid she was to be infatuated with a man who could actually marry a bitch like Lisa Jordan.

Crap.

Did that make her a bitch, too?

Twenty-four

EN ROUTE, JOHNNY CRYPTICALLY SAID TO Cole, "Tell Barry to meet us out there."

Cole nodded, and that was that.

Male ESP, Nicky decided.

Once Lisa and Chantel left the car and were being escorted to the plane by Vinnie and Cole, Johnny moved closer to Nicky. Leaning back, he exhaled a sigh of relief and turning his head enough to see her, grinned. "Problem solved. She's out of my hair."

"And solved without a shot being fired, I'm happy to say." Nicky gave him the thumbs-up.

He laughed. "That was only a remote possibility."

"You coulda fooled me."

"Sorry to put you through this, but I didn't know where we'd end up." He blew out a small breath. "And if I needed someone who spoke French—you were it."

"Happy to be of service—now, *after* the fact." She smiled. "There were times I wasn't so sure."

His answering smile was free and easy. "Don't worry—everything's good. Once Lisa's back in the States, someone else can pick up the slack if she needs protection. Hollywood is teeming with security." His expression took on a sudden earnestness. "I do have a favor to ask of you, though."

"What kind of favor?" she asked, her tone marginally wary after the recent events.

"If you don't mind *too* much, I'd like to go to Nice for a couple of days. Just until my pilots can get back. I know it's a huge imposition with your tight construction schedule, but I'd be willing to make it worth your while. Seriously. Anything you want."

A large engagement ring? A wedding in Capri? Lifelong fidelity? Jeez, where the hell did that come from? It just went to show how great sex, movie star looks, and tons of money could turn a girl's head. More realistically, she asked the question that could be the deal breaker. "A couple of days as in two? Or are you thinking more?"

"No, two days should be enough. My pilots will just need some sleep time before they make the run back to Nice."

Cole suddenly appeared at the car window, and Johnny hit the button to roll it down.

"They're here, and the charter's ready."

"That was fast. We'll be right out." Johnny turned back to Nicky. "Jordi and Vernie are here with Barry."

Nicky gave him an accusing look. "So your questions were rhetorical?"

"No. Look, if you can't come, I'll send you home. I just thought you might like to see Nice," he said, a promise of pleasure in every soft syllable.

He must know no woman could turn him down.

She could be the first.

She could give up seeing his villa and the beach life of the rich and famous.

She could be a complete idiot.

"Okay. Two days. Then I have to get home," she said, because she *would* be a complete idiot if she let herself be talked into staying any longer just because God's gift to women was beaucoup talented in bed. A way distant echo of concern, though, was what to tell Buddy. Even two extra days was gonna make him scream big-time. In the interest of adding two days of world-class sexual memories to her souvenir album, she'd have to promise Buddy something good. Like maybe time off for that fishing trip he'd been wanting to take.

"That's great. Thanks. I mean it."

Hearing Johnny Patrick say thanks, he really meant it, went a long way toward making it easier for her to say what she was about to say. "There's one little iffy thing though. I do have to check with Buddy—you know . . . see if he can deal with the work for a few more days. I have a feeling he's gonna go ballistic."

"If there's anything I can do to help . . ."

"Give me your phone. I'll call him." As she punched in the numbers she asked, "What time is it back home?"

"Five in the morning."

"Good. He's up." Then she waited for the ring, telling herself she was the boss, she owned the company, and if she wanted to have phenomenal sex for a few more days, she deserved it. "Hey, Buddy, it's me, and you're gonna go ape, but I'm staying for two more days." She held the phone away from her ear for a few seconds, before saying, "What do you think about going on that fishing trip when I get back? Take off a week. I'll cover for you."

"Tell him to use my place in Tahoe if he wants," Johnny interjected.

"Johnny says you can use his place in Tahoe. Okay, that won't work then. Yes, yes . . . absolutely. I won't ask for any more favors. Right after I get home, you take off. Make your reservations. Yeah, yeah, it's written in stone. Make your reservations." Nicky nodded her head and said yes or no to a number of questions, offered slightly longer answers to a few more, and after promising once again that two days wouldn't be extended any further, she hung up. "Buddy's going deep sea fishing, but he said thanks for the offer."

"So we're good now? Buddy's not too pissed?"

She smiled. "Not too much. I'll be paying penance for a while. But I'm figuring it'll be worth it."

"I can promise you it will be. You name it, it's yours."

"Meaning?"

"Anything."

"Anything sexual you mean?"

"Anything, anything—if it exists, you can have it."

"Jeez, you're kinda freaking me out with your blanket largesse policy. You're not crazy, are you?"

"No. I'm just really intrigued by your dewy fresh sweetness."

"Hey!" She wasn't sure about dew fresh with that teasing light in his eyes.

"It's a compliment, babe. You're sweet as hell." He studied the toes of his shoes for a moment before hitting her again with that cool gray gaze. "Look, you remind me of my life a couple hundred years ago—before I began living in this fabricated, plastic world."

"I'm not completely gullible just because I don't know movie producers and rock stars," she asserted. "I didn't fall off the last turnip truck."

"No one's saying you're gullible—or even thinking it.

You're just nice. Hey, there's Jordi." He waved at his daughter, who was running toward the car, then turned back to Nicky. "So we're good for a couple of days?" he said, like no one had even mentioned dew fresh or harbored any equivocal feelings. Like life was back to normal.

"We're good." She could do measured and calm, too.

In a flash, his mouth was against her ear.

"We're good in more ways than one," he whispered. Then reaching for the door handle, he shoved the door open. "Hey, baby girl," he said, greeting his daughter. "Did Vernie tell you we're going to Nice?"

The echo of his words sent a warm glow through her body, although, flip side, she was slightly intimidated by the ease with which Johnny Patrick bent the world to his will. She'd never known anyone who could bend even a teeny, tiny part of the world to their will. And now, she was traveling with a man who chartered planes like most people bought BART tickets, who rescued women from gangsters and walked into restaurants and hotels like he owned them. Oh, Christ, look at that. There was all their luggage being wheeled out on the tarmac. "Our luggage!" she blurted out. "Who packed it so fast?"

He was halfway out of the car, but he paused and glanced back. "The staff at the Castille is efficient. Although," he added with a grin, "it helps that I know the owner."

Of course he did. He fucking knew everybody. Although, that explained the excellent service, Nicky thought, and the excessive courtesy and lack of questions when she checked in. Not to mention, the view of the Eiffel Tower in her room.

After helping her out, he pulled her close for a second. "Thanks for coming along."

"Thanks for asking." She didn't have time to say more. Jordi was plucking at her father's sleeve.

"Daddy, Daddy! You won't believe how fast we drove here! It was *so* much fun! Barry said you were waiting and we had to *roll*! Didn't he, Vernie?"

"We could have raced in the Indy 500," Vernie noted, her cheeks still slightly flushed from the excitement. "I gather you were in a bit of a hurry."

Johnny met her gaze over his daughter's head. "It seemed like a good idea to leave. I felt like swimming in the sun. How about you, sweetie?" he said, brushing his fingers over his daughter's curls. "Are you in the mood for a swim on our beach?"

"Yes, yes, yes!" Jordi was fidgeting from foot to foot. "Are we going right NOW?"

"Right this second. You lead the way. Over there where Cole and Barry are standing."

"Lisa must have called you at lunch," Vernie muttered, keeping pace with Johnny and Nicky as they followed Jordi. "I saw your look."

"Who else precipitates a crisis wherever she goes?" He grimaced. "But everything's back on track; Lisa and Chantel are headed for the States. We're going to wait for the plane to return, so I thought Nice would be as good a place as any to sit it out. You'll have a couple of days to drink some of that local wine."

"Twist my arm," Vernie said, grinning.

Johnny chuckled, then glanced at Nicky. "You'll like the wine. It's a nice, smooth red."

She was figuring there were things in Nice she was going to like better than the wine, but Johnny Patrick's ego was already more than adequate. "Sounds good," she said, in lieu of the X-rated comment on the tip of her tongue. "I love red wine."

Twenty-five

SHE'D SEEN A VILLA LIKE JOHNNY'S ON TV once. It was on a program about some art collector who'd wanted to live like Monet and Matisse—you know, breathe the same air, absorb the same vibe, wallow in the life of an artist without actually doing the work. Not to mention this guy was like ten times richer than either Monet or Matisse—neither of whom had been exactly poor.

Anyway, it was one helluva villa.

Not that she begrudged Johnny his wealth.

He'd worked for it.

But, jeez, consider how hard it was going to be readjusting to her life once she was home again. A person could get real used to this splendor. Like, having a limo always waiting at the airport or something like this Garden of Eden surrounding your Mediterranean retreat. Splendor aside, though, she was mostly going to miss the surprisingly down-to-earth guy who'd just whispered in her ear before they'd gotten out of the car, "I'm glad you're here. I haven't felt this good in ages."

Not that she'd had time to do more than smile in return before they were greeted by a young woman wearing a hand-dyed sundress and sandals, who'd been waiting on the broad marble steps.

"Claire, I'd like you to meet Nicky. Nicky, this is Claire, who's nice enough to put up with our erratic schedule." Johnny smiled. "I apologize for the short notice. Things came up at the last minute."

"We're pleased to see you anytime," the young woman replied in slightly accented English. "Marie's at the beach, but I told her I'd send for her the minute you arrive. She's thrilled Jordi's going to be here."

"I'm going down to the beach right now," Jordi announced as she came around the car. "Is that okay, Daddy? Pleeease! Vernie'll come with me, won't you?"

Johnny looked at Vernie.

"Sure, kiddo." Vernie handed her purse to Johnny. "Send down some of that red wine when you get a chance," she added. "And my big hat"—she smiled— "and I wouldn't mind a snack."

Johnny glanced at Claire. "I'll get the hat, if you get the other stuff." He looked at Vernie again. "We'll be down in a minute. I just want to show Nicky her room."

"Andre will bring Vernie her things," Claire offered, with a smile for Johnny. "And we're having bouillabaisse for dinner, Vernie," she added, "so save your appetite."

Vernie grinned. "I must have died and gone to heaven. I don't suppose we're having Le Vacherin for dessert."

Claire laughed. "But, of course."

"I don't know why you can't set up your studio here,"

Vernie challenged. "Think how much work you'd get done without interruptions."

"Think how hard it would be to get anyone to work out here with all the distractions—topless beaches, great bars, great wines," Johnny noted, smiling faintly.

"Sure, rain on my parade."

"Ver-*nee*! Let's *go*! I want to see Marie!" Jordi insisted, pulling on Vernie's hand. "Daddy, stop *talking* to her!"

"Okay, okay, we're going." The nanny winked at Johnny. "Just think about it, that's all I'm saying."

"Will do. See you in five." He turned to Claire. "Nicky's in Victoria's room, right?"

"Yes. All is ready."

"*Victoria's* room?" Nicky murmured, thinking it can't be.

"Queen Victoria used to spend some time here."

His voice was so casual he could have been remarking on the weather. "Do you mean to tell me this is Queen *Victoria's* place?"

"Not anymore."

"But it had been."

"Yeah."

"Ohmygod! I'm going to be able to dine on this for*ever.*"

"It's not that big a deal. She only came here around Easter each year. And that was a helluva long time ago."

What could she say? She wasn't going to argue with him about time limits on historical personages. She wasn't going to say, Does anyone complain about sleeping in the Lincoln bedroom in the White House because the guy's been dead for over a hundred years? "I suppose you're right," she said, polite as hell.

"I'll show you the layout, and then we'll go down to the beach."

Claire nodded at their luggage. "Andre will carry your bags in after he brings Vernie her wine."

"I can carry my own bag," Nicky said. "Really, it's not a problem." Vinnie, Cole, and Barry had gone ahead in another car. Not that she needed them to shlep her luggage anyway.

"We'll bring them in ourselves," Johnny agreed, smoothly. "Thank you, Claire."

"I'll see you at dinner, then." The housekeeper met her employer's gaze. "Seven or eight?"

"Better make it seven." He handed her Vernie's purse. "Jordi gets hungry early."

AS JOHNNY LED NICKY THROUGH THE PALATIAL hallways and corridors, she inhaled the atmosphere of former royalty. Like really, who would have thought she'd be sleeping in Queen Victoria's bedroom! Never in her wildest dreams. Not that her dreams ever involved Queen Victoria, but the sheer *grandeur* of the idea was mind-boggling!

Since Johnny was carrying both their bags, when he stopped, nodded his head, and said, "That one," she found herself standing before a door that clearly was meant for queenly access. She'd never seen so much gilt and inlaid wood and carved marble in her life—at least not outside a museum. Even the door handle looked like—"Is this gold?" she blurted out.

"I'm not sure."

Jeez, he hadn't said no. Should she touch it?

"Want me to get it?"

"Huh." Coming out of her trance, she gave him a blank look.

"The door." He lifted his hands holding their bags.

"Sorry." Grabbing the ornate handle shaped like

some fish, she pressed down, shoved the door open, and immediately came to a standstill. The entire facing wall was floor-to-ceiling glass doors, framing a breathtaking view of the azure Mediterranean sparkling in the sun. "Wow," she whispered.

"I thought you might like this room," Johnny said.

It took her a moment to absorb the vast understatement and another moment to find the breath to speak. "It's awesome."

"We can have coffee or drinks on the balcony later if you like."

This was another of those pinch-me moments. She was in this authentic royal villa with *People Magazine*'s Sexiest Man Alive all because she happened to design tree houses. What were the odds of that happening? Then again, who was she to question good karma? "Drinks or coffee on the balcony sounds super," she said, as though such choices were offered to her every day of the week.

"We'll tell Claire later." He lifted his brows. "Do you want to go inside?"

"Sure," she quickly said, as though she'd not been doing the deer-in-the-headlights thing. Shit. Maybe she was dew-fresh after all. Taking a few steps into the sunlit room, her feet sinking into a pale, flowered carpet that was obviously custom-made for the space, she wasn't entirely sure she actually dared touch anything. The furniture was delicate rococo—built on a smaller than usual scale. But then Victoria had been really short. Even the canopied bed wasn't huge as beds went, although it was plenty big enough, she noted thankfully—a host of highly hopeful plans for the night on her agenda.

"I'll set your bag here," Johnny said, placing her carry-on atop a nearby marble table. "Are you okay?"

She hadn't stirred, lost in her survey of the spectacular room as well as in her reflections on the night ahead. "I'm fine," she answered, jettisoning her more lurid thoughts to concentrate on the present. "I have a question, though. Do you actually sleep in here?"

He shook his head. "I usually sleep in a terrace bedroom downstairs. It's easier to go outside from there. And it's closer to Jordi's room. She likes to be by the pool."

Uncertain after his answer, she debated whether she should voice her thoughts. Then, what the hell, she thought—screw politesse. She had plans for Queen Victoria's room. "So—are you staying *here* tonight or what?"

He smiled. "Unless you kick me out, I am."

She smiled, her world all rosy pink again. "No chance of that."

"Perfect. Although, I have to wait until after Jordi falls asleep. When she's around, I mind my manners."

His concern for his daughter only added to his sexiness. Although, maybe everything about him was sexy. From the way he took charge to the way he frigging stirred sugar into his coffee was a major aphrodisiac. "Not a problem," she said. "I can wait."

He checked his watch. "It's a goddamn problem for me, but I don't have a choice. So let's get out of here and go down to the beach. I gotta keep busy, or I'm going to jump you. Do you feel like a swim?"

She pretty much felt like doing whatever he wanted to do. She was in way, way too deep—when she'd only been around him a few days. When she knew it would be the height of stupidity to even consider falling for Johnny Patrick with his dismal track record of serial sexual encounters with the beauties of the world. "A swim's appealing," she said, blithely ignoring all the female skeletons in his closet. "But I don't have a suit."

"Jesus." He blew out a breath. "I don't need that picture in my head."

"Okay, so I'll keep my clothes on and just sit on the beach."

"Nah. That's crazy when the water's so great. I'll rein myself in and behave. I have to anyway with Jordi around. We'll have Claire find you a suit."

"Okey, dokey." Why shouldn't she take advantage of this little slice of paradise? She probably wouldn't ever be passing this way again.

"Damn, you're cute," he murmured, ruffling her hair.

"And you turn me on pretty much nonstop."

"Same here." His voice was ultrasoft.

She took a deep breath. "We probably should talk about something else."

"No shit." He brushed by her. "Let's go find you a suit."

Twenty-six

ANICKY HAD CHOSEN THE ONLY ONE-PIECE suit in the wardrobe of skimpy bikinis she'd been offered. She intended to do a few laps. As for the other women who may have enjoyed this beach before, she was guessing most of them weren't there to swim.

As Johnny led her down the stairway to the beach, he warned her, "I'm so horny, I'll embarrass myself if I see you in a swimsuit. Do me a favor and keep that shirt on until I hit the water."

"I'd have appreciated the same option, dude."

He looked back over his shoulder, his brows lifted in surprise.

"That European suit isn't exactly constructed for the prudish." He wore a skimpy black suit that rested low on his hips and displayed his gorgeous broad-shouldered, muscled body to the max.

"Sorry. I don't have anything else here. How about I keep my back to you."

"I'm not sure that's any better."

He dropped her hand. "Christ, talk about something else. I'm barely holding it together."

"Nice day if it doesn't rain."

"How's your stock portfolio doing?"

"Don't have one."

"Me neither. And now I'm out of conversation." All he could think about was fucking her, the part of his brain still functioning around that overriding thought operating at minimal levels.

"I like U2 a lot."

He flashed her a grin. "If only men could multitask as well as women."

"It's a gift," she said. "I'm undressing you with the rest of my brain."

"Jesus, stop," he muttered. "This hard-on is getting impossible to hide."

"Sorry."

"Yeah," he said on a suffocated breath. "Me, too. Mostly that it's four o'clock instead of ten. Okay, babe, we've got company coming into range."

She only had time for one last look as they reached the bottom of the stairs. Lordy, Lordy, those were buns of steel, his shoulders like a stevedore's, and she didn't even dare think of the front of him. *That* she *knew* was hard as steel.

"We have to behave now," he murmured, standing on the sand waiting for her. He waved at Jordi and Marie who were swinging their arms like semaphores from a distant man-made grotto midway up the rough escarpment bordering the private cove.

"I'll behave, if you will."

"Shit," he said. "I was counting on you to set an example for *me.*"

"I'm not sure I can promise that," she breathed, her insubordinate gaze on the tantalizing bulge in his swim suit.

"Hey, eyes forward. Vernie's watching us."

Her gaze flashed up, Vernie's command and control an effective deterrent.

"Hey, Vernie!" Johnny shouted. "We're going for a swim first!"

Vernie waved in acknowledgment from her seat inside a striped cabana that was fortunately a football field away.

"Race you to the water," Johnny said, and driven by necessity, he sprinted for the safety of the sea. Finally stopping waist-deep, he turned to watch as Nicky removed her long shirt and walked toward the water.

He was reminded of that classic scene from *10* with Bo Derek. Nicky even walked with the same fluid grace, her body supple and fit. As she smiled at him, he suddenly felt as though the subtlest shift in his universe had occurred. Nothing big—more like he was experiencing a new appreciation for life. Or maybe just a specific appreciation for one particular woman with long, slender legs, trim hips, a narrow waist, and fucking *great* tits. The kind of appreciation any normal, horny male would feel.

Not that he had to have more than the usual reason for liking her, but he also liked the fact that she'd chosen a functional suit. It set her apart from the women who were more interested in their decorative role around a pool. Not that the figure-hugging suit was *purely* functional. It was frigging turning him on, and first chance he had he was stripping it off.

Which, unfortunately, wouldn't be real soon. He groaned.

Maybe he should swim far enough out to take the edge off his lust. Perhaps strenuous exercise would calm the savage beast in him.

Good idea, his voice of reason agreed. "I'm going to swim out a ways. Be back in a while," he called out to her.

"I'll come with," she shouted. Already knee-deep, she dove in, and coming up a few seconds later, she moved into a smooth crawl.

He immediately kicked off, intent on putting distance between himself and temptation. It was a long, long time until ten o'clock.

But a half mile out, he slowed down to catch his breath and was surprised to find her only a few strokes behind. He was a strong swimmer. "Apparently, you've done this before," he said, treading water as she approached.

"Minnesota, Land of Ten Thousand Lakes," she replied as she reached him. "I've been swimming since I was four."

He smiled. "You're good at lots of things."

"Back at you," she replied, treading water effortlessly. "And might I add," she said with a grin, "tonight I'm looking forward to one particular thing you do exceptionally well."

"Speaking of which—have you ever been fucked in the Mediterranean?" His voice of reason apparently had drowned on the way out.

"No. Although, I expect it would be wise not to ask the same of you."

"Ask. I haven't." He'd never been that desperate before.

"You surprise me."

"Come closer, and I'll surprise you with something else. No one can see us out here."

"Except for that sailboat over there."

"I doubt it's anyone we know."

"For sure, it's no one *I* know."

"So, whaddya think?"

"I'd love to."

Christ, he loved her honesty. No games, no pretense. She said what she meant and meant what she said. An unprecedented phenomenon in his world where no one ever meant anything they said. "Let's see what we can do then about giving you an orgasm or two. Come here, I'll take your suit off."

He pulled off her suit, then his, slipped them up one arm for safekeeping, and holding her under her ribs, said, "Wrap your legs around my waist."

For a man who'd supposedly never done this before, he'd figured out the procedure without missing a beat. But with the head of his erection nudging her Mediterranean-Sea-bathed pubes, she wasn't about to take issue. And as he slid his ever-ready hard-on into her, it felt so good, so right, and really—so enormously gratifying—that she lost any sense of even mild resentment.

It was amazing how well they fit together, as though after only one night, their bodies had dovetailed, synchronized, and now fit to a *T*. It was equally amazing how strong he was—able to keep them both above water with just a leisurely kick of his feet. That the slow rhythm of his kick somehow matched the flux and flow of his hips resulted in a highly effective and fiercely arousing hard, steady penetration and withdrawal.

"Is that far enough in?"

As punctuation to his query, he drove in deeper.

She gasped, her legs tightened around him, and a kind of pleasure she didn't know existed suffused her entire body.

"More?" he whispered, as if he didn't know, as if she wasn't melting around him like hot fusion. "Answer me," he growled, needing the words, needing to hear she was as bad off as he, as insatiable.

"Yes, yes, yes . . . give me more . . ."

It was barely audible, the light breeze picking up the words and carrying them away.

He shouldn't have been so gratified. It shouldn't have mattered—one woman or another. Then again, why dwell on philosophical considerations when they were both grooving in some prodigal sexual wonderland.

He gave her more, and she greedily took it, rushing toward the finish line that first time so precipitously, he barely kept up.

But he did.

After years of fucking, he'd acquired a certain skill level.

And flipping on his back afterward, he pulled her atop him and floated in the aftermath of orgasm, the sun warming the sea and air, his body warmed by a heat of another kind.

How delicious it was, Nicky blissfully mused, resting on her own personal raft, to feel transcended, even dominated by such a superb example of male virility. Sexist it might be and insensitive to the issue of equality, but it was a world-class turn on, she had to admit.

Less introspective, Johnny was figuring he could do this a couple times before he drowned. But it felt so good right now, drowning wasn't a major concern—unlike that sailboat that had just put down its anchor.

But they were both so incredibly horny that issues other than immediate climax were cavalierly relegated to minor status. And fortunately, they'd both come so quickly the first time, the people on the sailboat had barely had time to get out their binoculars.

Their bodies still connected, Johnny gently ran his palms down Nicky's back. "You were quiet that time," he teased, getting used to her vocal orgasms. "Vernie can't hear way out here."

Nicky nodded toward the sailboat to their west. "They're kinda close."

"Don't worry about them," Johnny murmured, lazily kicking to keep them afloat.

Nicky's brows rose faintly. "You're way more casual than I."

"Believe me, I'm not in the habit of fucking in the water like some randy high school kid."

She grinned. "So I'm special."

"Damn right. Speaking of which—hold on, babe. We're gonna both feel special pretty damned soon again." And he said a little prayer that it was binoculars, not a camera that guy on the sailboat had up to his eyes. If it was a camera, this little escapade would be front-page news tomorrow. Not that it mattered with the state of his libido pretty much run amok.

But he kept Nicky turned away from the sailboat during their next frenzied coupling, and after they'd climaxed again, he figured they'd probably pushed their luck far enough. That they were both insanely fast in their prurient state of rut, at least kept the photos to a minimum—if that *was* a photographer on that boat. "Are you gonna be okay for a while now?" He'd have Cole check out the sailboat first thing when they got back.

She grinned. "How long is a while?"

"Sex fiend," he whispered, kissing her smile.

"Don't blame me. It's all your fault."

"I beg to differ, but let's have that argument on shore. I'm getting tired."

"Oh, dear, how selfish of me," Nicky quickly said, pushing away so he wouldn't have to hold her afloat. "Give me my suit. I can put it on myself."

If he wasn't damned near exhausted, he might have argued. But he was at that stage when he couldn't remember when he'd slept last. And even though the sea was calm and the current minimal in the lee of the cove, keeping them both above water had taken a certain amount of effort.

When they were both suited again, he said, "You set the pace."

Nicky swam slowly, mostly doing the backstroke because it was easy.

Johnny did a lazy breaststroke alongside, asking from time to time if she wanted to stop and rest.

He was so damnably polite, so obliging and indulgent, she found it becoming increasing difficult not to move from infatuation to something more serious, and let's face it—ridiculous. Although, she understood now why women in such numbers dogged his heels. If she wasn't careful, she'd be going through major, *major* withdrawal when this was over.

"Wanna take a break?"

"Maybe just a minute." She took his outstretched hand.

He just quietly held her, letting her rest, treading water with a minimum kick. "That was really nice," he said with a smile. "You and me—back there."

There was something in his tone of voice that touched her heart. Or maybe everything about him touched her heart. She was thoroughly confused, charmed, and fascinated, giddy, too, with she didn't know what—but *something*. "You betcha," she said, smiling back. "It was nicer than nice."

And then she shut up before she said something really stupid.

Something a man like Johnny Patrick wouldn't appreciate.

Something he'd probably heard too many times before.

*   *   *

"YOU TWO LOOK EXHAUSTED," VERNIE SAID, AS they walked toward the cabana a short time later.

"There's a bit of a current out there," Johnny said, curbing his impulse to smile. "It takes the wind out of you."

"Have a glass of wine and rest," Vernie offered, waving at the small table inside the cabana holding wine, glasses, and appetizers. "I've had my one-glass quota, and it was excellent. Tell me what your plans are while you're here. For one, Nicky should see the Russian chapel. It's spectacular."

Johnny looked at Nicky, his gaze studiously blank. His plans were pretty much limited to fucking 24/7. Not that it was possible, but tell his libido that. "Care for a glass of wine?" he asked.

"That would be nice," Nicky said, when the thought of returning to the house and sleeping for an hour was equally appealing. Particularly if she could share that bed with her host.

"If you're tired, go on up to the house," Johnny offered, politely. "I'll stay and visit with Vernie and the girls."

"I can rest here, and that wine sounds intriguing."

"Perfect. Sit down. I'll get you a towel and a glass of wine."

He seemed genuinely glad that she'd agreed to stay. She was surprised how moved she was by so small a thing. But post-orgasmic, she was feeling earnestly smitten and beguiled, wanting nothing more than to be near him, within sight and sound of him. Close enough to touch him. If she could. If it wasn't forbidden in public.

He was fast becoming a profound and heartfelt addiction.

And she a lovelorn fool.

Which wasn't sensible in the least.
Unless she wanted her heart smashed to smithereens.
Aaaagh.
She reached for the wineglass he was handing her.
Leave the bottle, she felt like saying.
I'm going to need it.

Twenty-seven

YURI RAPPED ON THE DOOR OF THE BED-room, then without waiting, pushed it open and walked inside a room that could have graced any *Architectural Digest* spread on French mansions. "Time to go," he said, curtly. "I had a call."

Raf glanced up briefly, panted, "No way," and resumed his rhythm.

"Make it quick. They want that ring delivered."

Yuri didn't move, and indifferent to his friend's presence, Raf continued pumping away. The woman beneath him—familiar with an audience—performed her duties with the vigor required of a three-thousand euro fee, and in short order everyone was satisfied. Raf was collapsed on his back, breathing hard, the beautiful woman was gathering her lingerie from the carpet, and Yuri was counting down the minutes until they could leave.

He waved the woman out. "We have to meet them at five," Yuri said brusquely.

With a groan and a string of curses, Raf rolled from the bed. "Couldn't you have rescheduled?" he muttered. "She was paid for all night."

"I didn't have a choice. The buyer has to fly back tonight. Something unexpected came up in Baku."

With a sigh, Raf reached for his shorts. "After this job, we're done—right? Because I've got better things to do."

"This is our last assignment here." Yuri smiled. "Consider it part of our internship."

"Consider it part of *your* internship. For me, it's a pain in the ass."

"Look, we're just paying our dues." Yuri had a modicum more responsibility than Raf, or maybe he was just more fearful of his father's wrath. Either way, he took the role of leader.

"I don't have to pay my dues. The business will be handed over to me regardless." Raf had a supremely indulgent father, an even more indulgent, equally connected mother, and as an only son, both a perceived and real sense of entitlement.

"Then you'd better make sure you have some damn good lieutenants."

Raf smiled. "I have twenty-two cousins. All loyal. Throw me my shoes, and we're out of here."

Minutes later, they were being driven to the Ritz.

"I don't suppose the girls will still be at the hotel." Raf offered Yuri a drink from his wine bottle.

Yuri waved off the bottle, his gaze scornful. "Since they bolted and then drove off with Johnny Patrick, I doubt it."

"Okay, okay, it was just a thought. I like Chantel."

"So go see her. You have her number."

"I might. What about you and Lisa?"

"There never was a me and Lisa, and even if there'd been, she's on my shitlist now. She tried to walk away with fifty of my black pearls. The bitch thinks the world is one big comp for her. I doubt she's paid for anything in years."

"Whatever," Raf said. "She *is* a damned fine actress."

"So? How does that affect me?"

"Don't blow smoke up my ass. You like to be seen with her. We both know that."

Yuri shrugged. "There are other actresses."

Raf let it drop, because he and Yuri had been friends a long time, and despite Yuri's nonchalance, he knew Lisa Jordan rang all his bells. And it wasn't just her A-list celebrity and dazzling looks. She and Yuri were both strikingly similar—in their self-love and swaggering egos, in their fondness for the spotlight. Soul mates as it were in the glossy world of swank and strut. "Those other actresses are probably better in bed, too," Raf noted. Yuri had always complained that Lisa liked drugs more than sex.

"Anyone's better in bed than her," Yuri muttered.

"Once we're done with this delivery, let's go to England for a change of scene. My sister and her friends are partying at some country house. We could do some shooting there."

"It's a thought." Yuri liked the English custom of shooting on private estates. He enjoyed the wholesale slaughter of game birds.

Raf lifted his brows. "So where are we supposed to meet this buyer?"

"Outside the Madeline."

* * *

TEN MINUTES LATER, YURI WAS SWEARING SO loudly, Raf shut the door to the bedroom so the Ritz security wouldn't come running.

"The fucking ring is gone!!! That BITCH had to have taken it!! I'm going to STRANGLE her with my bare hands!"

The bellowing invective continued unabated, as Yuri tore the bedroom apart looking for Catherine the Great's emerald coronation ring, which they were supposed to deliver in an hour.

Pawing through the disarray of clothing on the floor, he glared at Raf. "I could use a little help here, dammit!"

Raf looked up from the bed where he'd been lounging, his wine bottle still in hand. "You've emptied the safe, upended every drawer, and ripped apart the closets. Where would you like me to look?"

"Fucking up your ass might be an idea!"

"If only," Raf calmly replied. "Look, the ring is obviously gone, along with the ladies and their luggage. You can tear this place apart, but Lisa must have watched you open your closet safe. The jewelry wasn't in your luggage with the pearls. You and I both know it. But she didn't take it all—just the ring; it could be worse." Ignoring Yuri's incredulous look, Raf said, "It's true. What if she'd taken the entire set of emerald jewelry? Look, just give the buyer a call, postpone for a day or so, and we'll go and get the damned ring. *If* you think Lisa really has it."

"*If* fucking *if*? Who the hell else would have taken it! Mercenary BITCH!"

"Okay, then. Call your guy. Tell him you have to postpone."

"Jesus," Yuri muttered, suddenly faced with cold reality. "My father's going to shit. It wasn't just the ring." A look of fear crossed his face. "The key to our Zurich safe deposit box was under the lining of the ring case. I thought it would be extra safe there."

"Jesus." Even Raf who never worried about anything sat up and set the bottle down. "That key could be worth a lot to the wrong person."

"You think?" Yuri snapped.

"Especially if they know it's yours."

"Especially if Lisa hands it over to some of her druggie friends who always need money and aren't above ransom demands."

"Okay, okay, we have to stay calm. We're just going to have to postpone until we figure out what to do. There's no other choice. Look, I'll call my dad, and he can call yours. That way you don't have to talk to your old man, and we'll buy ourselves some time."

Dropping into a chair, Yuri ran his fingers through his four-hundred-dollar haircut and nibbled on his lower lip. He had a diminishing array of options. His father was not a reasonable man, although reason wouldn't get you very far in the Russian mafia. Violence and fear, dog-eat-dog vengeance was the orthodox model. "What the hell are you going to say to your old man if you call him?" he muttered.

"I'll say the bitch stole the ring and we're going to get it back. I won't mention the key. It should be simple enough to get them both back. It's not as though Lisa can refuse to give them to us." Raf's smiled tightly. "Especially with an automatic pointed at her head."

Yuri's frown eased. In dread of his father's fury, he'd panicked. But if Raf's plan succeeded, they'd have a few days to turn this fiasco around. "Okay. Call your father. Tell him we're on our way to get the ring. Tell him all the other jewelry is accounted for. In the meantime, I'll check with Lisa's friend Martine, who lives in Malibu; she and Lisa talk to each other a dozen times a day. She'll know where the bitch went." With his spirits reviving, Yuri gave a thumbs up. "Thanks for the cool head."

"You've saved my ass often enough. I'll tell my father it might take us a couple days and have him reschedule with the buyer." Raf grinned. "It'll be more official if the call comes from my father. And what the hell, I've never been to Baku. I hear it's hot this time of year."

A SHORT TIME LATER, THE BUY HAD BEEN RESCHEDuled for Zurich, since the buyer would be there next week. Raf's father had been amenable as usual, and Martine had helpfully informed Yuri that Lisa and Chantel were flying back to L.A. on Johnny Patrick's jet. To Yuri's heated query about whether Johnny was aboard, she'd been able to assure him that her friends were flying back alone.

Yuri checked his high-end watch, which colorfully displayed three time zones with or without alarm options. "They're four hours ahead of us, probably more like six by the time we get our plane off the ground. That's not bad though. We'll be in L.A. by midnight. An hour to her place and then"—his smile was malicious—"we'll see how good an actress Lisa really is . . ."

Twenty-eight

WHILE YURI AND RAF WERE GETTING BENT out of shape at the Ritz, the small party on the beach in Nice was enjoying the conviviality of good wine and pleasant company.

Vernie entertained them with stories of her travels, her position as nanny having taken her around the world several times. She'd been everywhere and seen everything. Jordi and Marie sat at her feet, enthralled by her descriptions of temples in Thailand and safaris in Africa, of the time she was flooded in Venice, or when she'd dined with an ex-ruler of Timbuktu.

During her narrative, Johnny and Nicky sat side by side on chaises and tried very hard not to look at each other.

And only partially succeeded.

But Nicky was cognizant of Johnny's relationship with his daughter and perhaps slightly intimidated by

Vernie as well. She tried really hard to behave with discretion and tact.

Meanwhile, Johnny was hard pressed to keep from spiriting Nicky away. Only sheer will and the constant reminder that at ten o'clock—give or take—he would be rewarded for his well-mannered restraint, kept him in check.

It was a taut and strained interval before dinner for two of the five people in the cabana. Fortunately, the other three seemed not to notice, engrossed as they were in the tales of Vernie's world travels. Or perhaps, Johnny and Nicky's acting abilities were demonstrably better than they thought.

Needless to say, dinner was equally difficult to pull off in terms of projecting the appropriate demeanor. Especially when the third bottle of wine was broached at dessert.

Nicky refused more wine at that point, even though it was a golden muscat she loved. If she had another drink, she couldn't guarantee her behavior. Johnny looked way too luscious, lounging in his chair at the head of the table—all tanned and virile in his cream silk, open-necked shirt, dark as sin and handsome as a god. And it didn't help that he casually handled the role of host as if to the manor born. He was gracious, charming, and affectionate to his daughter, erudite and discerning when it came to practically any topic. Although, the fact that he was a world-class stud seriously trumped even the most masterful of hosts in her current hot and bothered mood.

All Nicky could think of was sex, sex, and more sex. Overcome with an almost overwhelming need to touch Johnny, she flexed her fingers against the silky skirt of her green dress, which looked as good in Nice as it had in Paris. It would have been easy to reach out; he was so close. But she had to wait, she warned herself—for numerous reasons . . . most having to do with not embarrassing herself in public.

Maybe she should have a few quick cups of coffee. They might help mitigate her all-consuming, ravenous urges—further enhanced by alcohol, no doubt. Perhaps caffeine would assuage the need-an-orgasm-right-now mantra running through her brain and make her less inclined to throw herself at Johnny and plead for sex.

Even with three glasses of wine under her belt, she understood that doing that was strictly verboten.

Suppressing a shiver of desire, she stealthily glanced at her watch. "Shit." Oh, jeez, she'd said it aloud. "Sorry," she muttered to the table at large, everyone's gaze having swiveled in her direction. "My watch battery's worn out again."

"Doesn't that always happen when you're miles from a store," Vernie said, sympathetically.

"We'll get one in the morning," Johnny offered. "Let me take a look."

As she held her wrist out to him, he leaned over, whispered, "Hang in there, babe," as though he was a mind-reader. Unbuckling the band, he slipped her watch into his pocket, and said, "Let's take our coffee and dessert out on the veranda."

It wasn't a casual suggestion. With his erection becoming more and more difficult to restrain, he needed to get away from the bright lights in the dining room. The candle-lit veranda would better suit his need for concealment.

He wasn't usually so impatient. He must have had too much wine. Or maybe sex-on-demand was more of a constant in his life than he'd thought. Perhaps, Nicky simply engaged his interest more profoundly than other women.

Not a thought he particularly cared to pursue. But the lights had to go—that he knew. And quickly.

He waved the houseboy over. "We'll take our coffee on the veranda," he said, without waiting for a response from his companions.

"Bring the dessert, too," Jordi said. "Please," she murmured after a look from her father. "And thank you," she added for good measure.

He waited for the rest of the party to precede him, then followed them out to the veranda, grateful for the dusky shadows.

The summer night was ideal—balmy and warm, the stars twinkling in the velvety darkness of the sky, the full moon a brilliant orange above a calm sea.

Over dessert, Jordi and Marie kept up a steady chatter, while Vernie did her share of talking as well. Until, finally taking note of Johnny's desultory replies, Vernie said, "You must be tired."

"I am. I'll go to bed early tonight." He suppressed a smile at the tantalizing thought.

"Why don't I take the girls into town in the morning and let you sleep in?" Vernie suggested. "It's not as though they mind shopping."

"Sounds like a good idea," Johnny replied, when it actually sounded like sheer, unadulterated bliss. He had plans for the night, and Jordi was an early riser.

"Want to go shopping, girls?" Vernie asked, grinning at the raucous response to her question. She glanced at Johnny. "I gather that's a yes." And before long, although it seemed like eons to two adults with sex on their minds, Vernie began gathering up her charges. "We've had a busy day. Say good night, girls."

"Do we *have* to?" Jordi wailed, looking at her father.

"You two can watch a movie," Vernie offered. "You don't have to sleep. Just get in your jammies."

"Better do what Vernie says," Johnny agreed. "If you wake up early, you can go shopping early. How about that?"

"Can we watch *Jaws*? Please, *please*. Vernie'll never let me watch it. I'm nine now. It can't be *that* scary." Kids had that sixth sense when they could maybe get by with something.

Vernie looked at Johnny. "It's up to you."

"Why not," Johnny said, glad Jordi hadn't asked if she could watch a slasher film, because with his mind focused on getting Nicky into bed as quickly as possible, he just might have been tempted to say yes.

After good-night kisses were exchanged and several more dispensations had been wheedled out of Johnny, the girls and Vernie left.

Leaving a pregnant silence.

Johnny set down his coffee cup, the sound of the cup striking the saucer ringing like a thunderclap.

Nicky jerked in her chair.

Johnny blew out a breath. "Sorry."

"I'm a little on edge."

"Tell me about it. It seems like months since the beach."

"More like years."

He smiled. "We'll give everyone five minutes, then take the back way up. With this hard-on, I don't want to run into anyone."

"Except me."

"That's my plan," he said very, very softly.

"Just a word of warning," Nicky breathed, his plan and hers identical. "I might come the second you touch me."

"I'm about there myself. I almost lost it a hundred times during dinner. You must be some kind of witch," he murmured. "Definitely a good witch, though. Don't get me wrong."

She suspected he'd been the object of adulation so often and with such regularity, she didn't know if she should add her homage to the cast of thousands before her. Although, what the hell. It wasn't as though she was planning for any lengthy relationship. "All I know," she said, honest to a fault, "is that you turn me on like no one has ever turned me on. I don't know if it's magic or your talents in bed, but whatever—I'm more horny than I've ever been in my life. So—has enough time passed, or what?"

"Oh, yeah." After that blunt statement, no man in his right mind would hesitate. Leaning over, he took her hand and rising to his feet, pulled her up.

"Do we have to go upstairs?" she whispered, shuddering against him.

"I'd rather. Can you wait?"

"I don't know." Her voice was barely audible.

"Give me three minutes," he whispered, and knowing he could move faster than she, he scooped her up in his arms. Crossing the garden in long strides, he moved toward the back of the house at top speed. Had they remained on the veranda, they might be interrupted.

And he didn't want that.

At least not until morning—late morning now, thanks to Vernie's shopping trip.

In record time he was entering Queen Victoria's bedroom. Kicking the door shut, he'd barely turned the key in the lock with the tips of his fingers when she panted, "I don't think I can wait any longer."

"One second."

"Ohmygod," she breathed, not sure she could hold back the tide.

"Wait-wait," he whispered, moving to the bed in two swift strides, dropping her on her back, unzipping his fly, pushing her skirt up, and spreading her legs. Stripping off her panties in a blur, he climbed between her legs, and a second after that he was buried to the max right where they both wanted him to be.

His eyes shut tight against the agonizing jolt of pleasure.

She clung to him as though she were drowning—feeling him inside and outside with every ripe and ready, tingling, pulsating nerve in her body. His heart was pounding as wildly as hers. "Again, again, *please*!" she begged. There was no question whether she could accommodate him completely, her body unsparingly prodigal in its need. She was throbbing, drenched with longing, fevered and desperate.

As fiercely impatient, he willingly obliged her, quickly withdrawing, plunging back in, ramming in to the hilt, feeling as though he was caught in some powerful riptide that was carrying him along whether he liked it or not.

Over and over again in a mindless frenzy, he crammed her full.

Over and over again she breathlessly rose up to meet him.

And whether a few seconds lapsed or minutes or whatever heaven-sent interval passed, neither was entirely sure.

Although, Johnny was unconsciously monitoring Nicky's orgasmic progress, disciplining himself, waiting, watching. Damned near out of control, he wasn't sure he could delay his climax much longer when she suddenly went taut beneath him and whimpered frantically. As her orgasm broke over her and she sobbed in gratitude, he poured into her, deluging her slick cunt, ejaculating with such violence he forgot to breathe for a moment.

Just like he forgot to use a condom—*again*.

Fuck! Fuck! *Fuck!*

He *was* out of his mind. He was never so stupid, and with her he'd more or less forgotten the entire concept of using a condom.

She *must* be a witch.

Who the hell else could inspire this kind of craving? Not that he actually believed in witches; he was reachin' here. But whatever it was that was fucking with his head, he'd deal with it later. Right now, she was cooing and raining little kisses on his throat and feeling really soft and warm around his rising cock.

Right now, he was going to fuck his brains out.

"Oooooo . . . that's nice," she whispered, as his erection surged inside her.

Nice in flashing ten-foot-high neon, he thought, feeling the pleasure spiking up his spine and into the farthest reaches of his brain. Nice as in fly-me-to-the-moon without any visible means of propulsion other than steamy, flame-hot lust.

For a man who thought he'd seen it all, his eyes were being opened to an entirely new world of sensation. The kind that engaged something other than his cock's attention. The kind that knocked on doors he'd never opened before. Maybe even the kind that might make him think beyond tonight.

She arched fiercely up into his downstroke, bringing him back to reality, and he kept his mind on business after that because he liked to please her. And please himself in the bargain.

After an initial frenzy of orgasms, he left her sprawled on the bed and, stripping off his clothes, walked over to the French doors and opened them to the night. Standing in the doorway, he let the air cool his sweat-

drenched body, gave himself a few moments to come
back down, surveyed the moonlit sea with a new appreciation for its beauty.

As though prime sex heightened one's sensibilities.

"Don't be gone long."

He smiled and swung around. "As if I could."

Opening her arms wide, she wiggled her fingers.
"Bring me some moonbeams and yourself and *hurry*."

Ordinarily he would have resented such a command.
But nothing about this night was ordinary. "You already
have me," he said, softly. "How many moonbeams do
you want?"

"Just enough to warm me."

"I can do that better," he said with a smile, retracing
his path from the bed. "I can make you hotter than any
moonbeams."

"I know—I know, I *know*," she said, joyful and full
of play. "And it's early yet."

"That works out, 'cause I'm greedy as hell." Bending
low, he kissed her smile. "And talking of greedy pleasures, this dress has to go," he murmured, lifting her into
a seated position.

"I thought you liked it."

Her bottom lip settled into a delectable little pout
that made her look sweet and sexy at the same time. "I
love it." He grinned. "But not in bed."

She smiled, instantly mollified. "Oh, that's what you
mean." She turned her back to him. "Unzip me, then."

The way she said it, like it was a routine matter, like
he unzipped her dresses all the time, like they'd been
here like this in the moonlight many times before—was
strangely gratifying. A halcyon, cozy little moment. He
might have thought the word *cozy* foreign to his world.
But instead he found it charming. Unzipping her dress,

he bent his head and softly kissed the nape of her neck. "Is there anything else I can do for you?"

"Silly question," she whispered, turning back and smiling up at him. "Take this off for starters." She lifted her arms.

He pulled off her dress, tossed it aside, and suddenly grinned. "No bra. I like that."

"Practicality. I'm always in a hurry with you."

"But just with me." Fuck. Why did he say that?

"You want the truth?"

For a second he wanted to say, *No, no, forget it.* But he didn't. He said, "Yeah."

She hesitated, looked away, looked back. "I shouldn't say."

"Tell me." Clearly, he was deranged.

Her nose twitched like a bunny uncertain of what direction to take. Then she took a breath and said with a defiant tilt of her chin, "I only feel this way with you. Are you satisfied?"

"Definitely." This from a man who had always prided himself on his complete lack of possessiveness.

"So now you know." She made a small moue. "I've been trying hard to stay aloof, but there it is—I'm as adoring as all the other females you run across."

"You're not like them at all," he said, softly. "And I adore you right back—so there."

"Fucking smooth talker," she said with a grin.

"I believe that's in my résumé." He laughed. "But in this case it's no bull. And once you see the presents I bought you," he added, sportively, "you're going to adore me even more." Preferring playful banter to a conversation that had damned near turned serious, he walked to the dresser and picked up two packages the housekeeper had brought up. Returning a moment later, he handed them to Nicky. "Adore these, babe," he said, dropping into a sprawl beside her.

The two small boxes were wrapped in silver paper. "Here's where I say, you shouldn't have," she murmured, smiling at him.

He turned his head on the pillow and met her gaze. "And here's where I say, I hope you like them."

"How could I not if you bought them?"

He was surprised it mattered that she like them. After buying countless gifts for countless women, these simple and inexpensive objects should be irrelevant. But he found himself watching her face as she opened the first box.

"Oh . . . how wonderful," she exclaimed, pulling out a miniature, porcelain tree house. "This is what you bought at the toy store!"

He smiled, gratified at her expression of wonder. "I thought of you when I saw it. The door opens; there're people inside."

Carefully easing the small door open, she dipped her head and looked inside. The detail was startling, the execution phenomenal. A man, woman, and little girl were seated at a table, their arms and legs moveable, even their eyes opened and shut. "It's gorgeous!" Leaning over, she kissed him. "I can't thank you enough!"

He grinned. "I can think of a few ways you can thank me. But open the other package first."

"Ohmygod!" she marveled, unwrapping a small box of Roussel chocolates. "How did you do it?"

"One phone call and a messenger service. Do you like them?"

"Do fish swim? You're gonna have to wait while I eat these," she said, setting the tree house on the bedside table, fluffing her pillow up and leaning back with the box of chocolates in hand. "Don't interrupt me now," she murmured, a chocolate already halfway to her mouth.

"What happens if I do?"

"I won't even notice."

"Is that a fact?"

She looked up at his roguish tone. "Okay, I'll notice."

"Thank you. I wouldn't want to be outclassed by a few chocolates."

But she seemed not to have heard him, and he smiled to himself. Not that his ego couldn't take a little competition, not that he couldn't wait to fuck her for a few minutes. Not that he wasn't enjoying himself just lying beside her and watching her.

Maybe he was just so whacked-out from exhaustion, he was more easily disarmed by her winsome charm.

Or maybe her charms had more to do with hot sex than winsomeness, and he was caught up in some rare, lewd sorcery.

Or maybe it just felt good to lie here and watch her eat chocolates.

And wait his turn.

He laughed.

"What?" Her mouth full of chocolate, she looked at him.

"Nothing. Take your time."

She gave him a chocolatey smile.

Funny about chocolatey smiles, he thought. They were sexy as hell.

You learn something every day.

Maybe that's why men gave women chocolates.

Maybe it was all about giving something and getting something.

HE MUST HAVE DOZED OFF, BECAUSE HE CAME awake with a start and the realization that he was alone in bed.

Overcome with a sudden and novel moment of panic he quickly surveyed the room.

"You're awake."

She was standing nude in the moonlight by the balcony door, smiling at him. "Did I sleep long?" he drowsily murmured.

"Maybe ten minutes." She was moving toward him. "I didn't want to wake you. I knew you were tired."

"I feel rested now." He lifted his arms to her. "Come keep me company."

It was code for something else.

She knew.

He knew.

His rising erection was in on the secret as well.

"Are you sure you're not too tired?" she gently asked as she reached the bed. "I feel as though I'm more demanding than I should be."

His abs rippled as he surged upward and grabbed her. "I'm not tired." Lifting her off her feet, he set her on his hips, running his hands down her arms and hands, twining his fingers through hers. "I feel fine. Did you like the view out there?"

"It's gorgeous—like a scene out of a movie. Moonlight over the Mediterranean. A warm summer night, the scent of jasmine in the air."

"The view from here's even better," he murmured, sliding his fingers from hers. Raising his hands, he cupped her heavy breasts, the pliant weight resting on his palms. "Venus de Milo in the flesh."

At his touch her nipples had stiffened and swelled. It felt as though her breasts were enlarging just from the heat of his hands. Or the heat from his eyes. Or the heat from his testicles resting against her crotch and the tantalizing sight of his huge, rigid cock lying hard against his stomach.

Only inches away.

Close enough to touch.

She lifted her hand to reach for him.

"Wait," he said.

"Why?"

"Let's make this last a little longer this time."

"Why?"

He laughed. "You prefer instant gratification?"

"Always."

"Sometimes waiting makes it better."

"Don't tell me about your sometimes," she said, sulkily, as though she had the right.

"Sorry, I shouldn't have said that." Lifting her breasts so they mounded softly, he rose in an effortless sit-up and bending his head, took one of her nipples into his mouth, gratified to hear her sharp intake of breath as his lips closed over the taut crest. He sucked gently, first one, then the other, exerting the precise degree of pressure that soon had her squirming and wiggling, seesawing back and forth on his hips.

He took his time, as though he were intent on soothing her sulkiness, as though he knew exactly how to temper her mood and inflame her senses. When she began to pant, he whispered against her taut nipple, "Should I stop?"

Yes, she wanted to say. I want more than this; I want you. But the pressure of his mouth was sending waves of flame-hot bliss downward between her legs and caught between the reality of immediate satisfaction and the unknown, she whispered back, "Don't stop." As adjunct to her order, she slid her fingers through his dark hair and pulled his head closer.

Even if she *had* been unsure, he would have known better, her hot little cunt so wet she was slipping on his hips. "Do you want to come now or later?" he teased, lifting his mouth just enough to make himself heard.

"Cute," she said, her grip tightening on his head, her breathing frenzied.

And then as though in answer to his question, she instantly climaxed in a quivering, breathless, remarkably quiet, little orgasm.

When her eyes opened a few moments later, he was lying back on the pillow, a faint smile on his face. "You should slow down and smell the roses."

"Speak for yourself," she sweetly replied. "But thank you very much. Again." Leaning over, she touched the engorged head of his erection. "I expect you're thinking it's your turn about now."

"Not really." He was enjoying himself. She was a rare delight. Cheeky and naive at the same time. Independent as they come and small-town polite. "I'm having fun. You're so easy to turn on."

"It's you. It's all you. I'm ravenous, insatiable"—she grinned—"lost to all reason. And let me tell you, it's a damned good feeling."

He chuckled. "So now what?"

Her eyes widened. "You're asking me? How polite do I have to be?"

"Just so long as there's no animals involved, I'm good."

She smiled. "Would we disturb anyone if we sat on the balcony in the moonlight. I don't get to places like this very often."

"The others are sleeping on the pool side. We won't disturb anyone."

She leaned way down and kissed him, a soft, lingering kiss. "Thanks. For everything. I mean it. I'm really enjoying myself."

Her breasts were pressed against his chest, the warmth of her body soft as silk, her sweet good nature overcoming his usual reserve. Sliding his palms down her back, he held her lightly in his arms and whispered, "I should be thanking you. I've never felt this enchantment."

She replied with equal grace. "It must be the moonlight. Come, let's go outside." She didn't want to think of him saying things like that to other women. Call her foolish, but there it was. She'd fallen under his spell.

Like every other woman.

He slid his hands under her arms, swung her off the bed, and followed her to her feet in an effortless flow of muscled strength. He'd had his moment, too; he might have said too much. He didn't as a rule disclose his feelings so baldly.

They were both more careful after that.

Only playing at love.

Or sex. That was safer yet.

But it was unalloyed pleasure whatever you called it.

And their time together at the villa by the sea was bliss, pure and simple.

Twenty-nine

JOHNNY'S PLANE RETURNED TO NICE IN TWO
days as expected, and reality could no longer be
ignored. Their time together had been an idyllic
interlude beyond either of their imaginations, but it was
over now. They understood how mature adults were expected to deal with romantic interludes and were
scrupulously polite and practical.

After all, they both had very busy lives.

In fact, they worked during part of the flight home.

After landing in San Francisco, Johnny said to
Nicky, "Joseph took your car to your place, so if it's
okay with you, we'll go to my house first, and then I'll
drive you home."

She wasn't about to argue, inclined to play out the
dream as long as possible. It wasn't that she was naive
enough to have expectations. It was more about savoring every last drop of pleasure.

After Jordi and Vernie were settled in with Maria and her mother, after Nicky had said good-bye to all of them, Johnny took her home.

The trip was quiet, neither capable of glib small talk even though they both understood the pertinent rules governing temporary liaisons: Say good-bye politely; don't make any demands; pretend the future doesn't exist; never allude to anything even remotely personal.

One or the other would offer some innocuous comment from time to time in an effort to make conversation—like remarks about the weather, the flight, the weather on the flight . . . that sort of thing. Fortunately it wasn't a great distance between houses, for the bouts of silence became increasingly lengthy—and awkward.

When Johnny pulled his car up to the curb in front of Nicky's bungalow, they exchanged all the required thank yous and conventional phrases of leave-taking, the promises to see each other again. But no one mentioned anything specific. No actual dates were mentioned.

It reminded Nicky of the "We have to have lunch sometime" fiction. She finally said, "I have to go," because obviously he was too polite to kick her out of his car.

Johnny carried her bag to the curb.

They stood for a moment in another one of those dead silences, then Johnny leaned over and kissed her on the cheek.

"You'll be over for the tree house," he said. "I'll see you then."

"First thing tomorrow."

"If I'm not there, Jordi and Vernie will be—should you have any questions."

That sounded very much as though he would make certain *not* to be there. "Jordi knows what she wants. We're good. And thanks again."

"Thank *you*. I couldn't have managed the French without you."

Then he turned and walked back to his car.

Nicky picked up her carry-on, and as she moved up her path, she heard the low, throaty purr of his car fire up and drive away.

She didn't look back. What was the point? He was gone. She'd always known the trip to Paris had a finite limit. It was time now to relegate those gratifying memories to that souvenir album in the sky and get on with her life.

Dropping her carry-on in the front hall, she walked to her study and checked her e-mail.

Twenty messages since the plane.

With a sigh, she began dealing with them.

She checked her phone messages next. Aaaagh, there were fifteen new ones even after eliminating a couple dozen on the plane. Maybe she should get an unlisted number. Not very sensible when one ran a business, however. She clicked on the first one and began listening to some long, drawn-out question from Dora, her accountant. As the voice droned on, she hit the "save" button and prayed the next message would be short.

None of them were, of course, including the five from her sister since yesterday asking where the hell she was and why didn't she return her calls when she had some really good gossip about Jenny Grogin. Since that conversation looked to be lengthy, Nicky put off returning that call. She'd have to be in a better mood to listen to any gossip about Jenny Grogin anyway.

As for her mother's calls, they could wait, too. Her mom was always wondering if she'd met anyone *nice*. For her mother that meant someone *not* like her ex-fiancé, Theo, preferably someone who lived in Black Duck. She supposed she could tell her she'd met some-one really nice in bed, but she didn't think her mom would care to hear the details. On the rare occasions when her mother even mentioned the word *sex,* she would say *s-e-x,* like everyone was under five and couldn't spell.

By message ten, she was thinking of suicide by chocolate and had eaten four—okay, maybe it was five . . . at the most six—truffles she'd brought back from Nice. A few truffles more, though, the last message deleted, her mood was definitely on the upswing; life seemed worth living again.

News flash. Chocolate was not a viable agent for suicide.

She was even feeling good enough by then to deem her life well lived even if she never had sex with Johnny Patrick again. There were lots of other fish in the dating sea. Tons of them.

Like hell, the little voice inside her head refuted without a care for pragmatism.

Perish the thought! her selfish, little voice howled in affront.

"Oh, crap—let's face it," Nicky muttered under her breath, "there isn't enough chocolate in the world."

Work, work, work—fill your time with work—that's what she'd do. It was an excellent plan. She wouldn't even think about sex or pleasure or having fun. She'd give Buddy a quick call now, see if he'd survived her absence in good form, plan tomorrow's schedule, and then go to sleep so she'd be bright and alert and ready to face tomorrow.

IN JOHNNY'S WORLD, HE HAD THE ADVANTAGE OF having Jordi and Vernie for distractions, and the hours following his return home were busy. He played a game of chess with Jordi and Vernie, spent some time playing video games with Jordi, ate dinner, read his daughter a bedtime story—or she read to him, and as he tucked her in, they discussed what they were going to do the next day.

They'd agreed that Vernie would stay long enough to take Jordi school shopping. A task Johnny preferred not doing.

"And then when Nicky comes over to work on my tree house, maybe she'd like to go with us."

"We'll have to see," Johnny replied, not inclined to add Nicky to their family group. "Her project manager's going on vacation, now that she's back. She might be really busy." Christ, he hadn't like seriously considered her being around every day. Could he deal with it? Good question. Seeing the hotter than hot Nicky Lesdaux up close and personal every day could turn out to be a real problem.

"Why don't I call and ask her?" Jordi said.

"Let's wait. Nicky's probably as behind in her work as I am." Avoidance was his current plan, until he could think of something better; his libido wasn't up to any close personal contact with Nicky. "If you could stay for a few days beyond the school shopping, Vernie," he said, "I'd appreciate it. After losing almost a week, I should probably lock myself in my studio and get this album edited."

From her chair near the window, Vernie fluttered her hand in a shoo-away gesture. "Go anytime. I'll hold down the fort with Jordi."

"I might get started tonight." He dipped his head. "If you don't mind."

"Not at all."

"How about you, kid. Can you live without me for a day or so?"

Surrounded by a menagerie of stuffed animals in her

bed, Jordi gave her father a long-suffering look. "As though I need you around every minute, Dad. I've got a life."

Johnny laughed. "I'm not sure I care to hear that I'm disposable."

"If you gotta work, you gotta work. I know what it's like when I have tons of homework. And Vernie and me are going shopping anyway." She looked over at her nanny. "I want those purple boots, okay?" She gave her dad a mournful look. "Vernie thinks I'm too young, but I'm not. Abby Preston has some."

"Get the boots, Vernie. We can argue about propriety later."

"Whatever you say, boss."

"And I want that pink shirt with sparkles, too."

"Hey, kid, don't push it," Johnny said with a grin. "I can see from Vernie's scowl that pink sparkles aren't in the picture."

THAT NIGHT, WHILE NICKY LAY AWAKE A FEW miles away, Johnny locked himself in his studio and got down to business. He was even able to sustain his focus and motivation through the first four songs on the album, barely thinking of Nicky and sex. But it wasn't long before memories of Paris and Nice started undermining his defenses, and he began to fuck up. When he almost lost a masterful bridge because he was about to hit the wrong switch, he decided to pack it in. The last thing he needed was a major screwup at this stage of production.

Pouring himself a single malt, he opened the doors to the garden, pulled a chair up to the night air, sat down, slid into a comfortable sprawl, and took a sip of the golden liquor. He was looking to forget and find solace in some prime whiskey, open his mind to the sounds of silence. Funny thing about trying to relax, though. It only worked if you weren't wound up tighter than a spring.

He was way too fucking tense.

Too restless and agitated.

Although he wasn't about to admit why.

He'd only left her a few hours ago, for Christ's sake. This was crazy.

He had a second drink, then a third, but instead of peace and solace, he only ended up hungry at two in the morning.

And unfortunately, it wasn't just for burgers and fries.

HE AND NICKY COULD HAVE COMPARED AP-petites at two in the morning.

Nicky was zapping frozen mac and cheese in her microwave.

Johnny was ordering take-out at one of the only places open at that hour. So he ate Mexican. And ate and ate.

Maybe it was compensation for what he couldn't have.

At some level he was even willing to admit it. But not enough to pick up the phone and ask for what he really wanted. Because it wasn't just about sex with Nicky. That was the problem. And no way did he want to think about moving toward the next step. The thought of permanence made his blood run cold.

There was no *way* Nicky was going to make any calls. Even though she'd already given her vibrator a workout, twice. It was just one of those phone calls you couldn't make.

Not unless she felt like being shot down at two in the morning.

Thirty

THE NEXT DAY STARTED OUT SEMINORMAL.
If you consider two people without sleep capable of functioning in anything resembling a normal fashion.

Nicky was in the office before anyone else. It beat staring at the wall.

Johnny greeted his daughter and Vernie, bleary-eyed and unshaven, nursing an espresso at the breakfast table.

"You must have worked all night," Vernie remarked, giving him the once-over as she sat down opposite him.

"Sort of." No way was he going to tell the truth.

"Can I have pancakes, Maria?" Jordi called out.

"Me, too," Johnny added. He was craving carbs, which he never did. Getting up to run his third espresso, he wondered how he was going to get through the day. All he thought about was fucking—*one* particular woman with the sweetest cunt and the warmest smile and a body that made a man happy to be a man. He was definitely going off the deep end because nothing deterred him from thinking the same thoughts, seeing the same images in his mind, wanting the same thing. It was as though he was tripping.

And he hadn't done that for a decade or more.

BUDDY TOOK ONE LOOK AT NICKY WHEN HE walked into the office and said, "Tough trip, hey?"

"Not really. I just couldn't sleep last night thinking about work." Lies, lies.

"Go back home and sleep for a while. We don't have to see the Thompsons until eleven. And for that one, you'd better be on your toes. The wife has a fucking clipboard."

Nicky grimaced. "Rich wives have too much time on their hands."

"Tell me about it. That's all I see. Junior Martha Stewarts, with attitude. But I mean it. You look like hell. I'm not leaving until tomorrow. Go home and sleep."

"I would if I could, okay? It's not going to happen."

"Get a massage at Josie's. You'll look more rested."

"Since when do you care if I looked rested or not?"

"I never had to before."

"You're just going to have to put up with what you see," Nicky muttered, knowing damned well she wouldn't be able to sleep, no matter what.

"Suit yourself. It's your company."

"Thank you," she tartly said.

"Oooo, bitchy." Buddy grinned. "Here's where I could say something chauvinistic, if you know what I mean."

Nicky snorted. "Men have such a simple way of looking at life."

"It might help."

"Could we change the subject? Before I fire you for sexual harassment."

"Gotcha. Subject closed." Not that Buddy was worried about being fired, but Nicky looked fretful, and he didn't want to make her life any more difficult. They got along. They spoke their minds, but they both knew when to pull back. And this was one of those times. "So what's first on the agenda?"

"The Thompsons and whatever else you have scheduled. And we should check out Jordi Patrick's, too." Not that she wanted to, but she couldn't be a wuss.

"We're stalled there right now. The lumber we need for the decks is on back order. So that one can wait."

There was a God! She could feel her entire body relax. "Okay, then," she said, brightly. "That one's on hold for the time being."

PANCAKES DIDN'T HELP, A FOURTH CUP OF espresso didn't help, even being left alone after Vernie and Jordi went shopping only made him more restless. Christ, he felt like he'd taken a dose of Spanish fly. His mind was relentlessly one-track, focused on a single thought. He was going crazy.

He even thought of calling some of the women he knew and inviting them over to be his sex surrogates for the woman he really wanted. But he couldn't even bring himself to call. He didn't want some other woman. He wanted her.

He was screwed.

But there was no way he was going to enter into a relationship.

No way, no how.

Especially after knowing Nicky for less time than it takes a banana to ripen.

Christ, this craving was lunatic.

Get a grip.

Part of the reason he'd attained his success was due to his practical, hardworking, no illusions attitude. Those traits sustained him now in his hour of need, and forcing himself back into the studio, he sat down and got to work.

Funny how in the best of all possible worlds, work is both a passion and an avocation. With the sun shining into his studio, reminding him of new beginnings and better times, before long, he was lost in the music he loved.

NICKY ALSO FOUND HERSELF THOROUGHLY OCCU-pied that day—overseeing the thousand and one details integral to an architectural firm with eight projects under construction. She and Buddy surveyed two partially finished tree houses before meeting the Thompsons at eleven.

The interview didn't start out well, when Mrs. Thompson said, "I don't usually like to work with women, but you come highly recommended. I prefer working with men. They're more detail-oriented, and I'm a detail person."

Detail this. Nicky felt like saying, "I don't usually work with jerks." But she held her tongue and managed to say instead, "Why don't we see how things go? You don't have to make up your mind today."

Luckily, Buddy was smooth as silk during the interview, because short of sleep and already on the defensive, Nicky found it difficult not to snap off the officious Mrs. Thompson's head on about ten occasions. The lady with the clipboard felt that she knew more about designing tree houses than Nicky, and she didn't mind saying so.

"You were good, boss," Buddy said afterward in the car. "I could see the steam coming out of your ears, but you didn't blow up."

"Nerves of steel and the obvious fact that Mr. Thompson is going to be the one making the decisions. If we had to deal exclusively with his wife, I would have turned down the job."

"That's just because you're on edge this morning. You never turn down a job."

Buddy was right. She'd been too poor too recently to even think about turning away work. "I'd better go home early and take a nap," she said.

"Good idea."

Now what would really be a good idea was if she could go and take a nap with the very talented-in-the-sack Johnny Patrick. Since that wasn't going to happen, she'd have to settle for a pint of Ben and Jerry's and one of the chocolate bars she'd brought back from France.

A completely inadequate compromise.

Really, not even a compromise.

Just a totally inadequate act of sublimation.

AND AS IF SHE WASN'T AGITATED ENOUGH, SHE'D no more than walked into her house than the phone rang.

Shit, it was her sister.

After not returning her countless calls, Nicky had no choice but to pick up or take the chance of having the local cops show up at her door. Her mom had done that once when she hadn't been able to get hold of her for five days. Her family had figured she'd been lying in a pool of her own blood after being murdered by some crazed killer.

The simple fact was that there was no crime in Black Duck, unless egging cars on Halloween counted. So her mom, particularly, viewed any large city as highly dangerous and rife with crime, no matter how many times Nicky had explained to her how her tree-lined neighborhood was safe as can be.

But apparently, she didn't sound upbeat enough when she answered the phone, because she'd no more than said, "Hello," and her sister immediately asked, "What's wrong? We've been worried about you. Are you okay?"

Her sister's voice had taken on a anxious note at the end, and for the briefest of moments Nicky debated telling her the truth: that her life was in no way okay. That she was down in the dumps because she might be in love with a guy who didn't even know what the word meant. And even worse, if someone explained what it meant to him, he'd fucking die laughing. "I'm just tired," she said instead, lying through her teeth—not about being tired. About *why* she was tired.

"Just because you're tired doesn't explain why you haven't answered your phone for days," her sister, Belle, noted, with the cunning of a detective. "I'll have you know Mom almost called out the gendarmes."

How about that for Freudian, when she'd actually been in gendarme country for the past few days, Nicky nervously observed. Was it a sign that she should tell at least part of the truth? Was God trying to tell her something? "Actually, I've been out of the country for a couple days," she offered, figuring she couldn't afford to anger any gods with the shaky state of her nerves. She didn't need any more bad karma. Particularly from her family.

"Where in the world were you?" A wholly breathless query, each word punctuated with alarm.

"It was strictly business," Nicky said, lying like a rug. "I'm building a tree house for a family and they wanted me to see some stuff over in France."

"Who's building tree houses in France for God's sake?"

Okay, she should have thought that one through better. Belle knew as well as she did that her architectural speciality was extremely rare. "It wasn't precisely a tree house, just a site and stuff that they wanted to show me."

"Where was that?"

Oh, God, she was just digging herself a deeper hole. "Out in the country west of Paris. No place you'd know. How are Mom and Dad? How're the baby and Ed?"

"They're fine. Everyone's fine. So you're not going to tell me, your only sister, what you did?" Belle challenged. "I know when you're bullshitting. Spit it out. Where in hell were you?"

"I don't have to tell you." Nicky grumbled, resorting to a defense more appropriate to a six-year-old. So she was tired, her brain wasn't clicking on all ten cylinders.

"Then I'll tell Mom you won't tell me where you went, because it was too dangerous and you were almost kidnapped and—"

"I don't have to tell you anything, and you know it," Nicky doggedly muttered, figuring she'd stick with her stone-wall approach. "Mom's not going to do anything now that I'm back home anyway."

"Then how about you tell me because you sound really, really sad," her sister coaxed, the sympathy in her tone genuine. "I won't tell anyone, Nick. You know I won't. And if you want," she added, sweetening the pot, "I'll give you the gossip on Jenny Grogin. That will cheer you up for sure."

"Tell me about that first." The sisters knew each other's soft spots; they were extremely close, even though they didn't see as much of each other as they once had.

"Well, for starters," Belle declared, "she's mixed up with some married judge, if you can believe it. And believe it. It's true—Eva heard about it from a reliable source."

"No shit. Miss Goody Two-Shoes who does everything by the book is doing it with a married judge?"

"It gets better. The judge's wife is out for blood, and all the guy's money, too. So Jenny's straight-to-the-top career path, that's been planned and executed down to every last detail, could take a detour or at least be stalled for a while. Although, this is Washington, D.C., we're talking about, where scandal and corruption are routine, so who knows? But I thought you'd like to know Miss Goody Two-Shoes might have stepped into some shit."

Nicky laughed. "You were right. That's damned interesting news. Keep me posted on the gory details."

"Don't worry. Eva Monteil has her ear to the ground, and you know she can practically see through buildings, too. So if Jenny tells her mother anything more— however edited it might be—Eva will know about it."

"And in turn, the world."

"You got that right. Now spill your guts, sis, and I'll tell you not to worry, and you can quit being sad."

She and Belle had always offered each other that blanket assurance of perpetual happiness that solved nothing, but nevertheless made them feel better. "It's not a problem precisely," Nicky began. "I know better than to ask for the moon or expect Cinderella endings to relationships, but I'm sorta bummed out 'cause I'm missing someone. That's all."

"Anyone I know?"

"You might know *of* him. If you read the tabloids."

"You're kidding! You know some celebrity?"

Nicky went on to explain how she'd been asked to design a tree house for Jordi Patrick and all the events that had unfolded in the last few days. "So even though I know better than to expect anything but a fond farewell from someone like Johnny Patrick," she finished, "it still leaves me—*unhappy*—I guess would be the right word."

"You sound unhappy all right," Belle agreed. "And the guy's fucking unbelievably gorgeous, of course. Who wouldn't fall for him? Christ, he was the Sexiest Man Alive for a thousand obvious reasons! It's not as though you can just ignore a man like that."

"Are you being helpful? I don't think so."

"Sorry. But, wow, you've got to admit, he's a major player. Not that it matters when your heart is broken, I know. But consider, sis, how many women even have the chance to live the kind of life you lived the last few days. That's something to remember. And you know what they say about time healing everything. You know that's true. Look how you had to talk to that therapist after Theo left. And now you don't even think about him. You haven't even mentioned his name in I don't know how long. In a few months, the name Johnny Patrick won't mean a thing to you, either."

Nicky sighed. "You're making sense. Thanks. I knew as much, but it helps when someone else points out the obvious." And while she was talking to Belle, she almost believed that everything would work out just fine. She almost thought she might be able to get over Johnny in a few days or at the most—a few weeks.

But the moment she hung up the phone, she burst into tears. Fucking tears! She couldn't believe it. She hadn't even cried when Theo left, except when she'd found out he'd cleared out her checking account.

Jeez, if she was crying about this, she had to face

facts. There wasn't any simple solution to her wretchedness and her even more serious state of sexual deprivation.

It was definitely time for a punt play.

Walking into her kitchen, she selected one of the larger chocolate bars she'd brought back from Nice, moved to the freezer, took out a pint of Ben and Jerry's, found a spoon, and retired to her bedroom with her temporary solace.

Stripping off her work clothes, she put on comfort clothes—her *Simpsons* T-shirt she'd had since college and a pair of shorts from probably high school. Piling up the pillows on her bed, she arranged the chocolate bar and ice cream within easy reach, picked up her TV remote, and prepared to escape from her world of suffering and woe.

Now if only they'd make a new season of *Entourage* in the next five minutes, her life would be much improved.

Short of that miracle of technology occurring, she scrolled through her TiVo list and settled on reruns of the *Daily Show*.

She was in the mood for fake news to go, with her fake sense of acceptance that she could live without ever having sex with Johnny Patrick again.

And laughing was supposed to be good for depression.

Everyone knew that.

Thirty-one

A WHILE THE TWO MOST SEX-STARVED PEOPLE in Berkeley were struggling to put their lives back in sync, Yuri was bundling a protesting Lisa Jordan onto his jet in L.A.

"I don't know why I have to go with you! I gave you the ring back and told you what I did with the box for Christ's sake! Let go of me you damned brute!" she screamed, trying to shake off his bruising grip on her arm. "Let go!"

"Once I have that box back, you can go wherever the hell you want," Yuri muttered, pushing her down in a seat. "But until then, you're staying with me. I don't care how much you bitch. Buckle yourself in. We're taking off."

Under threat of violence, Lisa Jordan had admitted to taking the ring, but swore she'd only done it as a lark and had planned to give it back. That Yuri had come looking for the ring hadn't necessarily surprised her, although she'd only taken one little ring from all that jewelry in the safe. (And truthfully, she'd been hoping he'd overlook it.) But she *was* surprised he was interested in the empty box. Not that she was about to ask him why, when he was so pissed. But it was strange.

But strange or not, right now, she was really hoping that box was still in Johnny's little playmate's purse where she'd dropped it.

She'd never seen Yuri so furious.

He'd actually let Raf put a gun to her head. She tried to cry her way out of it at first. When that hadn't worked, she faked fainting. Unfortunately, when she'd opened her eyes again, the gun was still there.

At that point, she'd understood the seriousness of her predicament and had handed over the ring and given them Nicky's first name. "I can't remember her last name," she'd said, "but she builds tree houses. That's all I know, I swear."

Yuri nodded at Raf. He put his weapon away and after making a few calls to their offshore office, which had an efficient staff, they soon had Nicky's business and home addresses.

They were offered satellite photos of both locations as well.

Google and GPS in action.

YOU CAN IMAGINE NICKY'S SURPRISE AT BEING wakened at dawn by a rough whisper and the feel of cold metal on her forehead. Was this a nightmare? And then the unmistakable voice of the movie star who had awed the world in at least ten wildly acclaimed films said, "That's her. She has your ring box."

Nicky opened her eyes and said in as calm a voice

as possible with her heart beating at warp speed,
"What box?"

"One that belongs to me," a tall, dark-haired man
with Asiatic eyes said, gruffly.

"You must be mistaken. The only ring box I own has
Barbie on the lid."

"She's funny," Raf drawled. "And she's got great
tits, too."

His tone of voice was really scary, although up
against the gun at her head, Nicky wasn't sure which
was more terrifying. "I'm going to sit up now. Don't
shoot," she said, preferring not to be lying down with a
strange man looking at her like that.

"Keep your dick in your pants, Raf," the tall man
muttered. "We have more important things to do. Now,
where the fuck is the ring box?" he growled.

Nicky tried to display a certain calm reason, but the
name *Raf* was coming up CODE RED in her mind. Wasn't
he one of Lisa Jordan's undesirable—as in bad guy—
companions in Paris? "I wish I could help you," she
said, gently, like a hostage negotiator on TV might in
order to deflect hostility. "But I don't have whatever it is
you want."

"Unless she threw it away, she has it," Lisa declared.
"I put it in her purse."

Nicky's brain was racing, trying to figure out what
the hell was going on—why these people had broken
into her house (not technically, because she didn't lock
her doors) and what the hell they were talking about.

What ring box?

But the *I put it in her purse* phrase finally broke
through all the confusion in her mind.

Bingo.

All that fiddling Lisa did with her purse in the limo
before she came up with a cigarette and lighter. And

her own green tote bag had been on the floor, too. Okay, now she got the picture. These must have been the men Lisa was running from, and—just a wild guess—she'd taken something she shouldn't have. "My purse is downstairs," Nicky quickly offered. It was still on the chair where she'd dropped it when she'd come home, her tote bag too big to use for everyday. "I haven't unpacked it. If there's a box in there, feel free to take it."

Yuri gave Lisa a sharp look. "You actually were telling the truth."

"It was my forty-five," Raf murmured, his smile malicious.

"I *told* you I was telling the truth," Lisa murmured, ignoring Raf and giving Yuri the most sweet, sad-eyed smile Nicky had seen outside of the movie *Old Yeller.* As a kid, she always cried buckets when Old Yeller died.

"She's playing you for a sucker again," Raf sneered.

"Shut the fuck up," Yuri snapped.

"I'm soooo sorry, darling," Lisa murmured, managing to look both glamorous and childlike in her summer dress and sandals, her limpid gaze fully on Yuri. "You don't know how *awful* I feel."

Try ten times ten more and you'll know how awful *I* feel, Nicky thought, hoping she would be lucky enough to come out of this little visit alive. From every freaking angle, that trip to Paris had been nothing but trouble. Well—except for getting Jordi back. But other than that, it had been a major catastrophe. Not only was she in a serious blue funk over some guy who didn't give a damn about her, she was caught up in some major real-life danger with CRIMINALS WITH GUNS!

If she survived these gangsters, she was going to express some *serious* displeasure to a certain Johnny Patrick who had had the poor judgment to marry a thieving bitch like Lisa Jordan. She wouldn't be in this pickle if the woman could keep from stealing things. For sure, she wouldn't be in this pickle if the woman could keep from stealing from people WITH GUNS!

She didn't appreciate being awakened by a gun to her head. She didn't *like* being accused of stealing something, when she'd never stolen anything in her life. And if she wasn't afraid of having her head blown off, she'd say as much to these people cluttering up her small bedroom under the eaves. "My purse is on the chair in the front hall. It's green," she said instead, hoping to get them out of her house and out of her life without bloodshed. Hers in particular.

"Why don't you show us," Raf murmured, his gaze trained on her breasts.

Shit. She should have worn something less revealing to sleep in—like flannel pajamas instead of panties and her Simpson's T-shirt, which was a little too small after a thousand washings.

"Get the purse," Yuri ordered. His gaze flicked to Lisa. "We'll figure this out later. Although, you shouldn't have taken the ring in the first place."

"I was just playing a game, darling. It was silly, and I apologize."

"You've caused me a helluva lot of trouble," he growled.

One of the most beautiful women in the world gazed at Yuri and said, softly, "Maybe I could make it up to you somehow . . ."

"Get a room you two," Raf grumbled.

Preferably, far, far away, Nicky thought. And with the hope of expediting their departure, Nicky rose from her bed. Stay calm, she warned herself, knowing she would have to ease past Raf who was very close. Don't show fear. With luck, this could be over soon.

She tried not to flinch as Raf patted her bottom when

she moved past him. She just kept walking. Don't run, slow down, she told herself, as she left her bedroom and entered the outside corridor. Raf's gaze was on her, she could tell. Just ignore him. Walk slowly. Fortunately, Yuri seemed to be in charge.

Soon, she was at the bottom of the stairs and moving across the foyer. It took only seconds to rummage through her purse and come up with the red leather ring box. "Here," she said, holding it out, hoping Yuri would take it from her instead of Raf, with his frightening eyes. And then please go, she silently prayed.

Yuri plucked it from her fingers. "We're done here." Without another glance for Nicky, he nodded at Lisa and reached for the front door latch. "After you, sweetheart."

"I'll catch up with you later," Raf murmured.

Nicky's heart sank.

"There's no time for shagging, dammit," Yuri growled. "We have to deliver the ring. Come back later if you want."

How about if she wanted, Nicky resentfully thought, cursing Johnny Patrick for introducing her to this violent underworld. Maybe she'd have to move—like tomorrow. Or sic the FBI or CIA on Yuri and Raf, if either were actually worth a damn.

"I'll be back," Raf murmured, his gaze slowly traveling down Nicky's body, then up again, coming to rest on her breasts. His mouth twitched into a wicked smile, and his gaze finally lifted to meet hers. "Keep that cunt warm for me, babe."

Nicky was holding her breath; her heart was beating so loudly she was sure everyone could hear. But no matter how much the rational part of her brain told her to stay calm, look calm, don't show fear, she couldn't force herself to actually breathe.

Not until the front door closed.

Gasping like a drowning person, she gulped in enough air to restore her lung function, then slowly exhaled and literally shook despite the fact that the morning sun was streaming in her foyer windows, the birds were singing outside, and a beautiful summer day was beginning. Immune to the beauty of the day, her knees suddenly turned to rubber, and simultaneously hyperventilating and sobbing, she crumpled to the floor. She'd never experienced hysteria. She'd always been levelheaded. But she'd never had a gun pressed to her head before either, so maybe she was allowed to play the swooning Victorian lady just this once.

Breathe in, breathe out—slowly, slowly . . . count your blessings and Yuri's sense of responsibility to deliver some ring. Thank God. Although, if Lisa Jordan could have kept her sticky fingers off of other people's things, none of this would have happened.

Her rising anger at having become involved in something she never should have been involved in brought her sobs to an end sooner rather than later, and with her equilibrium marginally recovered, and her sense of umbrage reaching critical mass, she picked herself off the floor and marched into her study.

Dammit, she had a phone call to make!

Fucking A she did.

She had a few choice words to deliver to the man who had put her in this high-risk, highly dangerous position! Maybe more than a few!

And this time she wasn't worried about being shot down.

She was so pissed, this time *she'd be* the one doing the shooting.

*   *   *

AS THOUGH GOD HAD DECIDED SHE HADN'T BEEN suitably chastised yet, her phone suddenly rang. And guess who it was? At fucking six in the morning.

There was no way she couldn't answer, especially after having talked to Belle last night.

She picked up the phone on the fourth ring, just before the voice mail kicked in. "Hi, Mom. It's early, so if I sound weird, I'm just sleepy." She needed an up-front excuse, in case she lost it somewhere in the conversation with her heart still beating at triple time. With her near-death experience still fresh in her mind.

"I thought it was ten already out there."

"Other way around, Mom. We're two hours behind." She said this every time her mother called.

"Oh, dear—well, as long as you're up," her mother went on in the breathless way she had when she wanted to make sure she got her message across, "I just wanted to say that Isabelle told me you went to France and had the most wonderful time. Your clients were just the nicest people. So I don't have to worry for another second that you hadn't answered your phone for days. I just wanted to say we're glad you're back home, darling."

At the word *Isabelle*, Nicky's heart had practically stopped, even though it was going a hundred miles an hour. She was afraid her sister had squealed on her. But Belle had put out a great cover story instead. "It's good to be home, Mom, but can I call you back later? I have to get to work early this morning." She wasn't up to a long conversation with her mother. Not when she wanted to lash out at some celebrity she knew for his bad choice in a wife.

"You're working too hard, sweetheart. All work and no play—you know what they say . . ."

If her mother only knew the extent of her recent play, she'd blush to her dyed roots. "It's just an early client this one morning, Mom," Nicky lied. "I'll call back to-night, I promise."

"Not tonight, darling. Your dad and I have to go to Mabel and Bill Carlson's fiftieth wedding anniversary at the Legion. They're having prime rib. You'd love it; all your old friends are coming with their parents and grandparents. Practically the whole town will be there. I'll bet you're sorry right now you're way out in San Francisco," she said brightly.

"Yeah, Mom, San Francisco can't hold a candle to Black Duck."

"That's why we're such a tourist area, darling—especially for bear hunting."

Sarcasm was always wasted on her mother. "Tourism helps the economy, that's for sure," Nicky pleasantly agreed.

"We miss you, honey, and not just for Mabel's an-niversary party. Do think about coming home for a visit soon."

"I will, Mom," Nicky said dutifully. "As soon as I can. You could come visit me."

"Your father's bridge group is having some tourna-ment that lasts for God knows how long, and then every-one's going into high gear with the fall season, and the Christmas trees all needing to be shipped out early in November. Maybe after that, your dad and I will come visit you. Oh, I forgot, Dad won a cruise at a drawing at the feed mill. I think we have to go on that next."

Her mother always blamed her dad for their busy so-cial life, although she was the prime impetus behind every function they attended. Her mother thrived on small-town living. "Look, Mom, I'll be home for Thanksgiving for sure. I'll see you all then."

"Oh, that's wonderful, darling. We'll have the sleigh

out for you and the pond cleared off for skating and that favorite kind of what is it—some special vodka you like. Your dad orders it from the liquor store for you."

"Sounds good, Mom, but I really have to go. Gotta make money."

"If only that awful boy hadn't taken all your money, you wouldn't have to work so hard," she said with annoyance. "I still think you should have pressed charges!"

If only they could have A) found Theo in Bangkok, and B) found him before he'd spent all her money on good times, she might have thought about pressing charges. Oh, yeah, the United States and Thailand probably didn't have an extradition treaty, either. "You're right, Mom. I should have pressed charges. Gotta go, though. Have fun at the Legion tonight, and give Mabel and Bill my best."

"I'll give you a call tomorrow—tell me again what the time difference is—and I'll let you know how the party went."

"Call anytime. I'm always up." For instance this morning, she'd had a real *early* wakeup call.

"Oh, dear—aren't you sleeping? Your uncle Milt had insomnia, but then he drank. You're not drinking are you, sweetheart? Are you taking your vitamins and eating plenty of green vegetables?"

"Everything's good, Mom, I'm sleeping like a baby, I haven't had a drink in a month, and I eat as many greens as a rabbit," she lied. "But I *really* have to go now."

"You have *such* a busy life! I don't know how you do it. Go, go, go, every minute. But I know, I know, you have to. Have a nice day, darling!"

"You too, Mom."

* * *

NICKY'S ADRENALINE WAS STILL REVVING BIG-
time as she hung up the phone—what with her recent
visit by the slime-meisters of the underworld and then
having to lie, lie, lie to her mother.

She should probably count to ten or twenty, maybe
even a hundred before she made that phone call to
Johnny. One-one thousand, two-one thousand, fifty-one
hundred. Fuck it.

With nostrils flaring, she picked up the receiver and
angrily punched in Johnny's unlisted number, which
he'd given her in a weak moment.

Thirty-two

"DON'T SAY ANYTHING, JUST LISTEN," NICKY snapped as Johnny sleepily answered the phone. "And when I'm finished," she said, her voice rising into the shriek zone, "I want a groveling apology, or maybe a thousand groveling apologies. Do you FUCK-ING UNDERSTAND?"

"Gotcha." He'd not risen so far in the world of entertainment without knowing how to deal with tempera-mental artist types. His voice was smooth as glass.

"And I don't need any glib replies like that, either," Nicky screamed. "Do you know what JUST HAP-PENED TO ME? Do you know who just broke into my house and rousted me from a dead sleep, put a gun to my head, and fucking SCARED THE SHIT OUT OF ME?"

Johnny sat bolt-upright in bed, his adrenaline begin-ning to course through his veins, because he had a pretty good idea who she was talking about. "Are they gone?" he asked.

"Yes, no thanks to you! And no thanks to your lying, thieving ex, who wouldn't know how to tell the truth if the fucking Spanish Inquisition had her on the rack!"

"What did they want?" No longer concerned with appeasement, his voice was curt as he thrust the covers aside.

"Little Miss Kleptomaniac apparently didn't just take the black pearls, she took some stupid ring from this Yuri guy! And the bitch dumped the box into my purse on the way to the airport!"

"Don't move. I'll be right there." Johnny was out of bed and striding toward his closet.

"It's too late for the fucking cavalry," Nicky bristled.

"Too bad, I'm coming. Stay put. Lock your doors." Each word was crisp and decisive. "Are you upstairs or downstairs?" He stepped into a pair of jeans.

"Downstairs."

"Go upstairs with your cell phone; give me the number. I'll be over in ten minutes."

She should say no. She should tell him to go to hell. She should spurn his too-little, too-late help with bitter indignation. "Make it sooner," she said instead, because she needed someone to tell her everything was going to be all right. Preferably someone who carried handguns in duffel bags under the seat of his car.

"I'm so damned sorry to involve you in any of this," he murmured, as though he could read her emotional shift across the lines. "I'll make it up to you, I promise. Now, give me your cell number, lock the doors, and go upstairs. Okay?"

Jeez, now she knew what it felt like when the cavalry really did come to your rescue. The man was a fucking

virtuoso with the finesse of a diplomat and the macho
assurance of a Neanderthal.

She could practically hear the bugles sounding the
charge.

"Are you there?" he whispered, the concern in his
voice vibrating over the miles.

She blew out a breath, all the adrenaline draining
from her veins. "Kinda."

"I need your cell number," he said in the tone of
voice you'd use to coax a kitten down from a tree.

Some delayed reaction seemed to be setting in, her
brain turning to mush, her focus in chaos. It took two
tries to get the number right.

"Hang up now," he said, real softly, worried she
might fall apart before he got there. "Lock up. Go upstairs." He pronounced the words slowly. "I'll take care
of everything from now on."

Now, that was confidence, she thought, hanging up
the phone.

The kind of confidence that could take a man to
the top.

Sort of where he was, come to think of it.

Which made her feel a whole lot better. That was the
kind of can-do attitude she needed to hear to help her
stop imagining a thousand worst-case scenarios.

Yep. She definitely felt as though her life was improv-
ing. Like maybe it could actually return to normal. Like
maybe she wouldn't have to move after all. Like maybe
she wasn't feeling as mad at him as she did before.

Was he good at just about everything, or what?

THE SECOND JOHNNY SET DOWN THE RECEIVER,
he found his cell phone and scrolled down his directory
to a number under the listing: Malibu.

It wasn't a California number though. It was an international number, and as he hit the call button, he pulled a T-shirt from a dresser drawer.

When someone picked up on the other end, Johnny said, "I need a favor."

The conversation was short, cryptic, no names were mentioned.

"I'll have a driver at the airport to pick you up," Johnny said after exchanging the briefest of comments. "I appreciate your help."

Then he pulled the T-shirt over his head, slipped on some sandals, wrote a note for Vernie, and, dropping it on the kitchen table on his way out, sprinted for his car.

Thirty-three

AFTER SETTING A PERSONAL SPEED RECORD, Johnny pulled up to the curb in front of Nicky's house and gave her a call on his cell as he swung out of his Lamborghini. "I'm outside," he said.

By the time he reached the porch, she was standing in the open doorway.

He should have censored his comment, but the thought of her half-undressed in that way-too-small *Simpsons* T-shirt and panties with *them* wasn't conducive to self-censorship. "They saw you like *that*?" His voice was sharp as a knife, his scowl unmistakable.

"I'm very well. Thanks for asking," she tartly replied, not in the mood for any more male libido working overtime after Raf's loathsome overtures. Really, if Johnny didn't get a little nicer real quick, her good mood was going to go south.

"Sorry. Strike that last remark. I'm fucking groveling, okay?"

Groveling was good. He was immediately exonerated.

"I couldn't be more sorry, babe. Really."

Definitely a man with a golden tongue.

A second later, he'd leaped up the stairs and was pushing her back inside. "I shouldn't have spoken to you like that." His smile was up close and personal, as he shut the door behind him. "But, what can I say? You're just too damned hot for your own good."

She may or may not have heard him—something about hot. He was standing too close. All she could think about was throwing her arms around him, clinging to him with a stranglehold, and declaring her undying love. It must be nerves. She must still be hysterical. Even *thinking* the word *love* about a man like Johnny was pure insanity.

"You shouldn't have had to deal with assholes like Yuri and Raf. It pisses me off something awful." Taking her hand, he led her over to the couch in her living room. "Tell me what happened, now. Start from the beginning. I want to know what they said and how they said it. I want to know if they mentioned where they were going. As for Lisa, I'm too teed off to go anywhere near her. My lawyer will deal with her." Sitting down, he pulled Nicky onto his lap and held her in a gentle embrace. "I'll do whatever it takes to make you feel better about this. It's my fault that they even knew who you were. So, give me a list, or tell me what you want, and I'll do it."

With such a carte blanche offer, that dazzling engagement ring fantasy immediately took center stage in her consciousness. It was crazy, of course—and totally immature. But she was feeling all warm and cozy in his arms, and white picket fence fantasies always went hand-in-hand with that kind of storybook enchantment. Not having lost all reason, however, she didn't put in her bid for an engagement ring. She said, instead, "You're off the hook. No list required, but thanks for the offer. Mostly, I'd like if I didn't have to worry about people like them ever again."

"You won't. My word on it."

"How can you be so sure? They're not the type to live by your rules."

"Trust me. I just am. But with your safety in mind, why don't you come and stay with me for a while. I'd feel more comfortable." A startling statement if he'd acknowledged it. But he didn't. He conveniently ignored the implications of such an invitation. "What d'you say?"

"If you don't mind." She had to admit, the thought of staying alone in her house wasn't so attractive after having had a gun to her head.

"Of course I don't mind. Why should I mind?"

Maybe because he'd sworn off relationships since his divorce.

Or because he'd vowed to never become involved with a woman again.

At least not until Jordi was grown and gone—say in ten years.

But previous pledges were conveniently overlooked at the moment.

Who knows why?

Maybe the all-too-revealing *Simpsons* T-shirt was to blame.

WHILE NICKY WENT UPSTAIRS TO DRESS AND pack, Johnny made a few calls to augment his plans for some personal revenge.

But he was smiling and congenial when Nicky came back downstairs. Taking her suitcase from her, he kissed her and said, "I'm looking forward to waking up with you."

"Me, too," she answered, more grateful and relieved than she would have thought by his generosity. She was also half in love, but that was a separate issue and one she was seriously fighting.

For his part, Johnny never thought in terms of love. He never had—even when he'd married. Not that his wedding had been planned. It had unwittingly happened one out-of-control weekend. He and Lisa had flown up to Vegas from L.A., and when he woke up the next morning, he saw a marriage certificate on the bedside table. Lisa told him she was pregnant later that day, and his first thought was to ask if it was his. But he figured it was a little late for that.

When Jordi was born, he was glad he hadn't bailed.

She became the center of his life.

From that moment on, he'd stopped taking recreational drugs.

As for Lisa, once he'd detached himself from the drug scene, she'd become a real pain in the ass.

So, long story, short, since breaking free of Lisa, he'd avoided permanent women in his life.

Until now.

Thirty-four

"THE REMODELING STORY, THEN," JOHNNY said as he and Nicky walked toward his house a short time later.

"It works for me." She tried to smile and only managed to remind herself that she was still shaky from her early morning encounter with evil.

Johnny reached out and slid his fingers through hers, folding them into the warmth of his hand. "You're safe here. We have security on top of security."

The gate at the bottom of the drive did bring her comfort, not to mention all the security cameras she'd never noticed before. They all twinkled in the trees and bushes, like personal guardians of the peace.

She exhaled softly. "I should be back to normal soon."

"Sure you will. Not that my household is exactly normal, with Jordi keeping everything stirred up." He grinned. "In a good way, of course. I'm not complaining. But you might not be used to kid commotion."

"I'm the youngest of three." Her smile was real this time. "Believe me, I understand turmoil."

He was pleased to see that the haunted look in her eyes had dissipated. "Don't say I didn't warn you, that's all," he said, squeezing her hand. "Brace yourself. We're going in."

They found Jordi and Vernie having breakfast in the kitchen with Maria and Johnny launched into the agreed-upon story. "Nicky's having some remodeling done on her house, and the crew woke her up at the crack of dawn with"—he turned to Nicky with a grin— "did you say jackhammers?"

"It sure sounded like jackhammers."

"Anyway, I told her she might as well camp out with us until all the dust settles at her place. We've got plenty of room."

"And then Nicky can finish up on my tree house faster!" Jordi exclaimed. "Come, sit by me," she added, patting the chair next to her. "After we eat, I'll show you the most perfect swinging chair for my tree house Vernie and I found on the Internet."

Johnny met Nicky's gaze. "I don't know if Nicky's schedule—"

"That would be fun," Nicky said, moving around the table to take a seat beside Jordi. "After breakfast we'll check that out."

He hadn't been about to tell Nicky she should take the day off; he knew better. But he was pleased she'd decided to take a breather. Not that she was going to forget what happened to her in a few hours or a day.

Nor would he for that matter.

He already had a list of people who were gonna pay for what they'd done to her.

AS PREDICTED, JORDI KEPT EVERYONE BUSY. SEV-eral hours in the morning were devoted to the tree house, even though it was temporarily on hold. Jordi and Nicky selected some furniture on the Internet and went over the addition of fairy lights and a bunk bed to the plans. They even laid out a secret path to the structure, outlining it on the grass with washable pink spray paint.

They all ate a picnic lunch on the hill where the tree house was going up, the blue Pacific sparkling in the sun, the scent of eucalyptus pungent in the air, the specimen redwoods that outdated the state of California soaring high above them in all their stately splendor.

While they ate peanut butter and jelly sandwiches, chips, and cookies—Jordi's menu having precedence over this picnic luncheon—the adults shared a fine Riesling, a wine tolerant of such wide and varied food groups.

Johnny could see Nicky visibly relax as the meal progressed, liquor a useful tranquilizer. After lunch, they played Ping-Pong and video games in the pool house, then swam and finished the afternoon on Johnny's putt-putt golf course. Jordi upstaged them all playing putt-putt golf—at least Nicky and Vernie. Nicky wasn't so sure about Johnny. But then, he always let his daughter win.

No rainy days existed in Jordi's world.

Except for the occasional views into her mother's life.

Added reason, no doubt, why Johnny protected his daughter when he could.

* * *

DINNER THAT EVENING WAS *EN FAMILLE* AND DE-
lightful. She could really get used to this style of happiness, Nicky reflected, her gaze on her host, who was in
the process of teasing Vernie about the men in her past.
"The stories I've heard," he said with a grin. "Rumor
has it you almost broke the bank in Vegas one time."

Vernie was blushing and smiling at the same time. "I
happened to have a good friend who owned the casino.
Why shouldn't I win?" she lightly noted.

"And you bought yourself a house in the Hollywood
Hills. Smart girl," Johnny said, smiling.

"What can I say? Some people have more luck than
others." Vernie grinned. "Present company included, of
course."

As if on cue, Johnny and Nicky's eyes met.

"Affirmative from where I'm sitting," Johnny said,
winking at Nicky.

"Daddy winked at Nicky! He likes her!" Jordi's gaze
swiveled to Nicky. "Do you like Daddy back? Say yes,
say yes, Nicky! Come *on*!"

"Your father's very nice," Nicky said, blushing
cherry red.

"See, Daddy, she likes you back! He never hollers, and
he always lets you do whatever you want," Jordi noted,
her intent blue gaze on Nicky once again. "I hope you stay
with us *forever* . . . Tell her, Daddy, tell her she can stay!"

"Now, Jordi, that's enough," Vernie interposed, stepping in to defuse an awkward situation. "We don't have
to tell your father what to do. He and Nicky can work
things out for themselves."

Jordi was silenced but not inhibited. She smiled and
included Nicky in all her future plans, from her favorite

pep fest the first week of school to mall shopping and helping her practice her swimming.

His daughter's reaction to Nicky was definitely over the top, Johnny noted.

Especially since Jordi had only *tolerated* the few women he'd brought to the house in the past.

His daughter's vetting was significant.

Although he wasn't entirely sure how to deal with it.

Both pleased and uncomfortable, he did what every red-blooded male did in similar situations.

He blew it off.

FOR PROPRIETY'S SAKE, NICKY HAD BEEN GIVEN her own bedroom. It was conveniently next door to Johnny's, however, so later that night, when the house had quieted, she heard her bedroom door open and couldn't help but smile. "Are you sure everyone's sleeping?"

"They better be. Baby, I can't wait any longer." Johnny had found himself actually counting the hours since he'd last slept with Nicky. An unprecedented act for a man who often couldn't remember who, when, and where, with the number of women passing through his life.

"I've been thinking of you—*a lot*—since getting into bed," Nicky murmured, watching him approach in the moonlight.

"Sounds like you might be in the mood."

"Sorta, kinda."

"Is that equivocation I hear? Have I lost my touch?" He was stripping off his robe as he approached.

"It's not about you. It's about that stuff this morning. I'm having trouble getting it out of my head." Although the sight of such gorgeous male splendor was a start, she decided, her libido already taking note in spades.

"I wish I could make it all go away." And he would very soon if his plans all came to fruition. Lifting the covers, he slid into bed beside her. "You're safe here now," he murmured, bending to kiss her. "Nothing and no one can hurt you."

His kiss was soft and gentle, a balm to her anxieties, the scent of his cologne familiar and comforting, the warmth of his body a bulwark against all uncertainty. A kind of snug, agreeable security encompassed her as he took her in his arms and made the world disappear—or at least diminish to the sweet, restricted environs of blissful desire. "I'll make you forget," he murmured, easing his body over hers. "I promise."

"That would be nice." Sliding her hands over his shoulders, she pulled him close. "I could use some of your brand of forgetfulness . . ."

"Good, 'cause—"

"You can't wait," Nicky interposed, liking that they were both obsessed.

"*He* can't wait," Johnny corrected, his grin sweet and sexy at the same time, the head of his erection nudging her sex.

But as he entered her, he did so with abstemious forbearance, as though he understood how vulnerable she still was. He eased into her sleek passage slowly, delicately, as though she needed calming.

Although his cock forcing its way inside her was doing the complete opposite, and by the time he'd reached target point and she was gorged full, she was faint with longing. Not that his solicitude and concern for her feelings weren't equally powerful aphrodisiacs. She was warmed heart and soul, along with other more pertinent portions of her anatomy, which were pulsing and throbbing, awash

with lust, and craving more. Had her brain not been increasingly focused on those nerve centers immediately
adjacent to his erection—as in surrounding it—she would
have told him his skill at inducing forgetfulness was
prime. If only she weren't waiting breathlessly for his
next dexterous stirring inside her, she might have been
able to operate that brain-to-tongue mechanism required
for speech.

"How's this?" he murmured, sliding his hands under
her bottom, lifting her higher to meet his smooth downstroke. "Is this better?"

As if he didn't know, she thought, so overwhelmed
by spiking pleasure, she would have replied in poetic
verse if she could have formed the words.

She tried—because she adored the poet Hafiz who
knew all about passion—but her breathy reply was inaudible, incoherent, and definitely nonpoetic.

But Johnny understood, because he was feeling the
same speechless delight. After all the years of fucking
other women, he'd finally lucked out—all that screwing
mere prologue to this—the real thing.

Shifting into a languid rhythm, he set about memo-
rizing every tiny fold and furrow in her slick, silken
passage. It was an exercise in offering pleasure, but
perhaps he was marking her cunt as well—
performing the human equivalent of leaving his scent
so he'd be able to recognize her as his, eyes-shut in
the dark.

After having survived the fear and terror of the
morning, Nicky willingly gave herself up to sensual
bliss and oblivion, welcoming the waves of carnal pleasure as a benevolent gift.

A gift as wondrous and uncommon as the man af-
fording her that delight.

"You're the best," she whispered, her words infused

with the full impress of lust and tender emotion bombarding her senses. "The very best . . ."

What the hell did that mean? The best of what? he resentfully thought. A hundred other men? Raf this morning, if he'd been able to stay? Some guy next week or the week after?

Jealousy had him in its steely grip—this a man who hadn't understood the word existed a week ago.

"Tell me you feel this," he muttered, pulling her forcefully into his downstroke, impelled by male prerogatives previously beyond his ken, the thought of Raf and Yuri having seen her almost undressed suddenly filling his brain, the thought of other men *fucking* her— Jesus! "Tell me you're mine," he growled, as though he'd lost his senses.

"Yes, yes, yes," she breathed, her climax beginning to swamp her senses, willing to cede him anything as she trembled on the brink.

Gratified, he smiled—this man who had prided himself on never needing a woman. "Scream if you want," he murmured, giving her permission in his newfound role of authority. "No one can hear."

Immune to his novel, proprietary feelings, she only thought—How did he know she was stifling a scream? And then a second later it didn't matter, because he'd swung his hips out and back in again, harder this time, and then again and again—so violently her impending orgasm exploded in a flame-hot rush and her half-smothered cry was ripped from her throat.

Ecstasy flooded over her in ten-foot-high waves. Hot, foaming waves that picked her up bodily and held her suspended in a shimmering, glowing, outrageously hedonistic sensation of bliss.

Superlative control aside, Johnny wasn't completely selfless. Even with this woman who mattered like no woman had ever mattered before. He'd waited for her out of courtesy, but he caught up now, racing to join her, coming with her at the end in a dozen violent shuddering thrusts.

Like all good things, however, bliss was short-lived and no matter how rarified that pleasure, their obsession remained. A single orgasm wasn't likely to quench appetites too long deprived—a relative term—but powerful to those in the grip of carnal sorcery.

"What if I said you had to stay here with me," he muttered, still lodged inside her, yet discontent, driven by a curious need to possess her.

Her gaze—steamy hot—came up and met his scowl. "Here?" she whispered, shifting her hips in an explicitly lewd swivel and pivot that imploded through Johnny's rising cock and shot to his brain with the force of a pile driver.

"Damn right," he grumbled, wondering where she'd learned that little trick. "And here, too"—he slammed his cock into her—"and here"—a swift repeated crash dive and withdrawal—"and here," he finished on a caught breath, his cock at full mast and hard as a mallet bottoming out in her.

"Whatever you say," she purred, melting around him, her arms and legs spread wide in acquiescence, her gaze submissive. "I'll do whatever you want, whenever you want."

Impelled by such ripe and ready compliance, his erection swelled larger with shocking swiftness. Christ, he'd never been into domination, never even felt the urge. Sex had always been simple. Uncomplicated screwing—not him imposing his will. "You have to fuck me all night," he said, heated and gruff, taking her face between his palms, staring into the fiery green depths of her eyes, jettisoning his past without a qualm. "And then you have to fuck me some more."

"I have to go to work in the morning." The lust in her eyes was in direct contradiction to the servility of her tone.

"You can't," he said, brusque and low. "I'll have my cock in you." He measured the length of her cunt with a swift downstroke, the head of his penis hitting her womb so forcefully she gasped.

But when she spoke, her voice was as heated as his. "How long do you plan on staying inside me?"

"For as long as I want," he harshly replied, the thought of keeping her filled with cock adding inches to his erection.

She drew in a breath as he surged larger, only to offer him a sweetly seductive smile a moment later. "May I come, too?"

"Maybe—if you're good."

"What do I have to do to be good?"

"Fuck me—when, where, and however I say."

"What if I don't want to?" But she was so aroused he had to have felt it.

"You have to anyway." As if she wouldn't with a cunt that wet.

A shameful excitement pulsated inside her. "Perhaps I might want to after all," she breathed.

"With an insatiable pussy like yours, I'm guessing you do."

"With a cock as big as yours, why wouldn't I?" Quick as a flash, she was her old insubordinate self.

"So you'd fuck anyone with a big cock?"

His wolfish smile alarmed her, his tone no longer ironic. "What do you want me to say?"

"Guess." His voice was rough, brutal. "And you'd better be right."

"I only want *your* cock."

His smile was silken. "Smart girl." Inexplicably, her answer mattered. More incomprehensible, the thought of her fucking other men was anathema. "Put your legs around my waist," he ordered, gruffly, dragging her closer. "And make me feel that cunt of yours up and down my cock. Now, babe—get a move on. I want to see some action."

She shouldn't have responded to that growl. With anyone else she wouldn't have. But the pressure of his penis was producing fierce sensations of pleasure and longing she was powerless to resist.

She obliged him.

And he gave her pleasure in return—more deft and proficient than brutish.

The heated rush of his breath grazed her throat as he matched her rhythm. She could feel the tension in his arms as he guided her hips, moving her, holding her, easing his grip so she could glide more freely. Until wildly impatient, he abruptly pulled her legs from around his waist and raggedly muttered, "Wider. Spread'em wider."

And he plunged deeper with a desperation she eagerly met.

They were both in a fury that might have been alarming had they been capable of rational thought.

But neither were, helpless against the tempest, shaken and shaking, grunting and crying out, lustful and ravenous, the violence of their passions reaching fever pitch.

Until their mania reached climax and soon after they collapsed.

It was eerily quiet after the storm had passed.

Lying on his back, one hand over his eyes, Johnny

dragged air into his lungs and said on a breathy exhalation, "Sorry. I'm . . . never—like that."

Nicky's gaze was trained on the ceiling, her breathing labored. "Me . . . either."

"It was—just play."

"I—know."

"I apologize . . . for giving orders." He mostly wished he hadn't fucking meant them.

"I probably—said a few . . . things, too. Let's just forget it." *As if,* she thought, wanting him still without reason or rationale.

Lifting his hand away from his face, he turned, and feeling more in control, smiled at her. "Forgotten. Right?"

"Absolutely," she replied, meeting his gaze, hoping her lack of conviction didn't show in the shadowed room.

Abruptly rolling over her, he settled between her legs, as though having been exonerated he was suddenly free to indulge his desires again. "We're gonna need a bath or a shower soon. You're all sticky."

She could see his smile in the darkness. "It's not my fault we're sticky," she said. Keeping it light worked for her, too.

"I guess that means I'll have to do the washing up."

He didn't sound unhappy about it. And she could tell she wasn't going to be unhappy, either, his penis already rigid against her thigh. "It's up to you."

He liked the sound of that.

He mostly liked that she was in the bedroom next to his.

Available 24/7 he was thinking.

"Ready?" he murmured.

"Need you ask?"

"I was being polite."

"Is that so," she said in a skeptic's tone.

"I *said* I was sorry."

"I know." She grinned. "I was just making you squirm."

"Squirm on this babe."

Christ, was she lucky or what?

"Ummm . . . ummmm." Definitely lucky.

Thirty-five

THE NEXT MORNING, JOHNNY EXCUSED HIM-
self after breakfast. "I have an appointment in the
city," he said, coming to his feet. "I'll be back in a
few hours." He glanced at Jordi and Vernie. "You girls
have plans for the mall—right?" He turned to Nicky.
"Are you going to work?"

"Since I have a business to run"—Nicky pointedly
met his gaze—"yes, I am."

"Why don't I stop by your office after my appointment?"

"For?" She wasn't sure how closely she wished to be
monitored.

He grinned. "I don't know. Coffee break?"

"I'll call you if I leave the office. I wouldn't want you
to make an unnecessary trip," she said with just a hint of
crankiness.

"Good idea," he said, blithely ignoring her fretful look. "Sayonara, girls."

And with a wave he was gone.

UNBEKNOWNST TO NICKY, SHE HAD A BODYGUARD that day, although Barry had orders to stay out of sight. Johnny didn't want her to freak after their discussion, i.e., argument, over the issue of bodyguards and privacy late last night. But he was making his own rules on this one.

He wanted to make sure she was safe.

Yuri and Raf weren't the nicest guys in the world.

IN ONE OF THE MORE FASHIONABLE APARTMENT buildings on Russian Hill, Johnny gave his name to the doorman and was passed through the opulent lobby to a private elevator that served the penthouse. The doors on the elevator opened with a whisper as it came to a stop on the twentieth floor, and he walked into a large foyer paneled in golden teak. The floor was an intricate patterned parquet, the space lit with ancient torchieres, the room dominated by a brilliant red lacquer suit of Tokugawa armor centered beneath a glass domed ceiling. The centuries-old armor never ceased to dazzle him with the exquisite craftsmanship and magnificent splendor that overlay its purely functional purpose.

"This way, sir."

A white-coated servant had appeared seemingly from nowhere.

He gestured Johnny to follow him, and a few moments later, he swept open a tall, bronze-embellished door.

"Mr. Patrick," he announced, softly.

"Johnny, come in, come in," a familiar voice proclaimed.

Stepping over the threshold, Johnny walked into a sunfilled room with a breathtaking view of the bay.

"I've been expecting you," Fukuda Kazuo said with a smile. "Coffee, tea, or something more interesting?"

The man Johnny had called yesterday in Tokyo was lounging on a wheat-colored sofa, his arms spread wide along the back. He wore a gunpowder green silk robe, embroidered in a crane motif, his long black hair resting on his shoulders, his lean, wolfish face creased in a smile. He and Johnny had met years ago on the club scene in L.A., both handsome, young men enjoying the fast lane with reckless disregard for life, limb, and moral convention.

"Make it coffee," Johnny said, sitting down in a sleek leather chair. "I gave up the 'more interesting somethings' a long time ago."

A servant materialized from behind a screen in the corner.

"Just thought I'd ask," Kazuo said, as his servant poured Johnny's coffee. "Although, I know how much you value your family."

Johnny grinned. "I just figured Jordi deserves a dad who knows what day it is."

"My wife assures me such deprivation would do me good as well." Kazuo waved off the servant.

"I recommend it."

"I'm seriously considering it. I will soon have a son."

"Congratulations."

Kazuo smiled. "Thank you. My father is ecstatic." His gaze softened. "As am I. I have other interests now, so perhaps, I, too, will embrace a more conservative lifestyle. I'm funding an institute to study the impact of global warming on marine life." He smiled faintly. "My wife is a marine biologist, so I have an incentive."

"Whatever your reasons, it's great you're investing in the future. If you're looking for contributions, hit me up." Kazuo's degree in finance from the Sorbonne suited him to the role of CFO. A position he held in his father's organization as well.

"I may, although, it's a private concern at the moment." His brows rose. "My father prefers I keep a low profile."

"Got it." Kazuo's father ran the largest yakuza—organized crime syndicate—in Japan. And while government and law enforcement in Japan had a long-standing, live-and-let-live relationship with the yakuza, Johnny understood that discretion was required.

"So give me the details, *mon ami*. Where are we going; what are we doing?"

"I need to put the fear of God into Dutov's son. He terrorized a woman I know."

"Know?"

"Care about."

Kazuo's brows rose. "In what way?"

Johnny shrugged. "Don't know. But it pissed me off when they broke into her house and frightened her. I want him to pay."

"How much?"

"Just enough, I guess. I'm not unreasonable. I understand Dutov's power. That's why I needed your help."

"Because my father outranks Dutov."

"Yes."

Kazuo grinned. "And it doesn't pay to cross my father. You're talking about Yuri, I presume. He's a bully."

Johnny grimaced. "So I understand. He's a real prick from all reports. My ex got mixed up with him, involved me and, by extension, this woman. I wouldn't have bothered you, but I needed your clout."

"Don't apologize. What are friends for? Don't think I've forgotten how you saved me from that narc."

Years ago in L.A., Kazuo had made a deal for a delivery of ecstasy, and Johnny had tipped him off that his contact had been flipped by the DEA. While Jimmy Gordon, a fellow surfer, had said he'd been enjoying a month in the stews of Bangkok, he'd actually copped a plea with the DEA and had been doing time at the white-collar camp in Leavenworth.

"I'm guessing Yuri just needs a talking-to," Johnny murmured. "To set him straight."

"That should be enough. Without his old man"— Kazuo shrugged—"he's an empty suit, and his old man isn't going to take on my father. Do you know where to find him?"

"I'm looking into it. He has to deliver a ring somewhere." Johnny grimaced. "Which was the reason he rousted this girl in the first place. Fucking Lisa had stolen the thing and then dumped the box into Nicky's purse in my car."

"What the hell did he need the box for?"

"Good question. But obviously he did. Fucking prick."

"We'll have to teach him some manners," Kazuo said with a smile. "So, tell me, where did Lisa's little theft take place?"

"Paris."

"Ah, I love that city. Make my day. Tell me we're going to lean on Yuri there."

"I don't know yet, but my men are on it. I should get some info shortly."

"So tell me about this Nicky. You're going to a lot of trouble for her."

"She's an architect. She's building a tree house for Jordi."

"And?"

"And she turns me on, I guess."

Kazuo smiled broadly. "Why do I ask?" He half lifted his hand. "And yet, how many women have you known who've turned you on?"

"Why did *you* marry?" Johnny countered, not sure whether he was avoiding the question or asking a serious one.

"My father picked her out." Kazuo grinned. "But Chiyo's turned out to be an admirable choice. She's independent, intelligent, and not afraid of me. *You* wouldn't be thinking about getting married again?"

"God, no. Not after the fiasco with Lisa. I'm gun-shy."

"If you do, I'll expect an invitation."

"Don't hold your breath."

"Whatever." Kazuo didn't argue with his friend, but he'd known Johnny for a long time, and he'd never seen him go out of his way for a woman. If he was a betting man—which he was—he'd put some money on this Nicky. "Let me make a few calls and see if I can track down Yuri. My people might be able to pick up his trail."

"He travels with Raf Cartegna."

"Ah. A weakling and a playboy."

In contrast, Kazuo was honed to the inch, an expert in the martial arts. In his youth, he'd lived in the mountains, studied under a legendary master, and become a deadly force.

Johnny came to his feet. "If I hear something, I'll let you know. Cole's seeing what he can find out. Barry's guarding Nicky, but I want to check out her security myself."

"If my people come up with an answer first, I'll give

you a call. We should be ready to go by"—Kazuo shrugged—"evening at the latest, I'd guess." He grinned. "Unless you want to spend the night with your lady."

"Don't tempt me."

"Seriously, Yuri can wait. You have guards on your honey. He can't hurt her."

Johnny thought about disputing the term, *honey,* but decided against it. Why make a federal case over a casual designation. And if truth be told, she *was* sweeter than sweet. "I'll stay in touch."

"I'll be waiting by the phone, darling," Kazuo said with a grin. "And when this is over, you'll have to introduce me to this unusual woman."

Johnny's gaze narrowed. "You're not exactly trustworthy." The propensity for serial sexual encounters had been common with both men.

"I'll have you know I'm a married man."

"If you tell me you're faithful to your wife, I might actually believe in miracles."

"Let's just say, I'm thinking about it." Japanese tradition had always allowed men wide latitude outside marriage.

"Seriously?" Johnny's surprise showed.

"Seriously." Kazuo smiled. "My wife is better than all the rest."

As Johnny left the apartment, Kazuo's words— *better than all the rest*—ran through his mind. It wasn't a completely new thought. When it came to Nicky, he was beginning to feel the same way.

Although, damned if he knew why.

But there it was.

And the feeling wouldn't go away.

Thirty-six

JOHNNY STOPPED BY NICKY'S OFFICE shortly before lunch. Deliberately. After being introduced around, he said, "Do you have time for lunch at Chez Panisse?"

"No, but maybe I could make time, if you felt like paying me back later tonight," she said with a smile.

His plans were highly equivocal, but he lied and said, "Sure," because he wanted what he wanted. A bad habit, perhaps, but one of long standing.

And as though lying always required its reckoning, as they were eating lunch, Johnny's cell phone rang. Kazuo had information on Yuri. Johnny tried to keep the conversation short, but even though he spoke as vaguely as possible, by the time he hung up, Nicky was looking at him strangely.

"That was mysterious. Is some woman on your

trail? Not that it's any of my business," she hastened to add.

"It wasn't a woman," Johnny said, quickly. "Just a friend of mine I haven't seen for a while."

"A friend who's apparently going to Europe." The word *Zurich* had come up.

"Yeah."

"I got the impression he wanted you to go along."

Johnny debated his reply. Although, he'd have to tell her eventually that he was leaving—like soon, with Kazuo warming up his plane—would it be better or worse if he let her know now? Fuck it—what was he waiting for? "Actually, I might fly out with him this afternoon. He wants me to scout out a hot new band with him."

"This *afternoon*?"

"You'll be safe. Barry and Cole are on duty." He felt like saying Yuri was meeting his buyer in Zurich, so you really *are* safe. But that might give a clue to why he was traveling to Europe. And the less Nicky knew the better. He didn't want her involved in this. He didn't want her to ever have to think about Yuri and Raf again. Mostly, he didn't want her to worry. Like Jordi, he wanted to protect her from all the major and minor road bumps in life.

"On duty?" she hissed, her gaze heated.

"Look, it won't be for long. Just until things settle down a little."

"Until I met you, I didn't have to worry about things *settling down*," she muttered.

"I know, and I apologize. Believe me, people like Yuri and Raf aren't normally in my life, either."

"But these *honest-to-God gangsters are in your ex's life*! Don't forget that!"

The waitress who had come up with their desserts looked startled.

"We're discussing a movie script," Johnny said with a smile. "The crème brûlée is mine."

"You lie well," Nicky murmured, as the waitress walked away.

"Would you prefer I tell her the truth?"

"No, I suppose not," Nicky said with a sigh, knowing he'd prefer not dealing with his ex's friends any more than she. "It's just that all of this is so outside the normal context of my world, I'm not sure which way to turn."

"Eat your chocolate cake. You'll feel better."

"Do you mind? I'm not a child."

"Sorry; I didn't mean it that way. I promise this will all go away. Very soon. Guaranteed."

"What the hell does that mean?" Her voice had taken on an edge.

"I'm just trying to be reassuring." White lies weren't really lies, were they? They were just social necessities. "Look, I'll be back before you know it. In the meantime, though, I have a favor to ask. After work, would you mind going to that store with the rope swings with Jordi? She's been nagging me something fierce about taking her. She wants to pick out a rope swing for her tree house, and that's more your territory than mine."

Nicky gave him a jaundiced look. "Are you changing the subject?"

"No, I just thought of it, that's all." Add another lie to the lengthening list. "Vernie has my charge cards, so buy whatever looks good to you and Jordi." He smiled. "And thanks in advance."

"Don't think I'm falling for this diversion," she grumbled, her fork poised over her slice of cake. "But I'll do it for Jordi."

No way was he going to argue about diversions. "I'll

be back in a day or so," he said. "And if my friend, Kazuo, has time, I'll bring him around so you can meet him."

She didn't even want to know who someone called Kazuo was; not if she wanted to sleep tonight. Better to deal with the reality she knew. "I don't want Barry or Cole stepping on my toes. Agreed?"

"They'll keep their distance. It's just a temporary precaution anyway."

"So you say."

"Trust me on this one."

"It's not you I don't trust so much as your untrust-worthy ex."

"She won't bother you again."

Each word was cold as the grave.

And on that point, if nothing else, she believed him.

Thirty-seven

KAZUO HAD A TAIL ON YURI, SO HE CALLED to get an update as they were being driven to their hotel in Zurich. Setting his phone aside after a brief conversation, he turned to Johnny. "Yuri's still waiting for his buyer." He grinned. "You wouldn't be interested in Catherine the Great's coronation ring if the price was right, would you?"

"No thanks, Kaz. Play it safe—that's my motto."

Kazuo's grin widened. "What if Yuri wants to give it to you?"

Johnny laughed. "Somehow I can't see Dutov the elder going along with the deal even if his son caved."

"I could guarantee you ready compliance."

"Much as I appreciate your offer, I think I'll stick to shopping at Costco."

"I was just looking to make this more interesting." Kazuo's gaze was amused.

"While I was looking for this to go smooth and easy."

Kazuo dipped his head faintly. "You're the boss."

"Not really. Your father's the boss, and for that I'm supremely grateful. But let's not complicate things."

"Smooth and easy it is, then," Kazuo murmured, although it was obvious he would have preferred a little sport. "From last reports, here's what's going down. Yuri's to meet his buyer tonight at SINNERS. Once the transaction is over, I'm guessing the buyer, Gurbanly, will want to take his prize back to Baku, Azerbaijan, where laws are—shall we say—more flexible. That will give us an opportunity to speak to Yuri without fear of being overheard by Interpol or any of the other agencies tracking Gurbanly's lamentable activities. Not that Dutov, the elder, doesn't have a penchant for torture, too," Kazuo said with a shrug. "But his son's a nonentity as far as the governmental agencies are concerned."

"Fucking Lisa," Johnny muttered, words like *torture* way the hell out of his universe. "If not for her, we wouldn't even be here."

"I never did figure out why you married her."

"Who the hell knows why we did anything in those days," Johnny muttered.

"True," Kazuo grunted.

"And Jordi's more than a payoff for the train wreck of my marriage. Although her mother is beginning to really get on my nerves. I shouldn't be in Zurich chasing some lowlife. I should be home with Jordi and Nicky."

Kazuo's brows rose. "Did you say *Nicky's* at your *house*?"

"Just till all this blows over. Don't look at me like that. It's temporary, okay?"

"Whatever you say."

"That's what I say," Johnny growled.

"Relax. Marriage isn't so bad."

Johnny gave him a narrowed glance. "Don't tell *me* about marriage."

"Maybe if you marry someone who isn't into drugs next time."

"How about I don't get married at all?"

"Fine." But Kazuo was thinking he might have to begin looking for a wedding present after all—protests or not. Johnny was going out of his way for this Nicky woman. But obviously, this wasn't the time to have that conversation. "Would you like to meet my banker while we wait for the club to open? I have a little business to do with him as long as we're here and he could save you a bundle on your taxes."

Johnny grinned. "You don't know my accountants. But sure, why not? It doesn't hurt to listen."

The two friends spent a leisurely day, Kazuo's contact the stereotypical Swiss banker. Soft-spoken, well-dressed, an office like a movie set with manly furniture, real paintings, and expensive carpets. Over a lavish tea served by an in-house chef, he was able to offer Johnny the moon in terms of tax-free investments and high-interest bank accounts. But then Swiss bankers had been doing business with rich men for centuries. They understood balance sheets better than anyone.

The men had cocktails afterward in their hotel suite and a light dinner before setting out to square accounts with Yuri.

They walked the short distance to a large medieval-looking structure on the lakeshore that was flamboyantly illuminated with strobe lights. The building gave the appearance of having once been a church, the exterior exuberantly gothic from top to bottom, although the architectural detail was so crisp and clean it was more likely a nineteenth-century pastiche. But whatever its date, it was impressive.

Entering through monumental cast bronze doors, Johnny and Kazuo found themselves looking down into a large nave. The high, gothic-arched ceiling was supported by soaring, elaborately carved pillars, flickering torches on the wall bestowing a sinister, dungeonlike atmosphere to the interior.

A punk band on what once might have been the altar had their amps ramped up high, the sound shaking the colorful pennants and banners hanging from the ceiling. The crowd on the dance floor below was wall to wall, people at the bar three deep, the din earsplitting.

Johnny and Kazuo stood at the top of the broad stone steps descending to the main floor where bodies gyrated to the loud, energetic head-banger music. Every color of the rainbow emblazoned the bobbing heads below, heavy eye makeup apparently de rigueur for the predominately Goth crowd, body studs and tattoos, leather and chains the uniform of choice.

"See anyone you know?" Kazuo shouted above the raucous roar.

Johnny shook his head.

Kazuo made a drinking motion with his hand and pointed at the bar.

As they moved down the stairs toward the bar, Kazuo touched Johnny's arm and putting his mouth to Johnny's ear rapped out, "VIP section, first table on the left by the rail."

Three men were at the table.

Leaning in close so he could be heard, Johnny halfshouted, "Is the bald guy the buyer?"

"In the flesh."

Three men standing off to one side against the wall were obviously bodyguards: muscled, gimlet-eyed, casually dressed, each with a bulge under his armpit.

"Let's get that drink," Johnny said, feeling a rush. "And wait."

They had two drinks before the bald man stood up and walked away, one bodyguard peeling himself away from the wall and following him out.

"Now," Johnny said, pushing away from the bar.

Kazuo followed as Johnny shoved his way through the crowd. Taking the stairs to the VIP section three at a time, Johnny slipped the bouncer a large bill and stepped over the velvet rope that closed off the mezzanine level. The sound of the music was substantially muted in the area, as though money had the power to diminish long-term hearing loss.

Walking over to Yuri's table, Johnny pulled out a chair and sat down. Kazuo took the chair beside him.

"If it isn't the man who couldn't keep Lisa satisfied," Yuri jeered, swagger in his blustery tone and lounging pose.

"Everyone can't be a big-time supplier," Johnny silkily replied.

"Funny man. Hey, Raf, look who's here. Lisa's loser ex."

Johnny smiled faintly. "I doubt she's interested in you for your scintillating conversation or intellect. But we didn't come here to exchange compliments." He leaned forward slightly. "I came here to tell you to stay away from my girlfriend. I don't want scum like you anywhere near her. And while we're at it, stay clear of Lisa, too. I don't want you around my daughter." He sat back in his chair, his gaze ice cold. "I wanted to deliver the message in person so you understood my views. So everything was crystal clear. Stay away from them all. Got it?"

"You got balls," Yuri sneered. "I'll give you that. Obviously, you don't know who I am."

"I know who you are. You're a fucking pussy."

At the sound of the word *pussy*, the two bodyguards pushed away from the wall, but assured of his family's power, Yuri stopped them with a raised hand. "You must have a death wish, pretty boy. Apologize, or you're dead." He smiled tightly. "Or maybe you're dead anyway."

"I doubt it. For starters I could shoot your balls off right now if I wanted to. You don't have to look down. They're still there. But you might want to think about being polite to me or you'll be carried out of here on a stretcher. My Beretta is pointed right at your crotch." They were a little more casual about weapons in Europe, since no one could buy them or by extension carry them. Unlike in America. Johnny and Kazuo were both armed.

"There's four of us and only two of you," Raf defiantly challenged, although he glanced at their bodyguards for reassurance.

"You'd lose your gonads before your goons could get over here." Johnny shrugged. "Kazuo has you in his crosshairs. It's your decision."

"You might want to consider what Johnny said for another reason as well," Kazuo murmured, slipping a pendant from under the buttoned collar of his shirt, the jade seal a translucent glimmer in the torch light. "Johnny and I have been friends a long time." He turned to Johnny. "How long has it been, *mon ami*?"

"Fifteen years, give or take."

Yuri's face had gone ashen, Raf was openmouthed. Even the guards knew better than to move at the sight of the Fukuda insignia gleaming on Kazuo's chest. The Fukuda clan's reputation and reach were formidable. In the pyramid scheme of organized crime, they were top dog.

"We're waiting for your answer," Kazuo said, pointedly. "You hassled Johnny's girlfriend; you shouldn't have. We don't want it to happen again. I'm sure my father would also appreciate knowing she was safe from any further visits from you. You understand how it works—my friends are my father's friends."

For a brief, ominous moment the word *father* hung in the air.

"I—I . . ." Yuri swallowed hard. "I—I—it was a mistake," he stammered.

"And?" Kazuo softly challenged.

"I apologize for bothering her," Yuri quickly said, his eyes darting from side to side as though searching for a means of escape.

"You, too, Raf, darling," Kazuo ordered, his voice whip-sharp.

"Sorry," Raf swiftly responded. "We're . . . real—sorry."

"And it won't happen again?" Kazuo gently queried.

"No . . . no—of course not." Raf nodded at Kazuo. "We didn't—know . . . I mean, that she—he . . . was your friend."

"What about you, fuckhead?" Kazuo jabbed a slender finger at Yuri.

Yuri recoiled as though he were about to be beaten and, sweating profusely, whispered, "We didn't—know . . . we won't go near—"

"Any of them," Kazuo prompted.

"Yes, yes . . . never again." Yuri had found his voice.

"Now you darlings toddle along. We're finished with you. A last word of warning though—stay out of California, too. Understand?"

"Yes, yes . . ." Both men nodded their heads like bobble dolls.

"Now beat it," Kazuo crisply ordered.

The men turned and tripped over each other trying to flee, eventually disappearing down the stairs at a run, their bodyguards right on their heels.

Lifting his hand, Kazuo beckoned a waiter and ordered a bottle of Krug. Leaning back in his chair, he
tucked the pendant back under his shirt and smiled
lazily. "I'd say that went well."

Johnny grinned. "You've got the touch."

"With people like that"—Kazuo made a dismissive
gesture with his hand—"all they know is brute force. So
when in Rome . . ." He grinned. "What say we wind
down after our drink?" He paused as the waiter poured
their champagne and set the bottle in an ice bucket. "I
know a very nice brothel not far from here," he went on
as the waiter walked away. "It's discreet, quiet, excellent wines."

"Not me, but feel free."

Kazuo's brows rose. "Am I hearing right? Johnny
Patrick turning down sex?"

"I'm not in the mood."

Kazuo grinned. "Even more astonishing. Has darling
Nicky emasculated you?"

"Don't ride my ass. Everything's operating just
fine."

There was a don't-push-it in his tone, Kazuo noted,
and well-mannered and urbane, he remarked, "Come
to think of it, my wife is having a dinner party for some
distinguished scientists day after tomorrow. Something to do with the Arctic ice cap. I should probably
show up."

"I should get back, too. I owe you, Kaz," Johnny
said, understanding his friend had come to help without regard for his own schedule. "Next time, it's my
turn."

"Glad I could be of help. It's been a while, hasn't it?
Funny how life gets in the way of friendships."

"We both have more on our plates than we did when

we were hanging loose in our twenties. Kids"—Johnny grinned—"or soon-to-be kids, work"—he shrugged—"and more and more work."

"If you settle down with your tree house lady, maybe you'll take a vacation and come see us."

Johnny liked the way Kaz referred to his wife. Maybe Kaz was right about recognizing when a woman was the best. Maybe he should have sense enough to see the light himself. "You and your wife come and visit us sometime, too," he offered.

"Us?" Kazuo drawled.

Johnny grimaced. "Fuck you."

Kazuo grinned. "It happens to the best of us, bro."

"Piss off. I'm not even sure I can get my head around the idea."

"Tell me about it."

"That's not fucking helpful," Johnny grumbled.

"Do I detect an actual romantic state of mind?" Kazuo said with a smile. "Surely not."

Johnny blew out a breath. "Fuck if I know. But I do know if I decide to get married again, it's gonna be for all the right reasons. If it means figuring out this love and romance stuff"—he grinned—"I'm gonna have to figure it out."

"I recommend diamonds as a means to possibly solving your dilemma," Kaz offered. "I suggest you bring home a large one for Nicky. I know this very good jeweler."

"Forget it."

"It can't hurt to look. Gustav will open his store for us. I'm a good customer." He lifted his flute with a smile. "To the blissful state of matrimony."

Johnny raised his glass and grinned. "No way."

Thirty-eight

THE NEXT AFTERNOON, AS NICKY LEFT HER office at the end of the day, she saw Johnny leaning against her car, a handsome Japanese man with long black hair standing next to him. She instantly understood the man must be Kazuo.

Both the men were smiling.

Which meant, she hoped, she could stop worrying.

She'd been mega-tense in Johnny's absence, his phone call at Chez Panisse unsettling, even more so his lack of explanation and quick departure. What made it even worse was the fact that she couldn't call any of her friends or family and whine to them about her fears. If she even mentioned the word *gangster* to her family, they'd get on the first plane, fly out here, and drag her back home. *Gangster* was only a movie word in Black Duck. As for her friends . . . she wasn't quite ready to tell them she was maybe in love after a week. They'd think first, that she was out of her league, and second, that a man like Johnny Patrick wouldn't remember her name in another week.

Which might be true.

So she'd been forced to stew and fret all by herself.

And apparently all for naught, she cheerfully noted as she walked up to the men. They were both dressed casually in slacks and dark T-shirts. Johnny looked gorgeous as ever, and his friend could have been the Japanese Bruce Lee, he was so incredibly beautiful.

It just went to show that worry could be a real waste of time.

"You weren't gone long," she said, approaching them with a smile.

"I was in a major hurry to get home."

If ever there was a heartwarming smile, she'd just witnessed it, Nicky thought, all her apprehensions swept away in an instant by Johnny's smile.

"Nicky, I'd like you to meet Kazuo Fukuda, Kaz, this is Nicky. Nicole Lesdaux to be exact," Johnny added, curving his arm around her shoulder and drawing her close.

Kazuo grinned. "Johnny spoke of nothing else but you."

"You two must have gone to the same charm school," Nicky said, lightly. "But thank you. I adore flattery."

"Kaz just stopped by for a minute to meet you. He's heading back home."

At Johnny's lifted hand, Nicky took note of a black Mercedes and driver waiting at the curb.

"My wife has a dinner party I have to be back for," Kazuo explained. "I'm trying to talk Johnny into bringing you to Tokyo soon."

The casualness of his remark struck her with a far from casual impact. Her pulse began beating violently. Did that mean her relationship with Johnny was more than say . . . a weeklong affair? Or was Johnny's friend just being polite?

"I told Kaz we'd try to work something out," Johnny said.

She almost fainted. Work something OUT—like—WOW. Did this mean Cinderella dreams really came true? Did this mean she wasn't crazy to move from instant infatuation to instant something else *way more profound*? Okay, okay, take it easy. Johnny was just talking about a trip to Japan. Like a trip to Paris. He probably took trips with women all the time. "That'd be great," she said, ultra-casually, like she might respond to a comment about car insurance, say, or a Disney movie.

"Stay in touch, now." Kazuo glanced at his watch. "Duty calls," he added with a grin.

The men shook hands, then Kaz shook Nicky's hand. "It was a pleasure to meet you. I can see why Johnny wanted to get home." Then with a wave, Kazuo strode away.

"You sure know a lot of different people," Nicky said, as Kazuo stepped into the Mercedes sedan and the driver shut the door behind him.

"Yeah, I do."

Silence.

Okay. She wasn't going to get an explanation for either Kazuo or their trip.

"I don't know how much to tell you." Each word fell into the silence with grudging unwillingness.

She was thinking maybe she didn't want to know when his jaw was set like that and each word he'd uttered had clearly been said against his will. Then again that line about curiosity killing the cat wasn't just a baseless phrase. "How about the truth? You went to scout some new band, didn't you?"

"Not exactly. I can't actually tell you the complete truth." Disclosing Kaz's father's business was off-limits for one thing; there was no room for negotiation there.

"You're kidding—right? What about 'The truth will set you free?' "

" 'Truth is stranger than fiction,' would be more appropriate to this situation. Look, the whole incident and trip is over. I'd rather just forget it."

"Now, you're freaking me out. What kind of bizarre trip did you go on?"

"Are we going to have a huge fight about it if I tell you?"

"It depends on what you tell me," she said, the green of her eyes taking on a sudden coolness.

A tic fluttered along his jaw line, he exhaled an inaudible expletive, and understanding some explanation was required to temper that coolness in her eyes, he finally said, "There was no band to scout. We went to get Yuri off your back. I didn't want him to frighten you again. That was it."

"Why couldn't you just say that?" Although even as she said the words, she knew how she would have freaked out had he told her.

He shrugged. "I just didn't want to get into it after your"—he hesitated—"bad experience with Yuri."

"Because I would have tried to stop you."

"I figured."

"You were right. They have guns. Oh, God, don't tell me you had guns, too."

"We mostly just talked."

She was smart enough not to ask him to parse *mostly*. She'd always been susceptible to nightmares. But it would go a long way toward mitigating any future nightmares if she knew whether he'd been successful in convincing Yuri to stay away. "So is he off my back?" Like could she sleep in her own house again?

"Yep. He's out of your life."

"Wow. That's good news. And Kaz must have gone along to help."

"Yep."

"And Yuri just said okeydokey, and you came home."

"That's about it."

That wasn't a credible answer, not with a man like Yuri. Just to make sure, she said, "And no one was harmed in the encounter?"

"Nope."

"Crap," she said, half pissed that Yuri might still be in the picture and half pissed that Johnny thought she was that stupid. "You actually expect me to believe that Yuri rolled over as easy as that?"

"We were able to exert pressure on him. No violence was necessary."

"But you would have used violence," she said between her teeth, wondering if she'd gotten herself mixed up in a situation that could only end badly. Like with blood involved.

"No—I wouldn't have," he lied. "Relax." He started to reach for her, and she slapped his hands away.

Christ, was Johnny mixed up in a way of life beyond the music he produced? Should she start running like hell? "I don't feel like relaxing," she ground out, part snappish, and mostly sullen. "This is all messing with my mind big-time. I live a simple life, or did until—"

"I know. I'm sorry to get you mixed up in any of this," he quietly said. "And look, I don't want to fight about my going to Zurich. The trip was a one-shot deal—sorry, scratch that phrase. It was a set of circumstances that will never be repeated. Never. Okay?" He bent low so their eyes were level. "Yuri is out of our life. I promise. There's just a lot of people I have to protect, so I can't explain every little detail."

She really liked his unreserved promise about it being over, but all the rest about not being able to tell her everything and people to protect made her uneasy. "You're like—not connected, are you?" she nervously asked.

He laughed so hard and so long she was beginning to get rankled all over again when, fighting a smile and wiping the tears from his eyes, he said, "Word of honor, babe. I'm not connected."

"For sure?" Could she ask him to swear on a stack of Bibles or something equally inane?

"For sure," he said without a hint of a smile this time, without a glint of amusement in his gaze, with such earnestness, she knew he was telling the truth. About that at least, if not about the Yuri stuff. And if he was really protecting other people, she didn't expect him to jeopardize that trust? Did she?

The honest truth was that she *would* like him to tell her everything. Like bare his soul to her, like they did in really hokey movies.

The reality was she'd known him a grand total of seven and a half days and really couldn't expect much more from him than a certain civility given to a woman he'd slept with.

Jeez, that was one harsh reality when she was trying her damndest not to even think about being in love with him after so brief a time.

"Hey, are we good now?"

He was giving her that unbelievably sweet smile that could, like, charm the pants off of the world's biggest ice queen. "Yeah, we're good." She smiled. "And I should thank you for dealing with Yuri. Thanks."

"Don't mention it."

"Anyway, it was very brave of you." A vast understatement, but she didn't know where the line between fantasy and real life actually met in that scenario. And maybe he was right. Maybe she'd be better off not knowing. She'd lived through a real-life nightmare with Yuri once already. She didn't need a repeat.

All Johnny wanted was for this conversation to be over. So much so that he did another brave thing. He decided to give her what he had in his pocket.

"Kaz bought some jewelry for his wife while we were in Zurich," he abruptly said, his voice brisk and hurried, as though having made up his mind, he wanted to get through what he was going to say as quickly as possible. "This jeweler does some special work apparently, so as long as I was there, I got you this." Pulling a small velvet box from his pants pocket, he snapped the lid open with his thumb. "What'd you think?"

"Holy Christ!"

He couldn't get a read on her wide-eyed expletive, or maybe he wasn't up to speed when it came to giving out engagement rings. "Is that good—or not good?"

"It's huge!"

"Kaz says his wife likes huge, no pun intended," he said with a faint smile, feeling better because Nicky was grinning ear-to-ear now. "Try it on." Slipping the diamond ring out of the box, he lifted her left hand, and slid a ring the size of Rhode Island on her fourth finger. "I was thinking about maybe a long engagement though . . . so we can get to know each other, if you know what I mean. Like no sense diving off a high dock into shallow water and breaking our necks because we haven't given this a little thought. Although I'm sober and straight this time, so I'm guessing it's a whole lot different than last time—but"—he half-smiled again—"just in case."

Now she knew what was meant by flummoxed. It was part numbness, part hearing a voice from nowhere saying *You better check this one out,* part fantasy Hollywood script. She swallowed and said in what she'd hoped would be a normal tone of voice but turned out to be a whisper, "Is this a marriage proposal?"

A long, long, *long* silence this time. Apparently she wasn't the only one spacing out.

"If it's okay with you," he finally said, "yeah, I guess that's what you'd call it."

Even as the little voice inside her head was screaming *Will you shut the fuck up!!,* she attempted to rally her rational faculties. "We don't know each other very well," she pointed out. "Or hardly at all," she added, nudged by the small, incorruptible bit of her sanity that wasn't dancing in the streets shouting *Hallelujah!*

"What I know about you," Johnny softly replied, every syllable rich with sexual innuendo, "I really like. But"—he shifted his stance marginally as though responding to the significance of her statement—"I hear what you're saying. I suppose you should meet my parents and brother . . . somewhere down the road." The masculine code of family obligation in action. "And we'll go see your family, too. But Jordi's the only one that really counts as far as any decisions I make," he added, his daughter viewed through a very different prism. "And she likes you, I can tell. So we're good."

"I have the requisite seal of approval, you're saying."

"Hey, don't be mad. I didn't mean it the way it sounded." He paused. "Yeah, actually, I did. Jordi really matters to me. What can I say?"

Nicky smiled. "I'm not mad. I was being flip. And for the record, it's more than okay. I wouldn't like you if your daughter weren't important to you." In fact, it was the first thing she'd noticed about him—well . . . maybe the second, next to his drop-dead good looks that couldn't be ignored unless you were blind.

He blew out a breath. "So, are you saying yes?"

She wondered if there was a woman in the world who would have said no. "How about a maybe?" So perhaps she was a little bit crazy not jumping at the chance to be married to the Sexiest Man Alive. But that's what came from being semi-grounded. She wasn't gonna jump out of a plane without a parachute.

His brows came together in a scowl. "What the hell does that mean?"

She smiled, liking that he towered over her looking worried, liking that he really was the Sexiest Man Alive and wanted her. "It's a high percentage, mostly yes, maybe—okay? But marriage is a big thing. It's not a trip to the grocery store. You said yourself you wanted a long engagement. I'm just going along with the idea."

"Gotcha." He looked relieved. "And you're right to be cautious. There's too many serial marriages and fly-by-night love affairs in this business. I'm not looking for more of that, either."

"Speaking of love affairs . . ."

He took her hands in his. "We're good there for sure."

"It's the love part I'm kinda wondering about."

He didn't quite meet her gaze.

"Hey, don't panic," she murmured. "I don't know what I'm doing in that department, either. Especially after the state of my relationship with Theo, who I thought I loved and obviously didn't, because here I am pretty sure I love you."

His face lit up. "Same here. On that pretty sure stuff."

"That's all I really meant about maybe. I'm head over heels for you, and I just want to make sure I'm not completely nuts to feel this way after knowing you for not very long. I'm figuring I need a little time to stabilize my out-of-control-blind-to-everything-but-you passions."

"No shit. That first night in Paris something just clicked. And not in the usual way. It wasn't just about sex, although," he said with a grin, "I'm not discounting what we had going there. But this was different—*is* different."

"Whatever that means."

"Yeah—whatever." He smiled. "How about we figure it out together?"

Together. What a nice word, she thought. Simple, yet improbably complex. Warmhearted. Soft as a kitten. Cozy. Pink sunsets and walks on the beach. Whoa . . . she was moving into the Hallmark card shit. "I'd like that," she simply said.

"I almost forgot. I brought you something else, too." Reaching up, he pulled a shopping bag from the roof of her car. "From Jean-Paul." Johnny had placed a special order from Zurich and had it sent to the airport in Paris where they set down to pick it up. "He sends his compliments."

Nicky could smell the rich scent of chocolate from the guerilla-style factory in the fifteenth arrondissement before she pulled the large red box from the shopping bag. "How did you *think* of this?" she asked, ripping the ribbon from the box, her salivary glands already gearing up.

"You seemed to like his stuff," Johnny said with the casualness of a man who didn't understand the full spiritual mystique of chocolate.

Since she had neither the time nor the inclination to set him straight when she had a full box of Roussel chocolates in her hand, she simply said with feeling, "You're an absolute darling," and handed him the cover and shopping bag.

"OHMYGOD!!" She didn't mean it to be a shriek, but there was no other word for it. Wide-eyed, she beheld an arrangement of Jean-Paul Roussel chocolate kisses on a spun-sugar cushion, the kisses spelling out: I LOVE YOU. Two rows, two times I LOVE YOU—enough kisses to keep her in chocolate heaven for a blissfully long time.

Quickly popping a kiss into her mouth, she gazed up at Johnny and, smiling through her chewing, savoring, and swallowing, managed to say, "Maybe—we could discuss . . . this—long engagement . . . thing." Any man who was this unbelievably, incredibly thoughtful was the kind of man one should immediately lock down in a long-term, signed, sealed, and delivered contract. Okay, maybe it was the chocolate talking. Everyone knew how really good chocolate affected the pleasure centers and serotonin levels in women, but seriously, she was beginning to waver on this issue of long engagements.

"I'm definitely open to a discussion." He grinned. "Say, tonight in bed."

"That's another thing," she said, returning his grin with a chocolatey smile. "And I don't want to jack up your ego any more than it already is, but honestly, you're really hot—you know, sex-wise. So in terms of pure selfishness . . ."

"I'm way ahead of you there." He had this irrepressible, possessive impulse when it came to one Nicky Lesdaux. Don't ask him to explain it. He couldn't. But the feeling was definitely a full-speed-ahead, pedal-to-the-metal sensation. "You know, *long* could be a couple weeks." Male possessiveness operating at the max.

Nicky's eyes flared wide. "Really? I was thinking six months."

"How about a month?"

"Three months."

He grinned. "Deal. Now I need a kiss to seal the bargain."

Plucking a chocolate from the box, she offered it to him with a smile.

"Cute." But he took the chocolate, put it in his mouth and then bent low and kissed her the way he wanted to kiss her.

Chocolate to chocolate.

Body to body.

Flame-hot, impassioned love to love . . .